ALL THINGS MURDER

A VERONICA WALSH MYSTERY

ALL THINGS MURDER

JEANNE QUIGLEY

FIVE STAR

A part of Gale, Cengage Learning

Farmington Hills, Mich • San Francisco • New York • Waterville, Maine
Meriden, Conn • Mason, Ohio • Chicago

LIBRARY OF CONGRESS CATALOGING-IN-PUBLICATION DATA

Quigley, Jeanne.
  All things murder / Jeanne Quigley.
    pages cm (A veronica walsh mystery)
    ISBN-13: 978-1-4328-2812-7 (hardcover)
    ISBN-10: 1-4328-2812-6 (hardcover)
    1. Actresses—Fiction. 2. Homecoming—Fiction. 3. Murder—Investigation—Fiction. 4. Adirondack Mountains Region (N.Y.)—Fiction. I. Title.
  PS3617.U5353A35 2014
  813'.6—dc23   2013050385

First Edition. First Printing: May 2014
Find us on Facebook– https://www.facebook.com/FiveStarCengage
Visit our website– http://www.gale.cengage.com/fivestar/
Contact Five Star™ Publishing at FiveStar@cengage.com

For my mother, Oona, and in memory of my father, Bob, with love and gratitude.

CHAPTER ONE

Melanie and I clung to each other for dear life. Neither of us thought it would end like this.

"You've been a sister to me," Melanie cried as she tightened her arms around my neck.

"Likewise," I replied, choking on a sob.

"I'm sorry for all the catfights, Veronica. All those times I slapped you."

"All those times I pulled your hair."

"And I scratched your face."

"It's all right," I said as I dabbed at the tears in my eyes with a tissue. "They were scripted, you know."

"Yeah. You were really good at them." Melanie laughed as we released each other from our firm clutch. She sighed as one of the lights above us went off. "I really thought I'd leave on my own terms."

"And I thought the hearse would pick me up here. I feel like I'm stepping over my own dead body."

We both sighed dramatically, two soap divas milking every moment, and flopped onto the sofa of Melanie's fictional living room.

We had just finished the final scene of our soap opera, *Days and Nights*. Canceled after forty-two years, a medical talk show would soon take our time slot on the daytime schedule. I spent thirty-two years on the soap, having started just three months after "Pomp and Circumstance" played at my college graduation. I really did feel as if my career had become a corpse.

"When do you leave for Hawaii?" I asked Melanie.

"Sunday morning. I cannot wait."

I smiled, tamping down a surge of self-pity. Many of my cast-mates were looking forward to life post-*Days*. Travel for some like Melanie, retirement for several, and for a lucky few, new roles.

When I told my agent of the soap's cancellation, she told me she was retiring and moving to South Carolina. While a few of my younger castmates had offers from the four remaining soap operas, all filmed in California, my soon-to-be fifty-four-year-old unmarried self received offers to do commercials for hot-flash herbs, osteoporosis medication, and cholesterol-lowering pills. I couldn't bring myself to say things like, "This medication can cause explosive diarrhea," or "Sudden death may occur upon standing." I had to face the reality that the television movie roles and guest parts on shows I had gotten in my younger days were now going to actresses who were *in* their younger days.

After my best friend Carol gave me the great idea of writing my memoir, three editors told me, not in these exact words, that my life story was too boring. So my options for life after *Days and Nights* were limited: I could choose to hang around my house in New City, praying for an acting job, or return to my Adirondack hometown to work in my family's bookstore.

My leading man, Alex Shelby, champagne-filled glasses in hand, joined us. He gave one glass to Melanie, another to me.

Sitting beside me, he raised his glass and said, "To Diana, Rachel, and Cal. Long may they live!"

We touched glasses and took generous sips. We leaned back and had a moment of silence for our characters. Melanie's Diana, the undisputed queen of the show. My Rachel, Diana's sworn enemy. Alex's Cal, sometime husband of both.

"I have to give Maura a hug," Melanie said, getting up from the sofa. She dashed off set to where our head writer stood.

Alex turned to me. "It was a pleasure working with you, Ms. Walsh."

"Likewise, Mr. Shelby."

We touched glasses again and drank. Although Alex had said that golf was in his foreseeable future, rumors circulated that he was about to land a role on the soap *Passion For Life*. It burned me a bit that Alex, a year younger than I, could still get contract offers while I couldn't even get a six-week role.

"I enjoyed being married to you three times, Ronnie. Was I your favorite husband?"

I released a giddy laugh. "Rachel Wesley Jensen Lewis Lewis O'Neil Dixon Lewis. Oh how I'll miss that woman!" I said with terrific melodrama.

I tried my first option, hanging around my house, for three weeks. At first, it felt like vacation. I gave the house the best spring-cleaning it ever had, pulled together a few bags of clothes to donate, and even had the exterior of the house painted. And then reality dawned.

The day didn't come when I once again had to get up early to get to the studio. The long days of filming were over. There would be no more scripts to memorize. I needed a change in scenery, so to speak, so I moved to my second option. I packed my car and headed north to the mountains.

Chapter Two

I pulled into my driveway, that first sight of my northern home a soothing balm for my beleaguered spirit. Although I usually made the two-hundred-mile trip to Barton every six weeks or so, I hadn't paid a visit since the show's cancellation three and a half months earlier. In the wake of my job loss, I wanted to delay the inevitable wave of sympathy I'd get from my hometown.

I grabbed two of my suitcases and went inside. I drew back the living room curtains to let in the early afternoon sunshine and opened the windows to air the room. I found a vase filled with gorgeous flowers on the dining room table, courtesy of my mother and Carol. In the refrigerator I found a few provisions—a large dish of ziti, apple pie, milk, eggs, fresh lemonade—so I wouldn't need to dash to the supermarket.

I drank half a glass of the tart lemonade and then carried my suitcases to my bedroom upstairs. I opened the window that overlooked my backyard and moved to the side window that overlooked the driveway and my neighbor's yard. As soon as I opened it, I heard the clink of a china cup.

"I appreciate this, Tim," my neighbor, Anna Langdon, said.

"You're welcome," a stiff voice said. I immediately knew the speaker—my high school boyfriend, Tim Petersen.

"You're still upset with me, Tim? I thought we agreed we were just having fun." I detected a hint of scolding under her facade of concern.

"I don't remember that conversation. Sign here."

After a few moments' silence, Anna said, "I thought we were both adults, Tim. I guess I'm the only mature one here."

I wanted to run down there and punch the woman in the face for how she was talking to Tim. Instead, I stood by the window and continued eavesdropping.

"I'm not a child, Anna."

"Then stop pouting, Tim. We had a fling. I helped you get over your wife leaving you." She stopped speaking for a moment, and then continued in a know-it-all tone. "Oh, you're not over your wife. So why are you so upset that I've ended our relationship?"

"Was it really a relationship, or you just playing?"

Anna was cordial but not particularly warm. "Tim, I'm sorry. I hurt your male ego. I'm the second woman who's dumped you. You probably just want to get back together so you can end it."

"In the future, you'll have to come to the office to do business." I heard a chair scrape along Anna's stone patio. "Or perhaps it would be best for you to find another lawyer. I should have told you that before this mess even began."

"As if you're the first lawyer to have a fling with a client," Anna said with a derisive snort.

A moment later I saw Tim emerge from under the tree cover of Anna's yard and turn the corner of her house. I raced to the guest room that overlooked the street to watch as he got into his car and drove off.

The backstory on Tim: We dated from sophomore through senior year of high school. We hung on through our first year at college—me at Fordham University and Tim at Cornell. During our summer break, we both realized and acknowledged that, although still fond of each other, the distance had not made us more so. After graduation, I landed my role on *Days* and Tim went on to law school. He joined his father's law practice in Barton, married and had three children. Tim and his wife, Sue, had separated ten months earlier.

As for Anna, she became a wealthy woman working as a financial advisor in Saratoga Springs. She moved to Barton five years earlier when she married local businessman Edward Frazer, a childless widower thirty years her senior and owner of most of the business buildings along Barton's main thorough-fare, Orchard Street. He also owned the All Things Adirondack shop, a store that sold crafts and goods made by local artists. That was his sole purpose in opening the store. It wasn't to make more money, but to support the talent of his fellow Barto-nians and promote the village.

Mr. Frazer was a modest, wonderful man who loved Barton. When he passed away three years ago, Anna mourned by extensively renovating his plain (her words) Folk Victorian home. She also dropped Adirondack from the shop's name and changed the inventory from handcrafted products to elegant, expensive goods that promoted the comfortable lifestyle highlighted in women's magazines.

"Poor Tim." I sighed.

I walked the two short blocks from my house to Orchard. I love the hustle and bustle of Times Square, the thrill of Broadway, and the elegance of Park Avenue. But Barton's tree-lined Orchard Street holds its own unmatched charms for thousands of visitors lured to the Adirondacks each year. A number of the shops are family owned, third and fourth generations now tak-ing their turn at the reins. Ingerson's Men's Clothing. Alcott's, which sells women's and children's clothing. The Johnsons' stationery store, now run by their daughter Pauline Weber. And, of course, there's my family's Orchard Street Books and Carol's shop, Emerson Florist.

In addition to the typical drug store, jeweler, supermarket, and dry cleaner along Orchard, we also have three antique shops, a small art gallery, a furniture store, an ice cream shop, the elegant Farley Inn, and excellent restaurants like The Barton Hearth, Giacinta's, and Yau's. If the great shopping and food don't entice tourists visiting our southeast neighbors Lake George and Saratoga Springs, the local McDougal Brewery and nearby Arden College do.

I stepped into Orchard Street Books, comforted instantly by the cream walls, hardwood floors, and mahogany bookshelves. The shop never fails to rouse my best childhood memories. I spent many an after-school hour stocking shelves, conducting story time, and ringing up sales on the register. I'd listen as Mom would introduce Shakespeare and Twain to doubting teenagers and Dad enthusiastically described the latest bestsellers. In my mind my father, deceased fifteen years, was still here in the shop, shelving his beloved Le Carré and Clancy novels.

Mom stood at the register, assisting a customer. I waited until she finished and then stepped forward. Mom spotted me before I uttered a word.

"Veronica!" Mom said. She dashed around the counter and over to where I stood. Throwing her arms around me, she said, "You're home!"

"Still spry, I see," I teased, squeezing her gently.

Mom stepped back, kissed both my cheeks, and tweaked my nose. It was a ritual I enjoyed.

"You look wonderful," she said, beaming at me. "It's been a while."

I ignored her cheerful dig at my long absence. "Thanks. So do you."

We discreetly studied each other. For the last few years, every time I have seen my mother I've searched for signs of her advancing age—memory loss, balance problems, faltering eyesight, chin hair. At age seventy-nine, she passed with honors. Posture still steel-rod straight, no fewer white hairs than when I saw her at Easter, her step still steady.

For her part, I'm sure Mom was searching for depression, weight loss, and a body odor that would signal apathy for my appearance. Her smile signaled that I had passed her inspection.

Wendy Costello, Mom's very capable assistant manager, appeared from the office. "Veronica," she said as she breezed toward me.

We embraced as I said, "Hi, Wendy. Good to see you."

"Welcome home." Wendy pulled back and conveyed her sympathy over my predicament with a gentle "things will get better" smile.

"Thanks," I said.

Another member of the Orchard Street Books team, Todd Seaver, stepped from the storage room. Todd just finished his first year at Arden College. He started working at the shop when he was a high school sophomore and now works full time in the summer and as his class schedule allows the rest of the year.

"Hey, Veronica," he said. He hugged me tightly, saying a simple, "I'm sorry."

"Thanks. How are you? How's college?"

"Fabulous."

"He made the dean's list both semesters," Mom bragged.

Todd gave a shy smile and said, "Nancy, stop telling everyone." He turned to me and said, "You're back in time for the big meeting tonight."

I looked at the trio for explanation. They suddenly looked as if someone had died.

"What big meeting?"

Mom sighed, saying, "The thing that we've feared for years

has come to pass. Gary Pierce is going to sell the farm to a developer. We found out Thursday. They're going to build a mall!"

I gasped. "What?"

Wendy nodded, her jaw clenched. "Can you believe it? An open-air shopping mall."

For decades, Marjorie and Alan Pierce had run the wonderful Pierce Farm. They grew and sold delicious vegetables and had an orchard and pumpkin patch that spanned acres. Anyone who grew up in Barton had fond memories of the midnight pumpkin pick the Pierces had the Saturday before Halloween and the Great Apple Pick they hosted every fall. Marjorie continued to run the farm after Alan's death in 1995. When she passed away in 2008, their son, Gary, inherited the property. Rumors had flown for years about him selling the land for various uses—condominiums, a housing development, a park, and a dreaded mall.

"Thirty stores," Todd added.

Mom suddenly looked weary. "A Pip's among them."

As in Pip's Books, the boogeyman of all independent booksellers.

"Oh, Mom," I said, patting her arm. "Don't worry. You know it will be years before it's open, if it ever is. The Village Council will have to approve it. People will fight it. Conservation groups will fight it." Mom's frown indicated doubt. "So what's the meeting about?" I asked.

"A preemptive strike, we hope," Wendy said. "The Business Association is going to meet with the mayor and Gary to see if we can come up with an alternative. I personally think the village should buy the land."

"Wishful thinking," Todd muttered. "The mayor thinks the mall's a great idea. He's thinking of all the tax revenue it will bring in. It's all about making money, not spending it."

"The meeting's at eight," Mom said as she looked directly at me.

"I'm not in the Business Association."

"This bookstore is owned by the Walsh family," Mom said.

I knew from her tone and stern stare that my attendance was mandatory. "We'll have a quick dinner first? Someone left a ziti in my refrigerator."

"I wonder who would do such an awful thing. I'll be there at sixty-thirty." Mom placed her hand on my left cheek as she kissed my right. "It's good to have you home," she said.

I next dropped into the neighboring shop, The Caffs, a coffee place run by sisters Dana and Chloe Cafferty. A homemade sign, *STOP THE MALL!!!* printed in red across white poster board, was taped to the window.

I entered the shop at a quiet moment. The décor, bright yellow and white, gave me a momentary shock, as it always does. The sisters joke that if their coffee doesn't wake you, their paint job will. The honey blonde pair sat at a table by the window, enjoying cups of their own brew.

"Hi, Caffs," I said before giving each a hug.

"Oh, please tell us what happens to Rachel," Dana pleaded. She and her younger sister Chloe are my self-proclaimed number one fans. Dana even claims to remember watching my first episode. I wonder about that, since she was only five at the time, but I never argue with a fan.

"Please," Chloe said, clapping her hands. "Does she marry Cal again? Tell us what happens."

I arched an eyebrow, thinking back to the filming of the scene in which my character and Alex's married. "Sorry, you'll have to watch," I teased.

"Don't put us through this," Dana said with a pout before stretching it into a bright smile.

"Are you going to the meeting tonight?" Chloe asked.

"Yes. I can't wrap my brain around a mall on that land."

"It's awful. Stop the mall!" Dana shouted, pumping her fist into the air. "Did you see our sign?" she asked, pointing her thumb at the sign.

"Yes. Very nice."

"We thought it a good idea to be proactive," Chloe said.

"Very smart."

We chatted as Chloe made me two cups of straight coffee (I'm not hip enough for all their variations), on the house, and I headed for Carol's, waving at various shop windows in greeting to old friends. Several had anti-mall signs similar to the Caffertys' propped in their windows.

"I want twelve dozen roses to go. *Now.*" I mockingly demanded as I stepped into Emerson Florist.

"You'll get no such thing," Carol replied dully, her back to me. After a moment, she turned and hustled around the counter. "You're such a diva."

"I brought coffee," I said, holding up the two cups.

"Well then, you can have anything you want."

I set the cups on the counter and welcomed Carol's comforting hug. As my mother and I just did, Carol and I checked each other out. This time, though, we compared wrinkles, gray hairs, and sags.

"I was worried you'd go blonde again," Carol said.

"That was for a storyline," I said. Five or so years earlier, my alter ego went to prison after a wrongful murder conviction. Rachel escaped with another inmate and ended up working in a diner in Indiana. She disguised herself by cutting and bleaching her hair. The show's producer suggested a wig, but I wanted authenticity, so I had my hair colored and cut into a shag. The haircut looked great, the color not so much. I didn't have more fun; I just got odd looks.

"I know. But I thought with the situation, you'd make a change."

I knew her thoughts and declared, "I'm not depressed."

"Okay." The phone rang and she walked back to the counter. "I'm just saying, you're not you unless you're brunette."

"I promise no more blonde moments."

I perused the shop while Carol took the call, stopping to inhale the fragrance of every single bunch of flowers in Carol's realm. I even sniffed the flowers in the refrigerator. I can't do this in just any flower shop or I'd be marked down as a loon.

Two of her employees, Amy and Casey, came in from the back room.

"Hey, Veronica," Amy said. She's in her twenties and is as deft with flowers as Carol. Casey, a college student, does the deliveries, among other tasks.

"Hi, kids." I hugged both and chatted for a few minutes before Carol chased them back to their work.

"I left some deliveries on the worktable," she commanded Casey with a smile.

"Yes, Madam Dictator," he said. He saluted as they returned to the workroom.

"This news about Gary Pierce selling the farm is unbelievable," I said as I knelt to admire a bucket of tulips.

"I can't imagine those beautiful orchards not being there. Anna's having a conniption over the prospect of competition. She thinks a shopping mall will put many of her renters out of business. She envisions empty stores up and down Orchard."

"And no rent for her."

As I considered telling Carol about the conversation I overheard between Anna and Tim, the bell jingled and Mary Rutherford, our high school English teacher, entered.

"Veronica!" she exclaimed. She hurried to me and enfolded me in a smothering embrace. After several minutes of her denouncing the show's cancellation and proclaiming me the best actress ever (I patiently listened—she was still an authority figure), I thanked her and excused myself.

"I'll get out of the way so Carol can assist you," I said as I dashed from the store.

I finished my coffee as I strolled down the street. When I reached Johnson's Stationery, I decided to pop in for a quick hello to Pauline Weber.

No one was in the store when I entered. I thought nothing of it, assuming Pauline was in the back room, so I busied myself by perusing a display of pretty sun catchers and wind chimes that was right by the door.

"You're late again on your rent, Pauline." The severe voice came from the office in the back of the store and belonged to Anna.

"I'll get you the money, Anna. I just need a few more days."

"I'm tired of waiting. I have to wait every month. Now you're pushing the grace period. You're later and later, Pauline. And I'm tired of your excuses. I've let you get away with this for far too long. I'm not my husband. I'm not going to take pity on people because they're nice or because I was friends with their parents."

I could hear the sneer in Anna's tone. I could only imagine her accompanying facial expression.

"I'm sorry, Anna." Pauline sounded as if she were about to burst into tears. "I really appreciate your patience."

"Well, I'm out of patience. Someone else would have evicted you by now. I can rent this place in an instant to someone who will have no problem paying me on time," Anna snapped. "And paying more for the space."

I didn't want to hear any more of the unpleasant conversation. I crept back to the door, praying I could slip out undiscovered.

"I want that money in my hand by tomorrow morning," Anna demanded. "If I don't get it, you're out of business."

I slowly opened the door, cringing when the overhead bell jangled. There was no response to the sound when I entered but, to my bad luck, it brought attention on my attempted exit.

"Veronica."

I turned to find Anna, dressed in a crisp linen set of black pants and white tunic, strutting down an aisle.

"Hey, neighbor," I said meekly as I saw Pauline, shoulders drooping, step from her office. "Hi, Pauline."

"Hi, Veronica." Pauline walked around the counter and began to fiddle with the cash register.

Anna arrived at my side and gave me a one-armed hug. Her highlighted auburn hair brushed against my shoulder as I felt her manicured fingernails clutch my elbow.

"What a shame about your soap," she said. Anna towered over me like a fabled Amazon warrior, thanks to a pair of the high-heeled, expensive shoes she favored.

"Thanks."

"I can't talk now," Anna said. "But I do want to talk with you about a business idea that will be good for both of us." Her glance lingered over to Pauline. "Can you come over at nine-thirty tomorrow morning? We'll talk over coffee and Rizzuto's pastry."

"I have no plans," I said, wishing that I did. Anna only bothered with me when she needed or wanted something. She liked to use my fame to promote her store, often asking me to tell my castmates about All Things and to talk about all the great shopping in Barton in interviews.

"Terrific. I'll see you then." Anna slinked from the store without a word to Pauline.

I walked over to the counter, silently prepping for my first bit of acting since I left *Days*. "You look great, Pauline. How are

Glen and the kids?" I asked. I ignored the dark circles under her eyes and her pallid cheeks.

Pauline smiled gratefully. "Everyone's great. Glen just sold a house."

The Barton housing market, just like markets across the country, had been in a prolonged slump. I was happy to hear of her husband's success. With both running their own businesses as well as raising three kids, I knew the Webers were under a lot of stress.

"I'm sure I'm the one thousandth person to say this. I'm sorry about your show. You were so terrific. I can't believe they canceled it. So many people still watched." Pauline reached across the counter and lightly placed her hand on my arm. Her smile was genuine and warm.

It did feel that Pauline was the one thousandth person to say that, but her thoughtfulness in the face of her own troubles touched me.

"Thanks, Pauline. Your words mean a lot."

We chatted for a few more minutes before I left. I walked home, glad to be back in Barton, but troubled by the revelations of the day.

Chapter Three

Mom and I were among the last to arrive at the Village Hall. As I looked across the rows, I noted that every Orchard Street proprietor was there except for Anna. Gary Pierce, the cause of the meeting, sat by himself in the second row.

We settled into seats Wendy and Todd had saved for us. I spotted Tim a few rows up at the same time he saw me. We acknowledged each other with friendly waves. I waved to Pauline and Glen, and nodded to insurance agent Myrtle Evans. She sat with Ella and Madeline Griffin, the grand dames of Orchard Street. Although their family's inn is no longer in operation, the sisters hold a place of honor in the business community as the descendants of one of Barton's first business owners.

I chatted with Carol and her husband Patrick, who were right in front of us. After a few minutes Mark Burke, a former classmate, came in and took the seat beside me.

"Hi, Veronica. I'm surprised to see you here."

"I've been drafted for the war," I joked as he kissed me and we clasped hands for a moment. "And what are you doing here?"

"I'm a recruit, too. Your mother called me in as backup. If they can't convince Gary to change his mind and not sell, I'm supposed to stand up and shout that a Revolutionary War battle took place on the land and therefore the farm is a historic landmark."

"It is?" I asked, very curious because I had never heard of

such a battle happening in Barton.

"Not that I know of."

"And you would know," I said with a smile. Mark was a history professor at Arden College.

"I lose all credibility if I don't. It's good to see you. How are you?"

Of course, Mark knew about the soap's cancellation, but he was a gentleman not to mention it. That's no surprise since Mark has always been a sweet guy. Our history goes all the way back to Mrs. Fisher's kindergarten class, where we began our twelve-year journey together through the school system. Along with Carol, we went to Saint Augustine grammar school and then on to Sacred Heart High. Mark was the kid who never teased the girls, never got into fights, never caused the teacher grief.

"I'm good," I said with emphasis. "I'm home on an open-ended visit."

"Great," he said, his smile reaching his green eyes.

From the corner of my eye I saw Anna enter, trailed by her store manager, Claire Camden. Anna wore a wrap dress in a woman's power color of choice, red. She completed the look with a pair of blazing red stilettos. The two took seats in the front row, right in front of Gary Pierce. Anna nodded at Gary and began a conversation with him.

"I wonder if Anna is trying to change Gary's mind," I said.

The chatter in the room ceased when Mayor Jason Quisenberry entered. He walked in, accompanied by a man dressed in a navy blue suit and tie. The man took a seat in the front row as the mayor, dressed casually in beige khakis and a white Oxford shirt, smiled at all of us and clasped his hands together as if praying. At twenty-nine, he is the youngest person to serve as mayor of Barton. Tall and lanky, his boyish face belies his organizational skills and ability to manage the village.

"Thank you all for coming this evening," he began. "I'm happy to see you all here. I know you've had a long day, so I'll get right to our reason for meeting. As you all know, Gary Pierce has decided to sell his farmland to the Thompson Development Corporation. Mr. Thompson has built a number of shopping centers in the Northeast and has designed a plan to build a shopping center on the Pierce property. Many of you have already expressed your displeasure with this plan to me. I understand your concerns. I do believe a shopping center would bring Barton tremendous benefits in the form of tax revenue and jobs. And I don't believe it would threaten your businesses on Orchard. Many visit Barton every year in large part because of the unique goods you sell. I don't believe for a minute that a Target would put any of you out of business."

"Yeah, right," Wendy muttered.

"Many residents have already voiced their excitement over a new shopping center. And I believe once you hear about the project, you'll be more open to the idea as well." Jason paused for a moment and scanned the crowd. "Now Vic Thompson, CEO of Thompson Development, would like to say a few words."

The mayor took a seat in the front row as the blue-suited man stood and stepped into the center aisle. Tall and in his mid-fifties, he glanced across the crowd, nodding in greeting.

Carol turned around and whispered to me, "He's really working the power suit."

"Thank you, Mayor Quisenberry," the deep-voiced CEO said. "It's a pleasure to meet with the fine business leaders of Barton tonight. I hope to allay your concerns over the shopping center I'd like to build in your village. As the mayor said, I think it will bring decided benefits to your community."

He went on to name those benefits—high tax revenue for the village, jobs, more choices in shopping—as we listened politely.

It was obvious he wanted to persuade us, but his delivery was rather cool and arrogant. He was certain he was right and we were just naive small-town folks averse to change. As he spoke, I glanced at the faces of the audience. No one seemed receptive to what he was saying, no one convinced by his argument. No one applauded when he finished, and he stood awkwardly until the mayor joined him.

"I'll open the floor now to all of you. Please share your thoughts, concerns, ideas," the mayor said.

Pauline expressed concern over a Lamb's Greetings and Gifts knocking her out of business. My mother voiced the same worry about a big-chain bookstore. Anita Rizzuto suggested the crime rate would rise. Charlie Ingerson added increased traffic to the list. Wendy stood up and declared it a sin to destroy such fruitful land and insisted the village buy the property and preserve it. Todd cheered and echoed her concern.

"Why do we need a mall when the outlets are just a few miles down the road in Lake George?" furniture store owner Denny Chester asked.

"Some want their own piece of the pie," baker Nick Rizzuto said. "Actually, they want the whole pie."

Finally, Anna turned around in her seat and asked Gary, "Is it true Mr. Thompson has offered you one million dollars for your land, Mr. Pierce?"

Gary shifted in his chair. He nodded and said, "Yes."

"I will give you one million, five hundred thousand for it," she said. Anna beamed with pride.

Many of us gasped as Dana shouted, "Take it!"

"Do it for Barton," Charlie said.

"Be a hero," Todd called out to some laughter.

Cheers erupted as more encouraged Gary.

"We have a deal," Vic gruffly said to him.

"Nothing signed," Gary said.

Anna turned in her chair to face Thompson. "Just because you two have a deal doesn't mean you'll be allowed to build your mall. The Village Council would have to approve the rezoning," she said. "And I promise you, Mr. Thompson, I will fight against that for as long as it takes. I have a lot of money and I always get what I want. I will not let you take over my village."

A few in the crowd gasped at Anna's braggadocio. Others applauded her defense of Barton.

"I can give you a check tomorrow, Gary," Anna said.

"A million five?" Gary asked.

"Yes." Anna rose and extended her hand to Gary.

After a moment's consideration, Gary stood and shook it. Our exuberant applause and cheers celebrated his decision.

Anna smiled sweetly and said, "I'm sorry, Mr. Thompson, but you'll just have to find another place for your steel and concrete. Mr. Mayor, I'll turn the meeting back to you." She turned on her heels and walked from the room, followed closely by Gary and Claire.

"Well," Jason said. "I guess that concludes our meeting and the matter entirely. Thank you all for coming. And thanks to Mr. Thompson for his time."

Thompson shook his head and walked over to the mayor. They shook hands as the mayor patted Thompson on the back. Thompson looked okay, not irate over the deal's collapse, though not ecstatic. He's certainly had other deals fall through, I thought as I scooted from our row.

"All's well that ends well," Todd sang.

"But now we'll have to call her Saint Anna," Wendy tartly said.

In the entry hall, I spotted Tim by the water fountain. He waved at me to join him.

"What's a girl like you doing in a place like this?" he joked as he kissed me on the cheek. We exchanged greetings over everyone's excited chatter. "That was something," he said.

"My neighbor certainly has a flair for the dramatic." I nodded toward Anna, who stood at the end of the hall, deep in conversation with Gary as Claire stood by, listening.

"Sorry that your *drama* has ended," he said with a wince.

"Nice way to put it. Thanks."

"Care to get a cup of coffee? Or something stronger?"

"I have Mom-made apple pie at home. Care to have some of that?"

"You can't beat Mom-made. Let's go."

We began to walk down the hall to the exit. As we passed Anna and Claire, Anna grabbed my arm and said, "Remember our breakfast meeting." To Claire she said, "Pick up a box of pastries at Rizzuto's and drop them off before going to the shop."

"Will do," Claire said rather coolly. I didn't know Claire too well, but we were always cordial to each other, so her stony expression surprised me.

"Hello, Tim," Anna said.

"Anna," Tim replied without looking at her.

Wendy came up behind us. She made a dramatic show of bowing to Anna, loudly proclaiming, "Hail, Queen Anna!"

Anna sneered. "You should be thankful, Wendy. I probably just saved your job."

"I am, Anna. I'm just getting a jump-start on the adulation because I know you'll be lording it over us how you saved Barton from the big, bad mall wolf. Good night."

Wendy left, leaving our little group in uncomfortable silence. I broke it, saying, "Good night," as I tugged at Tim's arm. He needed no prompting to move.

We walked toward the exit, where Mom and Mark stood talking.

"Hello, Mrs. Walsh," Tim said, his good cheer returned. "Hey, Mark."

"Good to see you, Tim," Mark replied as the two shook hands.

"The old high school gang, together again," Tim said. "A little lighter in the wrong places," he added. To emphasize his point, he ran his hand through his thinning black hair and then patted his soft belly.

"We're all too busy to spend our afternoons playing ball," Mark said.

"Look who's talking," Mom said. "I think you have a portrait done by Oscar Wilde in your attic, Mark."

She was right; time hadn't done much damage to Mark. A few gray strands streaked his dark blond hair, but otherwise he looked like he could still capably play the hot corner for the Sacred Heart High baseball team.

"It helps that my office is at one end of campus and my classes at the other."

"Walking is good for the body and soul," Mom said. "Are you ready to go, Veronica?"

"Tim's going to give me a ride home."

"Wonderful," Mom cooed. "I'll save some gas."

"Oh, yes," I said dryly. "All three drips you use driving the four blocks between our houses."

"You laugh. A penny saved," Mom scolded. And then she smiled. "And I'm going to save more pennies not making those long-distance telephone calls to New City."

"I guess I will, too," I teased.

As we walked outside, Mom asked, "Mark, will you walk me to my car?"

"It'd be a pleasure. Good night," Mark said to Tim and me.

I was about to invite Mark back to my house as well, but Tim grabbed my elbow and guided me away from Mom and Mark.

"She was quite serious about the gas," I said as we walked to his car.

"And it's that diligence that has made Orchard Street Books the success it is."

"*Touché.*"

Tim and I caught up with each other's lives as we made the short trip to my house. "Caf or decaf?" I asked as he parked at my curb.

We were on my back porch within fifteen minutes, content with pie à la mode and decaffeinated coffee.

"So, do you have any offers of new roles?" Tim gingerly asked.

"No." I sighed, tired of the question and of my negative answer. "I'm coming to grips with the fact that an actress my age, which you know so I won't declare it, does not have many prospects."

"Sorry," he said.

"Thanks."

"So you're having breakfast with Anna?"

"Yes. She says she has something to talk about that will be good for both of us."

"Be careful," he said. "She might want you as a silent partner in her purchase of Pierce's." Tim chuckled, but his warning was stern.

"I'll get everything in writing, and have you go over it with your legal fine-toothed comb before I sign."

As we paused to drink our coffee, a car pulled up Anna's driveway. The hedge between our properties obstructed my view, but I could see the car's headlights shining against the door of her detached garage. Just moments later, we heard another car pull in. Two car doors slammed and footsteps slapped against the driveway.

"I'm sorry about that, honey," Anna said.

Tim stiffened and set down his mug. I prayed for a sudden thunderstorm to chase us inside.

A sharp voice answered. "You could give a guy a little notice." Jason Quisenberry. AKA The Mayor.

"It was spontaneous," Anna giggled. "Oh, come on, Jason. It's just business."

"Why do you have to get in the middle of everything? A shopping center would not hurt your store, and you know it. It could even help it." No laughter from Jason; he was all business.

"Come here."

We heard the distinct puckering sound of a couple kissing. I could not bear to look at Tim.

"I'm not sure you've made a wise purchase, Anna."

"Well, it's only money. I'm protecting my business interests."

"A shopping center would serve Barton's interests. It would bring jobs. And tax revenue."

"You and your tax revenue. Don't worry about the money."

"Oh, really? Do you have a top-secret plan to bring in revenue?" Jason asked.

"Maybe," Anna said, stressing the last syllable for a few beats.

"And what are you going to do with a farm?"

"I don't know. Roll in the hay," she said. "Maybe I'll hire people to run it for me. Or maybe I'll sell it for a profit to someone who will farm it, or turn it into a park or something. Or condos! That will bring in more revenue."

"It must be nice having money to throw around."

"It's wonderful."

"I wish you hadn't flirted with Thompson. I don't like that."

"Oh, Jason. That's the way I am. It's how I got you." Anna's heels clicked across the driveway. "Are you coming inside?" she called with a soft, seductive tone.

Jason replied a stern, "You should have discussed the purchase with me."

I swept up the back porch steps to the kitchen entrance. The door was ajar. I tapped on its frame, calling Anna's name.

Hearing no response, I again said, "Anna?"

I pushed open the door and took a step into the kitchen. The breakfast table, usually parallel to the island, stood at an angle, one corner shoved against the wall. Two chairs had been overturned. Scattered across the floor between the table and island were shards of china, cloth napkins, silverware, and a dented box from Rizzuto's, its red and green string still tied around it. The napkins soaked up coffee spilled from a smashed glass carafe. The damage reminded me of the "redecorating" Melanie and I would do to a set during one of our characters' famous brawls.

And then I noticed one of the red stilettos Anna had worn the night before on the floor between the stove and island. A cast-iron skillet lay beside the shoe.

I stepped to the right of the island to avoid the mess and instantly knew I wasn't in a television studio. Anna lay sprawled on her side, her hair splayed across her face and her right arm extended across the floor.

I rushed to her. "Anna!" Kneeling, I pulled back a few locks of the hair covering her face, flinching when I saw blood around her nose and on the floor.

I pressed my fingers to her neck to check for her pulse. "Come on!" I pleaded as my fingers swept across her skin searching for rhythm in her heart as my own heart hammered a frantic beat.

I rose and raced out to the backyard. My hands trembling, I yanked my cell phone from my pocket and called nine-one-one.

"This is Veronica Walsh. I'm at ten Willow Lane in Barton. It is Anna Langdon's house. I found her unconscious. She's not breathing. I think she's dead!"

I answered the operator's questions and then waited in Anna's driveway for help to arrive. My hands shook and my legs felt like jelly as I paced from her lawn to the hedge.

A patrol car pulled in front of the house within five minutes. I had not realized I had been barely breathing until I released a relieved sigh at the sight of police officers Tracey Brody and Ron Nicholstone. Though acquainted with the pair, both in their early thirties, I had never dealt with them in an official capacity.

The officers took long strides to where I stood. Tracey's brown ponytail bobbed under her cap as she asked, "Where is Ms. Langdon, Veronica?"

"In the kitchen," I said.

I trailed them to the backyard. As Tracey jogged up the porch steps, Ron said, "Please wait here, ma'am."

I obeyed as he followed Tracey into the house. I walked back and forth over Anna's well-tended lawn, taking deep breaths and praying.

Tracey, standing just beyond the wide open door, said, "Chief, we have a one eight seven at ten Willow Lane. Anna Langdon."

She came outside a few minutes later. I met her at the bottom of the porch steps and asked, "Anna's dead, isn't she?"

"Yes. What time did you arrive at the house, Veronica?"

"At nine-thirty. We were to meet at nine-thirty for breakfast."

"Did you enter from the front door, or the kitchen?"

"The kitchen. I first rang the front doorbell, but no one answered. So I walked back here."

"Was the kitchen door open or closed?"

"Open. Slightly."

"Did you notice anyone in the vicinity?"

"No," I said. "I saw no one."

Another police cruiser pulled into the driveway. The chief of police, Bill Price, got out and hustled into the yard.

"Ms. Walsh," he nodded as he reached us. "Where's the body, Officer Brody?" he asked.

"This way, sir."

Again, I waited in the yard. A few minutes later, Tracey returned.

"What's going on?" I asked. "What exactly happened to Anna?"

Tracey put a hand on my arm and gently led me down the driveway. "I'm very sorry, Veronica," she said, her voice soothing. "I can't say right now."

"This is stunning," I sputtered. "Barton is so safe."

"Yes," she said. She released my arm as we rounded the hedge and headed up my driveway. "Chief Price will be over in a few minutes to speak with you."

"All right."

"And you'll need to come down to the station later to sign your statement. Can you come around three?"

"Yes."

Tracey's soft hazel eyes flashed with concern. "Are you okay alone? Would you like me to call your mother?"

"I'm fine," I said. I surely did not want my mother to get a call from the police on anything that involved me.

"If you have any questions or concerns, please call me at the station."

"I will."

I watched as she dashed down the driveway and around the hedge. Then I went inside, locked the front door, and ran up to the medicine cabinet for two aspirin. The three conversations I had overheard the previous day shot through my mind. Tim. Pauline. The mayor. All, to varying degrees, had trouble with Anna.

The doorbell rang just as I gulped down the aspirin. As I jogged down the stairs, I coached myself on how to talk with the police chief. I would answer his questions with exact responses, giving nothing more.

Chief Price politely asked me how I was when I opened the door. "Shocked, but okay," I replied as I led him into the living room.

He then drilled me with questions. Had I seen anyone at Anna's that morning? Had I seen anyone in the neighborhood who didn't live there? When was the last time I spoke with Anna? Saw her? Did I see anything? Hear anything?

"Did you leave your home at any time before you went to Ms. Langdon's at nine-thirty?"

"No."

He stared at me for a moment. I wondered if he was assessing my honesty. I maintained steady eye contact with him.

"Is there anything else?" he asked.

I told him about the backfiring car and at what time I heard it. "Do you know what time Anna died?" I asked.

Price gave me a peeved look. "We don't know that information instantaneously, like on your TV shows," he said.

I held my tongue. I hold the police in high regard; their work is vastly more important than that of an actress. But it was just a question.

"Do you have anything more to ask me?" I asked instead.

"No. But I may." He stood and ambled toward the door. "How long will you be in Barton?"

"For a while," I said.

He turned and gave me a long look. "That's right. I read about your show being canceled. It was on the front page of *The Chronicle*."

"Yeah, well. That doesn't seem so important now, does it?"

"No," he said. "But I'm sorry."

"Thanks, Chief."

"You'll have to come to the station to sign your statement."

"Officer Brody already told me. I'll come later."

He turned and walked to the door. "Let us know if you see or hear anything. Even if it seems trivial to you."

"I will."

"And make sure your doors and windows are locked."

"I will. Thank you."

I went into my living room and watched as the chief walked across my lawn. He met Tracey in Anna's driveway. They talked for a few minutes, and then the officer left in her patrol car. A few minutes later, another car arrived. A man in plain clothes got out and walked into the house.

I made a strong cup of coffee and sat drinking it at the kitchen table for a long while. As I sat in my clean, orderly home, I flashed again and again to the scene next door. Finally, the ringing of my house phone dragged me back to the present.

"Veronica, are you safe?" my mother said when I answered. She was close to tears.

"I'm okay, Mom."

"Oh, thank God. We just heard that Anna was found dead. Haley came in here, frantic and in tears."

"I know. I found Anna."

Mom was silent for a moment, and then she said, "You found her?"

"Yes."

"What happened? Why were you there?"

"I was supposed to have coffee with Anna. Mom, I'll come to the shop and tell you all about it."

"Be careful," she said.

I hung up and went upstairs to put on my sneakers. Back downstairs, I dropped my keys into my pocket and headed outside, twice checking the door lock.

Both the chief's and the plain-clothed man's cars were still parked in front of Anna's, as was the ambulance. A sheriff's car was parked across the street. I hurried past the grim scene, anxious to get away. Anxious to know who murdered Anna.

Chapter Five

I walked to Orchard Street, appreciating the beauty of the day more deeply than usual. I yearned to be back at *Days and Nights,* play-acting the drama of life rather than living it for real.

I considered Anna's murder and who could have committed it. Was it the result of a lovers' quarrel, or the consequence of a sour business deal? Passion could turn to anger and violence in both scenarios.

Or was it completely unrelated to what I knew? Could it have been a simple robbery gone horribly wrong?

I worried about Tim. Was he hurt enough over Anna's rejection to confront her again? To hurt her? Was Pauline in such financial dire straits that she could harm Anna to avoid losing the family business? I had to add the mayor to the list; he wasn't too happy about the deal she made with Gary.

Vic Thompson. Could he have been more upset than he looked? And what about Gary? Perhaps Thompson came back with a better offer and Gary reneged on the deal with Anna. Could they have argued? If only I had overheard the fourth conversation that preceded Anna's death. Maybe Anna would still be alive if I had heard something. But Anna had not opened her windows, and I had slept like a baby.

Parked cars lined Orchard, typical for a summer day. Visitors walked along the sidewalks, stopping to window-shop and step into stores to do some actual buying. I glanced toward All Things. It appeared as if business was going on as usual. I could see a few customers standing by the window and two leaving, carrying the store's forest green bags, the shop's name written in elegant script on each.

Through the bookstore's window, I saw Mom pacing along the aisle of mystery books.

"Did you *walk*?" she asked when I entered.

"Yeah."

She shook her head and then hugged me, squeezing so hard I lost my breath. Todd dropped an armload of books on a nearby table and rushed to my side.

"What happened? Haley said that Anna was murdered."

"Shh," my mother whispered.

I glanced to the register, where Wendy was ringing up a customer's purchases.

"Let's wait for Wendy," I said.

Mom and Todd impatiently waited for the transaction's conclusion. Wendy hustled around the counter as the customer left and the three bombarded me with questions. I answered them all, until three customers entered.

"It's lunch time," Todd said. He took sandwich orders and ran out to the deli while we assisted the shoppers.

We were again alone fifteen minutes later, eating our sandwiches and discussing the case.

"Vic Thompson is the prime suspect," Todd said.

"I don't think it has anything to do with the mall," Wendy said. "I think it was personal. A lot of people had trouble with Anna and the way she went about things."

"Hush," Mom said. "We can't accuse anyone. Let the police investigate. I'm sure they'll have it solved very quickly."

"I'm sure they will," I said.

"Maybe you should stay at my house until they do," Mom said.

"I'll be fine," I said lightly. "Don't worry about me."

I knew she would from the distressed look on her face and decided I would not share with her my theories on Anna's murder. Mom certainly wouldn't want me getting involved if she didn't even want me next door to the crime scene.

That left me with Carol, the person to whom I had told all my secrets since kindergarten. She called me just as I was leaving the bookstore.

"Veronica. I just heard."

"I *found* her, Carol." I stopped and leaned against the brick wall below the shop's window.

"How are you? Are you all right? What happened?" Carol's questions came rapid-fire.

"I'm fine. I found Anna in her kitchen. She was hit on the head. Apparently with an iron skillet."

"Oh." She was quiet for a minute. "May she rest in peace."

"I was just coming to see you."

"I want to talk, but I'm really busy today. How about we have dinner?"

"Okay."

"The Hearth at six?" she asked.

"I'll see you then."

"Are you okay?"

"Yeah. I'm okay."

"Take care, Veronica."

I slipped my phone in my pocket and continued down the street, not sure where I was going. Dana and Chloe rushed from their shop as I passed.

"Veronica!" they screamed in unison as they group-hugged me. I feared suffocation as the sisters, tennis stars in high school who maintained their athletic physiques by lifting gym weights and heavy pots of coffee, not so gently squeezed me.

"How scary!" Dana shrieked.

"The killer could have still been in the house," Chloe wailed.

"Poor Anna," Dana cried.

"Are you okay?" Chloe asked.

I extricated myself from the Caffertys. "I'm fine."

"A murderer is on the loose," Chloe whispered. She pressed her hands against her cheeks as her pale blue eyes filled with tears.

I lightly patted her arm. "Don't worry. The police will find the killer very soon."

"Poor Haley is a wreck. She ran into our shop, absolutely hysterical," Dana said as several customers walked past us and entered the coffeehouse. "We need to get back inside and help Nate," she said to Chloe as she nodded at the group. "Do you need coffee, Veronica?"

I shook my head. "No, thanks."

They hustled inside as I went next door to the bakery. Two women sat at a table eating slices of pound cake. Anita Rizzuto was setting a tray of cookies into the display case. She blessed herself when she saw me.

"May God have mercy on Anna's soul."

I gave a respectful nod. "I guess everyone on Orchard knows."

"Oh yes. Haley told the Caffertys. Chloe ran in here. And I made a few calls. We all need to be on the watch."

I leaned against the counter and lowered my voice. "Anita, I know Claire was going to get pastries this morning and bring them over to Anna's. Around what time did she pick them up?"

"After seven," Anita responded. She paused and leaned her chin on her fist. After a moment of consideration she said, "Yeah, about seven-fifteen, seven-thirty."

"I see."

"Do you think she saw something?" Anita whispered. "Claire couldn't have killed Anna."

"I'm sure not. Let's not think that. I'm sure she'll talk to the police and tell them everything she knows."

I left the bakery and walked to the corner. Tim's office was one street up Orchard. I needed reassurance that he was not involved. I crossed the street and hurried to the converted house that served as headquarters for the Petersen Law Office.

"Hi, Helen," I said as I crossed the threshold and stepped into the waiting area.

Tim's longtime secretary looked up from her computer screen. She smiled, and then frowned, when she saw me. "Oh, Veronica. Claire's told me the horrible news about Anna." Helen stepped around her desk and gave me a warm embrace. "It is horrible. I guess she'll be re-telling it all day."

"Yes. She's very composed though. I suppose it will sink in later, when her duties are complete."

"I suppose."

"You're here to see Tim?"

I nodded. "Yes."

Helen shook her head. "He's not here."

"When will he be back?"

"I'm sorry, but he's out for the day. He called this morning and said he was taking the day off. I just tried to call his cell to tell him about Anna, but I got his voice mail."

"Oh."

"If he calls, I'll tell him you dropped by. Do you want to leave a message?"

"No, thanks. I'll catch up with him. I was just stopping to say hello."

"All right. It's good to see you. This isn't a very nice welcome home, though."

"It isn't," I agreed.

I left the office, doubly worried about Tim. Why did he suddenly decide to take the day off?

I abruptly stopped, chastising myself for suspecting a good guy I had known for decades. As I proceeded, I reminded myself of the dark side of passion. I had played it, many times on the soap. I just never imagined it would happen in real life, right next door.

CHAPTER SIX

I arrived at the station to sign my statement at ten minutes to three. I thought it best to be fashionably early. I walked into our tiny police station, fighting my nerves as I walked down the entry hall and turned into the main room. A reception desk was right inside the door, separated from the rest of the workroom by a half-wall. There was a hallway beyond the room that I knew led to the chief's office, an interrogation room, the evidence room, and a room with two holding cells. I knew this from a long-ago class field trip.

Tracey was the lone officer present; she looked up as I entered and smiled. "Hello, Veronica," she said pleasantly. "Thank you for coming."

There was a door in the half-wall. I stood behind it, saying, "I'm a little early. I can wait, if you're not ready."

She walked over and pushed open the door. "That's fine." I walked through and she closed the door. "I have your statement ready," she said as I followed her back to her desk. She gestured at the chair beside her desk. "Please, sit."

I sat and asked, "Do you know what time Anna died?"

"According to the coroner, she was dead between ninety minutes and two hours, give or take, when you found her."

That would make the time of death between seven-thirty and eight. "I'm guessing that cast-iron skillet had something to do with it?"

"Yes," she nodded. "Ms. Langdon was killed by a blow to the head."

"Does it look like a robbery gone bad?"

She shook her head. "It doesn't appear to be that."

I waited for her to say more. When she didn't, I said, "Okay."

"Veronica, do you remember anything else since we spoke this morning?"

"No. Sorry."

"That's okay." She opened her drawer and removed a sheet of paper. "I typed up all that you told me this morning." Setting it on the desk before me, she continued, "If you could read it please, checking that everything is accurate and that nothing is left out. When you're done, please sign it, right here." She picked up a pen and pointed to the signature line. She then set the pen next to the paper.

"Okay." I read the statement three times as Tracey typed on her computer keyboard. An officer came in and sat at the reception desk. I looked up and we exchanged nods of greeting. Finally, I picked up the pen and signed my name, surprised that my hand slightly shook.

"Thank you, Veronica," Tracey said when I put down the pen. She took the paper and placed it inside a manila folder.

I took a deep breath and relaxed. "I didn't think I'd be so nervous."

"I understand," she said. "We really appreciate your help."

"Did you get any fingerprints off the skillet? Do you have any persons of interest?"

"I'm sorry, Veronica, but I can't discuss the case with you."

"Okay."

She stood. "Thank you again for coming in," she said, indicating it was time for me to leave.

I stood and we shook hands. "Thank you, Tracey. Or should I call you Officer Brody? I've always called you Tracey, but I've never dealt with you on official police business. Should I be more formal?"

"Tracey's fine. And please let me know if you remember anything, or if you need anything."

"I will."

I left, saying goodbye to the officer at the reception desk, and hurried outside.

"Veronica!"

Hustling toward me was Charlotte Farrell, a reporter for our local paper, *The Chronicle*.

"Hi, Charlotte," I said.

"I'm covering the Anna Langdon murder case," she said, giving my hand a quick, firm shake. "I hear you found her body. Do you have a few minutes to talk?"

"Okay. Sure."

Charlotte gestured to a nearby bench. As we settled, she said, "Did you give your statement to the police?"

I nodded. "Yes. I just signed it."

"Are you all right? You're a bit pale." Charlotte opened her messenger bag and took out a note pad and pen.

"I'm okay, just finding this all surreal. I simply can't believe this happened in Barton."

"I can't, either. I've been with the paper ten years and this is my first murder. And it's stunning that Anna Langdon is the victim. I just spoke with her the other day about the mall. She was adamantly against it. It's interesting she was murdered just hours after she killed the deal." She paused and then said, "Poor choice of words. But it is interesting."

"It is." I shut my mouth; I certainly wasn't going to discuss possible motives with the press.

"So why were you at her house this morning?" she asked, her pen poised over a blank page.

I recounted the morning's events once more. Charlotte took

copious notes and when we finished, she thanked me and handed me her business card.

"Please call me, anytime," she said. We stood and shook hands again. "I hope our next interview is for something positive," she said.

You and me both, I thought, as I watched her hurry into the police station. This wasn't the kind of press I wanted.

CHAPTER SEVEN

"You need a strong one."

Carol said that to me as we huddled at our table at The Barton Hearth restaurant. As much as I wanted to have an alcoholic beverage, I thought it best not to indulge.

"I think I'll just have a ginger ale," I said.

"After the day you've had?" She gave me a long, almost disapproving, look.

"Especially after this morning," I replied. "I want to have full awareness, just in case."

"Maybe you shouldn't stay at your house. Come stay with Pat and me."

"I'm joking," I said. "Not that there's anything to joke about. But nothing's going to happen." I smiled and patted her hand. "Thanks."

We were silent for a few minutes as we read our menus. After our waitress took our order, I took a quick glance around. We sat at a corner table; a young couple fully absorbed in each other and three families with young children sat nearby. No one I recognized.

"I have to tell you something," I said in a hushed voice.

"What?" she whispered.

"Tim and Anna had—" I searched for the proper title for what they had. Affair? Fling? I really didn't know. "There was something between them."

Carol's eyes widened. "You're kidding? Anna and *Tim*?"

I nodded. "Yeah."

She leaned back, her face slack with disbelief. "How do you know? Did Tim tell you? Did Anna?"

I recounted the overheard conversation. "About five minutes after I arrived. Whatever happened between them, it was over and Tim wasn't happy about it."

"What did Tim see in her? She was such a shrew." Carol immediately looked chastened. "I shouldn't speak ill of the dead. May she rest in peace."

"Maybe Tim was lonely and needed companionship. Maybe there was a side to Anna she didn't let anyone see."

"Maybe. But wow."

"Anna made it clear that it was all just for fun. It didn't mean anything to her. And then last night, Tim and I overheard Anna and the mayor."

Carol's eyes became like huge round saucers. "Are you telling me Anna and Jason Quisenberry were *involved*? She was old enough to be his mother! And where were you and Tim?"

I quickly explained that set of circumstances. And the kiss between my fifty-year-old neighbor and the twenty-eight-year-old mayor.

"Tim left right after that. And he really didn't look happy."

"Poor guy. But wow. Anna and the mayor?"

I nodded. "Carol," I started and then saw our waitress coming with our drinks. I leaned back in my chair and waited. Carol anxiously played with the napkin in her lap. I leaned forward the second the waitress left. "I'm worried Tim's involved in Anna's murder."

Carol glared at me and snapped, "You can't be serious. Veronica, you can't really suspect Tim?"

"I don't know what to think. Tim was upset about the breakup, and then hours later he finds out it's because Anna's going out with Jason. A much younger man, may I emphasize."

Carol grimaced. "Tim? *Tim,* Veronica? You've known him for decades. Most of your life." She lowered her voice until she was barely audible. "You know he wouldn't murder someone. Certainly not because of a failed romance."

"I'm so worried about it. Carol, he wasn't in his office all day. Helen said he took the whole day off. What lawyer does that?"

Carol scratched her forehead and then rested her chin on her fist. "Well then call him and ask him."

"If he murdered Anna?"

"Where he was this morning. Just casual. You can say you wanted to go out to lunch. Or have dinner or something. And he wasn't around. Maybe he'll offer up the information."

I chewed on my lip as I considered the suggestion. "I could."

"You're making a big soap opera out of this," she joked. When I didn't respond, she became serious and asked, "Are you thinking of getting back together with Tim?"

Carol's suggestion startled me. "No. That hasn't even crossed my mind. He's just a friend. I care about him."

"Would it be so bad if you were a couple again?"

"I'm still looking for a new role," I responded fiercely. "This isn't a permanent visit."

"All right," Carol said, taking a sip of her white wine.

"So what about Jason? Do you think he could have killed Anna?"

Carol almost spat out her wine. She grabbed her napkin and blotted her lips. "Are you prepping for a role as Miss Marple?"

"I'm too young."

"Not so much. Just let your hair go gray." She smirked. "Now you suspect Jason?"

The waitress arrived with our salads. Carol and I waited in silence until she was gone.

"He didn't seem too happy about the deal Anna made with

Gary." I forked a cherry tomato and put it in my mouth.

"But angry enough to kill her?"

"Who knows?" I swallowed the tomato as a conspiracy came to mind. "He was also upset that Anna flirted with Thompson. I don't know when that happened. Maybe," I whispered, "he and Thompson had an under the table deal? As in money changing hands."

Carol arched her eyebrows as she chewed. I could tell she was beginning to take my suspicions seriously. "Perhaps," she finally said. "He is very pro-mall. I wonder if this means Gary's deal with the developer is back on."

I pointed my fork at her. "Another suspect."

"Gary or the developer?"

I considered that for a moment and said, "The developer. What does Gary care about what a buyer does with the land? He was obviously ready to sell it to a guy who would pave it over. And Anna was paying him fifty percent more."

"And how do you plan on investigating Thompson?" she asked.

I shrugged. "I'll figure something out. If it gets to that. But I bet the police will get to Thompson first. I'm sure they know what happened at last night's meeting. He's probably prime suspect number one."

We ate quietly for a few minutes as a toddler at one of the family tables became rambunctious.

"There's one more person," I said after the child's mother took the boy outside. Carol gave me an "Are you kidding?" glance and then leaned in, curious.

"Who?"

"This is the person who worries me most." I leaned forward and whispered, "Pauline."

Carol dropped her fork. "Pauline! I think she's capable of murder even less than Tim is. Why do you think she did it?"

"She owed rent. She was late on it every month. And yesterday I heard Anna tell her that if she didn't pay by this morning, she'd be evicted."

"Poor Pauline. How did you hear that?"

"Yesterday afternoon, in her store. Pauline and Anna were in the office when I got there." When Carol gave me a look as if I intentionally walked around the village eavesdropping, I added, "I swear, I tried to get out of the store. But Anna saw me."

Carol leaned her elbows against the table and clenched her hands, as if in prayer. "She and Glen must be in serious money trouble. He hasn't been selling houses. And I guess the store's not doing too well, either." She rubbed her temples. "I don't want to even think about it."

"Not happy thoughts, I agree. But if Pauline was at her wits end . . ."

Carol narrowed her gaze. "What did you tell the police?"

"Nothing," I said. "No way am I going to share what I know with the police. I'm not going to point the finger at people who could very well be innocent."

"Good."

"I just have to figure out how to get alibis from all of them without them knowing I'm asking for alibis."

"You've been on a soap too long," Carol chastised, shaking her head. "Come back to reality, Veronica. This is a murder investigation. That's no place for you."

"A little nosing around won't do any harm."

Carol glared at me. "Yes, it could."

I set my fork on the plate. "If only I had come home a few days later, I wouldn't be involved in this at all."

"If only. Let's not talk about this anymore."

"Agreed."

"We'll talk about your job situation. And then you'll go home and get a good night's sleep. And tomorrow morning you'll call

Tim. He'll have a perfectly sensible explanation for taking the day off. And then everything will be fine and you can let the police do their job."

"From your lips," I murmured.

Carol and I enjoyed a delicious meal and said good night in the parking lot behind the restaurant.

"You're sure you don't want to stay with us tonight?" she asked.

"I'll be fine," I assured her. We hugged and she headed to her car. My phone rang as I reached my car at the other end of the lot.

"Veronica!" Mark exclaimed when I answered.

"Hi, Mark," I said, surprised because I didn't think he had my cell phone number.

He quickly explained, saying, "Your mother gave me your number. I heard about your morning and was concerned. I went by the bookstore, thinking you'd be there."

"Thanks, Mark," I said, touched. "That's so sweet. Some news, isn't it?"

"It's unbelievable. Are you okay?" he asked. "That's not a very nice welcome home you got at Anna's."

"No, it wasn't. But I'm all right. I'm over the shock."

"You're sure?"

"Yes. Thank you."

"Are you staying with your mother tonight? You won't be in your house alone, will you?"

"I'm not worried about being alone," I said. "I bet the killer is already long gone from Barton."

"If you're sure," he said. "But let me give you my number, in case you need anything."

I smiled at his thoughtfulness, grabbed a pen and a scrap of paper from my purse, and jotted down his number. "Thanks for calling, Mark. I appreciate it."

We said good night and I dropped the phone back in my purse. It felt good to have so many people worried about me.

Dusk was about to turn to night when I turned into my driveway. A chill went down my spine when I saw the police tape across Anna's front door. A patrol car and two other cars stood in front of Anna's house. Ron Nicholstone stood on the front lawn with Jason and Charlotte Farrell.

Interesting. I pulled up to my garage, wondering if anyone in the village knew about Anna and the mayor.

I glanced in the rearview mirror to spy Jason walking up my driveway. I braced myself and turned off the engine.

"Hi, Jason," I said as I slid from the car.

"Veronica," he said.

I shut the car door and took furtive peeks around the area, searching for Charlotte and Ron. I could hear their voices drifting up from the street.

"Do you have a moment?" he asked.

"Sure," I said. Normally I would turn into my backyard and go into my house through the kitchen. That was when a murder investigation wasn't taking place yards from said kitchen.

I casually strolled down the driveway, leading the mayor to my front porch. The police car would be within my view, and I would be within view of the police officer, reporter, and my neighbors. My voice would be within their hearing range, if circumstances necessitated a scream.

"How are you?" Jason asked as we climbed the porch steps. "This is quite a shock."

"It is," I said. I crossed the porch and settled in a wicker chair. "I'm fine. And you?"

"I'm stunned. I can't believe this happened in Barton. And to someone so prominent in the village," he said as he sat in the chair beside mine.

Two cars drove slowly past Anna's house, braking for a few seconds right in front of it. Jason and I shook our heads at the drivers' rubbernecking.

"Do you know if the police have any leads? I asked when I was at the station this afternoon to sign my statement, but of course they won't tell me anything."

He shook his head. "Not yet." He paused and then asked, "There's nothing you heard or saw?" He turned to me, a plaintive look on his face.

"Just a car backfiring. It woke me early this morning. It may be connected, it may not."

Charlotte said goodbye to Ron and walked to her car.

"Nothing else? Did you notice anything in the last few days?"

I paused as Charlotte started her car. There was much I wanted to blurt out, like "I know you visited Anna last night after the meeting. I heard you two arguing about the farm deal. I heard you kissing."

But authority is a funny thing. Even though Jason was young enough to be my son, he was the one with the clout. A whisper to the cops from him would more quickly cast suspicion on me than vice versa, I knew. If he really wanted to put the screws to me, he could raise my taxes in the snap of a finger.

"I got home yesterday," I told him as I studied his expression. Was he quizzing me to learn if I knew about him and Anna?

"Oh," he said. "Some welcome home."

"Yeah."

Charlotte finally pulled away while Ron walked to the back of Anna's house. Another car came down the street, slowing for a moment to check out the crime scene.

"We should close the street off," Jason mumbled.

We sat in silence for a few moments. Jason broke it by asking, "Are you staying here tonight?"

I nodded. "Yes."

"You'll be all right alone? Or will someone be with you?"

I softened, touched by his concern. I then toughened, my overactive imagination considering he might be asking for details to come back and kill me, the sole (sort of) witness to Anna's murder.

"Yes," I said. He could take that either way. Yes, I would be alone. Yes, someone would be with me.

I wondered if the animal shelter was still open at that hour. I had a sudden need for a huge German shepherd.

"Thank you for talking with me, Veronica," Jason said as he rose.

I stood. "You're welcome, Jason."

He held out his hand. Taking it, I looked into his eyes and saw a look I couldn't quite interpret. Was he heartbroken because someone he cared for was dead? Or was that a look of guilt?

Or was I seeing something that wasn't there? I was a drama queen for thirty-two years. I have a talent for heightening the suspense. Backed by excellent writing, line reading, especially in between, is what I do.

Jason descended the porch steps, stopping at the bottom to turn and say, without irony, "Welcome home."

"Thanks."

I watched as he crossed my driveway and around the hedge to Anna's backyard. My neighbor, Ellen Gleason, came from her house and caught my attention with a wave and call of my name. I walked down my lawn as she hurried across the street.

"What did the mayor have to say?" she asked.

"Nothing, really. He just asked how I am and said how stunned he is."

"An understatement," Ellen said, her eyes widening. "I feel so guilty I didn't hear or see anything." Tears welled in her eyes.

I patted my sixty-year-old neighbor's arm to comfort her. "I didn't hear anything, either."

"That frightens me," she said. "I like to think we look out for each other, but when we were needed the most, we were completely unaware."

I nodded. "The police will make an arrest very soon, I'm sure."

I glanced over to her house. Her husband, Ted, stood just inside their screen door. We waved to each other.

He opened the screen door and called, "Are you all right, Veronica?"

"I am. Thanks, Ted."

Ellen looked up at the sky. "We should get inside before it's pitch black. Would you like to stay with us tonight?"

I appreciated her invitation, but declined. "You're very kind," I said.

"If you change your mind, just come over."

"Thanks."

As Ellen walked back to her house, the slam of a car door and the hum of an engine pulled my attention back to Anna's just as Jason pulled away from the curb. He waved as he passed my house.

A sudden chill went up my arms. Did I really want to spend the night alone?

I dug my cell phone from my pocket and called my mother.

"Is my old room available for the night?" I asked when she answered.

"Of course," she said.

I went inside and packed an overnight bag. I wasn't going to take chances on how Jason had interpreted my "yes."

CHAPTER EIGHT

I pulled into Mom's driveway, blocking in a car that wasn't hers. Four more cars took up the space that stretched between Mom's walkway and the neighbor's driveway.

Mom stepped onto the porch as I climbed the steps. "What's going on?" I asked.

She clicked her tongue and said, "Anita, Nick, Evelyn, and I were going to say the rosary for Anna."

"That's very nice," I said, ready to join the prayer circle.

"But just as we got started, Wendy knocked on the door, wanting to talk about Anna. And then Chloe, Dana, Jessica, and Andrea from the hair salon showed up."

"Why?"

My mother gave me a look. "We're the elders of Orchard," she said. "Evelyn told Jessica we'd be here, so they all came here for comfort. They're scared."

"They're not the only ones," I said, holding up my overnight bag.

"You, I understand." Mom linked her arm through mine. "Hopefully they won't stay too long."

The group sat in the living room, some drinking coffee and tea, others wine. When I entered, they all jumped from their seats and hurried to give me a hug. When we all settled, Wendy handed me a glass of red wine, while Mom put a mug of chamomile tea on the table in front of me. I accepted both without comment.

"Did the police interview all of you?" Andrea asked.

Heads nodded and there were a few "uh-huhs."

"They talked with all of Anna's tenants," Evelyn Alcott said. "I'm sure they've talked, or will talk, with anyone who did business with her. They want all the information on Anna's life they can get."

"Veronica, what have the police told you?" Nick asked. "You must know more than we do."

I shook my head. "Not really. They don't think it was a robbery, and there were no fingerprints on the skillet."

Jessica shuddered. "It chills me to think Anna knew her killer. That means we may know the person, too."

"It's likely," Wendy said, her expression grim. "Even though Barton is large enough that we don't know everyone, we're still a small village."

We were quiet for a moment as we contemplated Wendy's words. Andrea gave me a darting glance, and then moved her stare to Wendy, and then Jessica. Jessica looked over to Dana, who shot a look at Nick.

"Don't look at me," Nick said.

"Nick was in the kitchen from five a.m. until eleven," Anita said, her sharp eyes fixed on Dana. "Shame on you for even thinking of him."

"I wasn't!" Dana said.

Chloe hugged herself. "I can't bear to think that it's someone we know. I don't think I'm going to be able to sleep until they find the killer."

Dana put her arm around her sister. "It could have been someone from her past," she said. "We really don't know much about Anna's life before she moved here."

"Maybe she had a secret lover," Andrea said.

"Someone she jilted to marry Mr. Frazer," said Jessica.

"And he waited all this time to seek revenge?" Wendy asked,

her tone dripping sarcasm.

Jessica shrugged. "Maybe."

"Or maybe she had two lovers, and she dumped one for the other," Chloe said.

Her words hit very close to the mark. I stared at my two beverages, hoping there would be no further digging.

"There's a lot about Anna we don't know," Dana said.

"So we should stop speculating," Mom said. "And stop making this a drama fit for a soap opera."

Everyone laughed as Mom gave me a deferential nod.

"I agree," Evelyn said. "An innocent person's life could be ruined by baseless accusations."

"Veronica," Andrea asked, "was there anyone working at Anna's this morning? A lawn service? Plumber?"

"Not that I know of," I said. "I didn't see anyone around her house."

"That happens a lot," Jessica said. "Women are assaulted by men they let in to do work in their home."

Chloe brightened. "It could have been someone who does work at her house. They didn't necessarily have to be working there this morning."

"I don't even have my own voice on my home answering machine," Andrea said. "I left the prerecorded response with a male voice on so that people think a man lives in the house."

"Those factory messages are annoying," Wendy said. Andrea glowered at her. "I always think I've called the wrong number."

"Nick recorded our message," Anita said.

"That's good," said Andrea. "Does everyone know self-defense? You must know it, Veronica, having worked in the city all those years."

"The city's not that dangerous," I said. "I used my common sense. I didn't walk down dark alleys. I didn't roam the streets at three a.m."

"You were never mugged?" Andrea asked. She seemed to want danger to lurk at every corner.

"No. Though I would have followed Mom's advice and just handed over my purse."

"That's my girl," said Mom.

"You wouldn't defend yourself?" Andrea asked, incredulous.

"Not if I had a gun pointed at me. But I know how to fight. I've been in plenty of catfights. Scratch at the eyes. Kick the kneecaps. Pull 'em down by their ankles."

Mom, Evelyn, and Anita laughed as Chloe said, "You rocked those scenes."

"Those were staged fights. But what if someone grabs you?" Andrea asked, looking around the group. "Does everyone know what to do?"

"I carry my car key so that if someone grabs me, I can poke his eyes out," Wendy said.

"I carry a bottle of perfume, to use like mace," Evelyn said.

"Very clever, Evelyn," Mom said.

"That's great," Andrea said dully. She stood. "I can show everyone a few moves right now. Nick, you be the aggressor."

Nick, a gentleman in his sixties, was taken aback by her request.

"Oh, no," his wife said. "He's the baker. Nothing can happen to him."

"I'm not going to hurt him."

"No," Anita replied.

I was on the couch; Nick sat across the room in a corner chair. Our eyes locked for a moment and Nick smiled, obviously happy with his wife's interference.

"Wendy," Andrea said.

"It's been a long day. I'm worn out."

Andrea rolled her eyes in exasperation. "Dana, will you be the bad guy?"

"Sure," Dana said. She set her wine glass on the table and jumped from the sofa. "Just be careful with my right arm. That's my coffee-pouring arm," she teased.

"I certainly wouldn't want to injure my barista's arm. You supply my caffeine fix every day," Andrea said. "Now stand behind me." The two moved to the space between the couches and fireplace. "And put your arm around my neck."

Dana did as Andrea directed. "I've got you, my pretty," she said, cackling.

"Very funny. Now, when you're in this situation," Andrea said to our group, "you want to injure the person where it will hurt the most. So you do this."

Andrea lightly jabbed Dana in the stomach twice with her left elbow, and then used her left arm to push away the arm Dana had around Andrea's neck. Andrea then used her elbow to knock Dana in the jaw.

"Wow," Chloe said.

"What about the family jewels?" Dana asked.

"You can do that, too," Andrea said. "After you smack him in the jaw, you can do this with your knee." She grasped Dana's shoulders and gave her a *faux* jolt to the groin.

"That will teach them who's boss," Jessica said.

I saw Anita give Nick a look that quite clearly said, "Look what I saved you from."

I turned my attention back to Andrea, who was demonstrating the self-defense move in the case of someone grabbing you by the wrist.

"Everyone got that?" she asked after she had shoved her knee in Dana's groin and pushed her away with a palm to the chin.

"Uh-huh," several said.

"Okay. Now Jessica, you attack Dana. And Wendy, I know you're tired, but attack Chloe."

Wendy sighed, but did as requested. As everyone got into

position, I grabbed my mug and wine glass and made a beeline into the hall and down to the kitchen. I wasn't in the mood to attack or be attacked, even if only in simulation.

I put the wine glass in the sink and took a sip of the lukewarm tea. I leaned against the counter and closed my eyes, anxious for the day's end.

The floor creaked and I twitched, opening my eyes to find Dana coming into the kitchen.

"Sorry," she said.

"That's all right. I'm just hiding out."

Dana shook her head. "Some people think a serial killer is on the loose." She took a mug from the mug tree on the counter and crossed to the coffee maker.

"I certainly hope not."

"I think it was personal. Most murders are, aren't they?" She picked up the half-full pot of coffee and filled her mug. "What I'm more worried about is who is going to buy the buildings. Anna was a difficult landlady, but at least we knew what to expect. Better the devil you know."

"It will take time. Don't worry until you have to."

"Easy to say, hard to do. What if the new landlord raises my rent?" She set the pot down with a thud as a panicked look froze her face. "What if that mall developer buys the buildings, and does a whole re-do on Orchard?"

"Dana, stop getting yourself into a frazzle over the what-if's."

"Uh-huh. Easy for you to say, hard for me to do." Dana sipped her coffee as we stood in silence for a few moments.

"It's all right," I heard Wendy say from the hall. She entered the kitchen, massaging her shoulder.

Chloe followed. "I'm sorry, Wendy. Are you sure you're okay?"

"Yes. You were just a little too enthusiastic." Wendy patted Chloe on the back and gave her a smile. "The bad guys better stay away from you."

While Wendy added tap water to the kettle and set it on the stove to boil, Chloe poured herself a mug of coffee and took a few big gulps.

"Don't you think you're jittery enough as it is?" Dana asked her. "That's only going to keep you awake."

"No it won't. This is just what I need to calm my nerves."

"Okay," Dana replied. "I think I'll go back and learn some more self-defense moves."

Chloe topped off her mug with more coffee and followed her sister back to the living room.

"People need to get a grip," Wendy said.

"Dana's worried about what's going to happen with Anna's properties," I said. "She's concerned her rent will be raised."

"She has a point." Wendy gave me a curious look. "What Chloe said about Anna having two lovers. Do you know something?"

"What makes you ask that?"

"You just had an odd look on your face when she said it."

"The guessing game bothered me. Like Mom said, let's stop the speculation."

Wendy stared at me for a moment and said, "It would be better if we all stopped trying to guess who did it. We don't want anyone else to get hurt."

"No, we don't."

The kettle whistled. "Would you like more tea?"

"No, thanks."

Wendy poured water into her mug and dunked a tea bag in the water several times before dumping the bag in the garbage can.

"I'll chase everyone out of here in a bit so you can get to bed. You must be exhausted."

"Thanks."

She left the kitchen, leaving me to consider all the speculative arrows that had been shot that night.

Chapter Nine

I had a fairly good night's sleep, considering the day's events. The familiarity of my childhood home certainly comforted me. Mom and I had a quick breakfast before she headed to the bookstore.

"Why don't you stay here until they find the killer?" she asked as she rinsed her coffee mug.

"Thanks, Mom, but I'll be fine at home. I'm over my jitters."

"Are you sure?" she asked as her mouth drooped into a worried frown.

"I'm sure," I said, giving her a hug.

I returned to my house to drop off my overnight bag. Gone was the police car, remaining was the crime scene tape across the front door.

I parked at the top of the driveway, grabbed my bag from the back seat, and began to walk toward my house. A few steps into the yard and my curiosity got the best of me. I turned around and looked up at Anna's house, debating whether or not I really should go over there. Just to see what I could see.

I dumped my bag on the picnic table and walked back to my driveway. I noticed there was no police tape blocking the space between the hedge. So I darted around it.

Easy enough, I told myself as I took a deep breath. I stood on Anna's side of the hedge for a moment, ready to run at the first sign of anyone or anything. Maybe I wasn't completely over my jitters.

Finally, I crossed her driveway and stepped onto the lawn, my eyes fixed on the kitchen door. Yellow tape blocked it as well. I stopped at the base of the porch steps, glancing all around me. I guess I thought a crime-solving clue would suddenly appear. Or that I would be caught and arrested for tampering with a murder scene.

Since neither a clue nor a law enforcer materialized, I slowly stole up the steps and across the pine boards. A Roman shade covered the door's glass pane, so I turned to the window. The drawn lace curtains shaded the kitchen from light, but did not provide complete privacy from a Peeping Tom (or Veronica). I braced myself before looking in, thinking of every scary movie I had ever seen. If this were a movie, I would not see my reflection in the window, but the terrifying visage of a killer.

"Nonsense," I mumbled.

With one knee leaning on the wicker chair under the window and my face inches from the glass, I squinted to see into the kitchen.

Everything was as it had been twenty-four hours earlier, except two things had been removed—Anna's body and the murder weapon.

"Hello."

The simple word of greeting so startled me that I jolted, lost my balance, fell forward against the chair, and slid down it. I recovered quickly, turning to find Tracey standing at the foot of the steps, her hands on her hips. She gave me a good-natured smile.

My face burned with embarrassment. "Good morning, Tracey," I said as calmly as I could as I stepped away from the window. I prayed she'd be so distracted by my scarlet blush that she wouldn't hear my heart pounding.

"How are you this morning, Veronica?"

"I'm fine. And you?" I hoped that if we exchanged enough

pleasantries, she would completely forget what she just saw me doing.

"Very well. Thank you for asking. I'm here to let the cleaner in. He'll be here in a few minutes."

"Okay." Surely she expected me to explain my presence. Instead, I scampered across the porch and down the steps. "I'll get out of the way."

Tracey climbed the steps, pulled the tape from the door, and unlocked it with a key taken from her pocket. She turned and regarded me, flashing the same polite smile.

I hastily offered my apologies. "I'm sorry, I just—"

She held up her hand, saying, "I understand. You have a particular interest in the case."

I nodded my gratitude.

"But you should stay away."

"I know. But I couldn't . . . help myself. Do you have any leads?"

"No."

"Any suspects?"

"No."

A van pulled up the driveway; I turned to see that it was the Adirondack Cleaning Service. A nice, nondescript name for a crime scene cleaner.

"I guess you won't answer any of my questions," I said.

"No," Tracey answered.

"I had to try," I said, shrugging. Then I added, "It was so much easier on the soap."

"TV makes everything look easier," she said. "Even reality shows. Except the soaps always drag the storyline out. It takes months to find the killer, when in real life, the case is usually solved quickly."

"It's all about the ratings," I said dryly.

"True."

The door to the van slammed shut and a man appeared from around it a few seconds later.

"I'll get out of the way," I said, starting to walk across the yard. "Thank you for your understanding."

"Don't worry, Veronica. We're going to find out who killed Ms. Langdon." She took a few steps toward me. "If it eases your apprehension, we don't believe it was random. There was no forced entry—"

"So Anna knew the killer and let him, or her, in?"

"We think so."

It did make me feel a bit better. "Thank you, Tracey."

"You're welcome. Hello, Mr. Campbell," she said to the cleaner, who had just walked into the yard.

"Good morning, Officer Brody." He nodded to me and said hello.

I gave him a polite nod and retraced my path across the driveway and around the hedge.

Back in my own yard, I grabbed my bag, unlocked the kitchen door, and hustled inside. Walking through my house, I dropped the bag at the foot of the stairs and went back outside through the front door. I slackened my pace as I headed down the path, in case Tracey was watching.

I had a sudden thought as I turned onto the sidewalk and headed for Orchard. Anna had a housekeeper. As of my last visit home, Sandy Jenkins was the woman who cleaned Anna's house. She surely still was, and she just might have a tidbit or two of information.

I landed on Orchard and rounded the corner of All Things just as Claire was approaching the shop. She carried a tall cup of coffee from The Caffs.

"Hi, Claire," I said.

She stopped, regarded me for a moment as if I had said

something rude, and then smiled. "Veronica. Hello."

"How are you doing?" I asked, noting her wan cheeks. Her copper hair, normally pulled into a bun or ponytail, hung loose around her face. Her casual attire of chinos, a blouse, and loafers, normal for Orchard Street, was unusual for Claire. Per Anna's dress code, Claire normally donned pantsuits or skirts in her job as manager of All Things. Now I was looking at the real Claire, the woman who was Edward Frazer's right hand at All Things Adirondack.

"All right, all things considered. It's still hard to believe Anna's gone. I'm processing it." She fingered the collar of her blouse.

"I guess you're getting all the phone calls and dealing with . . . things," I said.

"Yes. I'm helping until her family arrives. Her brother will be up later today to arrange things. They're going to bury her in Saratoga, in her family's plot."

"Will there be any type of service here?"

"There will be a memorial service. I think we'll wait until things have calmed down and the police have made an arrest."

"I just saw Tracey Brody. She said they have no leads."

"I'm sure they will soon," Claire said, looking away. I followed her glance across the street; Pauline was unlocking the door of her shop.

"Hi, Pauline," she called.

Pauline's shoulders twitched and she turned. She seemed to force a smile and waved.

"Hey, Claire. Hi, Veronica."

I said good morning and asked how she was.

"Plugging along," she said. She waved again and went into her store.

I turned back to Claire. "Do you know why Anna wanted to talk with me yesterday morning? You knew we were going to have breakfast."

Claire shook her head and stared into the street. "I have no idea."

"She said yesterday she had a business proposal."

"Oh, really? I don't know anything about it."

We regarded each other for a moment. "You were at her house yesterday morning. To drop off the pastries."

Claire clenched her jaw. "Yes. I saw Anna very briefly. I just dropped off the box and left. I didn't even go inside."

"And was anyone with Anna? Did she seem okay?"

Claire laughed. "Are you starting a new career as a detective, Veronica? Or are you doing research for a role? Method acting, right?"

I smiled and said, "Oh, no. I'm just curious. Anna was my neighbor. And I did find her."

"That must have been terrible," Claire said with a click of her tongue.

"It was. So you have no thoughts on who would kill her?" I looked at her squarely, trying to convey compassionate interest rather than plain old nosiness.

Claire shrugged and shook her head. "There are a few people who didn't really like Anna. She had a very forceful personality. She turned some people off. I'm sure you know that. But I don't think any of them would have killed her." She pointed at the shop door. "I need to get inside and get ready for the day."

"Of course. I'm sorry I kept you. Thanks for talking. If there's anything I can do, please let me know," I said.

"Thanks," she said as she turned and hurried into the shop.

"Hmmph," I declared. "Either she knows nothing, or she knows everything."

I continued along the sidewalk, crossing the alley that separated All Things from the building that stretched the rest of the block. I passed the pet shop, pausing for a moment to look at the beautiful exotic birds in the window. As I approached the bookstore, Wendy stepped outside, lighting a cigarette as the door closed behind her.

"Good morning, Wendy," I said.

She jumped and spun on her heels to face me. "Veronica," she said. "You caught me."

"Doing what?" I asked.

Wendy took a long drag on the cigarette and blew the smoke away from me. "Anna never liked me smoking on the sidewalk. She insisted that I smoke out back, in the alley. She was such a bit—" She stopped before completing the insult. "I shouldn't speak ill of the dead. She was a real pest about it. She didn't care about my health, like Nancy does. Anna just didn't like how it looked. So I humored her and smoked out back. But there's more to see out front and it's quicker to just step out here. But I'll think of Anna, with love, when I do it," she ended with a smirk.

"Aha."

Wendy took another puff. "I thought it was rich of Anna to tell Thompson she wasn't going to let him take over *her* village. She thought of Barton as *her* village. And acted like it was."

"Well . . ."

"I'll stop," Wendy said. "And be nice."

"Good idea."

She took a final puff of her cigarette and extinguished it in the "sandbox" on top of a nearby trashcan. "Now I can start the day," she said.

"I hope it's a good one," I said.

"For you, too."

She went back into the bookstore and I hurried along, anxious to get to Tim's office.

"Good morning, Veronica," Helen greeted me as I stepped into the waiting area.

73

"Good morning, Helen. Is Tim here?" I asked, trying to keep my tone light.

"Yes, he is. I'll tell him you're here." She walked down a short hallway, turning right into the last office. I waited, taking deep breaths to calm my nerves.

Helen returned in a few moments. With an amiable smile she said, "Tim will be with you in a minute, Veronica. Please, have a seat."

"Thanks, Helen."

I sat on the firm beige couch under the window and began to tap my feet to the rhythm of Helen's typing. It was as if I were at the doctor's office, awaiting news of my fate. Or at an audition, awaiting news of my fate.

Tim appeared a few minutes later, grinning broadly as he strolled down the hallway. "Hey, Veronica."

I stood, relieved by his relaxed demeanor. He put his hands on my elbows and kissed me on the cheek.

"Are you okay? I heard you found Anna . . ."

"I'm fine. Do you have a few minutes?"

"I'm overloaded with work since I was out yesterday," he said. "How about we have lunch?"

"Okay," I said. I hid my disappointment over having to wait a few more hours for answers. Anticipation is sometimes wonderful, sometimes not.

"How's twelve at The Hearth?" he asked.

"Perfect."

"Great. I'll see you then." He patted me on the arm and then trotted back to his office.

"Have a good day," I said to Helen as I headed for the door.

"Why do I have to wait?" I whined to Carol ten minutes later.

"That wasn't long," she said, thinking I was complaining about the call she was on when I entered her store.

"No, not you." I explained about Tim.

"So do something to take your mind off it," she suggested. "Go to the bookstore and help your mother."

"You're no help," I complained.

"Oh, well."

"And Claire is of no help, either. That girl says nothing." I told her about my conversation with Claire.

"She's tight-lipped, that one," Carol said. "Always plays it close to the vest."

"How unhelpful." I considered telling Carol about my conversation with Tracey, and the embarrassing start to it. If I couldn't tell my best friend, whom could I tell?

"I also talked with Tracey Brody this morning. I met her in Anna's backyard," I tentatively began.

"What were you doing in Anna's backyard?"

"Looking in the window," I said. "I fell on the porch furniture."

"I think this is a sign that you should stay out of this," Carol said when she stopped laughing. "Tracey didn't make a big deal of it, but you know Chief Price would had he caught you. I'm not going to think about what the killer would do if you got too close."

I nodded at her sage advice. Glancing out the window, I spotted Sandy Jenkins rush by, as if she were running a marathon.

"Gotta go," I said as I slid from the stool. "I'll see you later."

From the amused expression I glimpsed on her face as I hurried out, I knew that she knew I wasn't taking her advice.

"We really need to find you a job," she called to me.

"From your lips!" I yelled in reply.

I jogged up the sidewalk, dodging pedestrians as I looked for Sandy. I spotted her, dressed in jeans, a loose polo shirt, and snow-white tennis sneakers, ducking into the dry cleaner's.

I waited outside, catching my breath. A woman in her early seventies came up to me.

"You're Veronica Walsh, aren't you?" she excitedly asked me.

"Yes," I nodded, my gaze flitting between her and the shop door.

"I'm going to miss *Days and Nights* so much!"

"Me, too," I said. I tried to give the woman my full attention as I waited for Sandy.

"I've watched the show from the very beginning," she gushed. "I've always loved you!"

"Thank you. Thank you so much," I said, meaning it. "What is your name?"

"Alice Weaver. May I get a picture with you?" Alice asked just as Sandy came from the dry cleaner's. She carried several items wrapped in plastic.

"Of course," I said. "Sandy!" I yelled before she could make her getaway.

Sandy turned, exasperated until she saw it was me. "Veronica!"

"Can you take our picture?" I asked as Alice pulled her cell phone from her purse.

"I'm so excited. I can't wait to tell my friends back home in New Jersey," she said. She quickly showed Sandy how to take a picture.

I put my arm around Alice's shoulder and smiled as Sandy took the photograph, and then a second at Alice's request.

"Thank you so much, Ms. Walsh!" an excited Alice said. She threw her arms around me.

"Call me Veronica," I said as she squeezed me. "Sandy, I need to talk to you." I waved as Sandy made to leave.

"Then hurry up," she said with a hiss.

I extricated myself from Alice's arms. "Thank you, Alice."

"Good luck to you, Veronica," she said, pleased to call me by name.

"Thank you," I repeated, touched by her good wishes. I realized such fan encounters would now be sparse to nonexistent. "And thank you for watching all these years." Over Alice's shoulder, I saw Sandy give me an impatient look. She tapped her watch and shook a finger at me.

"God bless you," Alice said, patting my cheek.

"And God bless you," I said. "Sweet lady," I said to Sandy as Alice left.

"Yes. Now if you want to talk, you're going to have to come to the Food Mart with me." She restarted her supercharged walk up the street.

"All right," I said, already needing to jog to catch her.

We burned sneaker rubber past Carol's. She happened to be standing at the window as we passed; I waved and gave her a big smile, giggling at her bewildered response.

When we reached her mini-van, Sandy arranged the dry cleaning in the back and then practically shoved me into the front passenger seat.

A shiver of apprehension raised goose bumps on my arm as I fastened my seat belt. I had no fear that Sandy had anything to do with Anna's death. There is no way she would have left the scene in such disorder. Rather, after seeing her charge down Orchard as if shot from a cannon, I worried that I was riding shotgun with a kamikaze pilot at the wheel.

CHAPTER TEN

Two years younger, I followed Sandy through twelve years of school, her reputation trailing her like a comet's blazing tail. She was The Neat Freak, a moniker that changed to the more elegant The Meticulous One in her adult years. She was then, and remains, a powerhouse of cleanliness.

In grammar school, two cloth napkins spread across her desk served as a lunchtime tablecloth. In high school, she Windexed the outside of her locker every day, and the inside on Fridays. The nuns adored her and her mother was one of the most rested women in Barton, for all the housework Sandy gladly did. Sandy taught third grade for a few years until she and her husband, Sam, started their family. When it came time to go back to work, Sandy decided to skip the "sticky-fingered, runny-nosed" tykes and follow her natural calling, house hygiene. She has almost single-handedly kept Barton squeaky clean.

On the way to the supermarket I learned Sandy and Sam had an event-planning daughter in Boston and another daughter, a forensic accountant, in Albany. Plus a cocker spaniel named Daisy who knew not to look in the direction of the living room, for a lock of fur might separate from her body and infiltrate the carpet or cling to the Queen Anne sofa. Sam boasts that his car, no matter how old, always has that "new car" smell.

We arrived at the Food Mart a few minutes later, after rolling through three stop signs, turning a sharp corner sans brake application, and narrowly missing a woman pushing her groceries and a three-year-old child in a shopping cart. I slid from the car, my nerves a bit jangled, but okay.

"I have a lot to get and little time," Sandy said from her side of the car. "I hate when people leave their carts in the middle of parking spots." She grabbed the offending cart and pushed it toward the entry. She corralled another cart and gestured for me to push it. She dropped a canvas bag stuffed with several more on the seat of her cart.

Sandy pulled a folded sheet of paper from her purse. When she unfolded it I saw that there was print on both sides, words typed into sections separated by bold lines.

"Wow!" I exclaimed. "That's some shopping list."

"I shop for several families," she explained. "The Mastersons. Montgomerys. Griffins. The Collins, who have six children. I do it all in one fell swoop."

I wondered what the employees of Food Mart thought of her swoop. Sandy was great for business, but I pitied the cashier who had to checkout and bag two cartfuls of goods. "Sandy, can we talk about Anna?" I asked as I kept up with her pace.

Sandy stopped and grabbed my arm. "It's so disturbing, isn't it? And in her own home." She resumed walking, turning the corner at the checkout lanes and heading to the produce section. "Some say she was very tough. I never had a problem with her. We had the same standards of excellence. We got along great."

"Good."

"I heard the kitchen is a mess. You saw it. Is it?"

"Yes," I said, surprised that she didn't fuss and fret over any trauma I might have suffered from finding Anna's body. I was glad. "Her china was broken and scattered across the floor."

Sandy clicked her tongue. "That's a beautiful set."

We stopped in front of the tomatoes. As Sandy tested them

with firm squeezes, dropping several into a plastic bag, I said, "The crime scene cleaner came this morning to clean up."

Sandy gasped and looked at me with a fierce stare. "Are you kidding me?" She put the bag in my cart.

"No," I said, swallowing hard as I realized I had uttered the very thing that should have remained unsaid.

"I told the police I would do that. Chief Price said a professional would clean, but I insisted I would do it. I'm a professional." She stomped over to the bananas. "He was just humoring me," she said bitterly. She grabbed a few bunches of bananas and put them beside the tomatoes.

"Maybe he was just sparing your feelings. He probably felt it would be too upsetting for you."

"Phht," Sandy uttered. "Now I'll have to clean up after the cleaners."

I changed the subject as we headed to the meat case. "Sandy, do you know anyone who had a problem with Anna? Someone who would want to harm her?" I hoped that Sandy had overheard something while cleaning the toilet, or found something incriminating, like hate mail, while dusting the mantel.

"I can't think of anyone who would *really* hurt her," Sandy answered. "I mind my own business when I'm cleaning someone's home," she said with pride. "I want people to know they can trust me with their personal stuff."

"That's a good rule," I agreed, mentally snapping my fingers and silently saying, "Drats!"

"Usually, Anna wasn't home when I was there. But, as we all know, Anna had friction with just about everyone," Sandy said. She grabbed a few packages of chicken, checked the date, and tossed them into her cart. She hurried over to the steaks and did the same grab, check, and toss. "Maybe someone just finally had it and snapped."

"Maybe," I muttered.

"And with that skillet. She only used that pan to tone her arms."

"Huh."

I went through the store with Sandy, divulging the secrets of the last show of *Days and Nights* as she loaded both carts. It was either that or listen to her expound for four aisles on the merits of every cleaning item on the shelves.

My chance for escape came after we had loaded all the bags in her mini-van. "Where are you going?" Sandy asked. "Do you want me to drop you off at the bookstore? I could drive you home."

I interpreted "dropoff" as more of a push from the moving vehicle. "No, thanks," I replied. "It's such a nice day, I'll walk."

"All right," she said. "Thanks for keeping me company." She slammed down the car's back door and gave me a quick hug.

Two minutes later, as I was still crossing the parking lot, her van screeched onto the street and roared out of view.

"God bless," I murmured. I walked down Orchard, disappointed that Sandy didn't have anything to tell me about Anna, but grateful that she occupied some time as I waited to meet Tim. I spent the rest of the morning at the bookstore shelving books. Mindless work, yes, but welcome after my workout with Sandy.

CHAPTER ELEVEN

I arrived at The Hearth early and waited about five minutes for Tim. He breezed through the restaurant to our table in the corner, a wide smile on his face. He looked handsome in his white starched shirt and pale green tie. I smiled as he took the seat across from me.

"Hi," I said.

"Hey. I heard a rumor that you were spotted in a mini-van with Sandy Jenkins at the wheel." Tim wore a mischievous grin.

"True."

"What were you thinking?"

"I was catching up with an old friend. The time just flew by."

Tim chuckled. "You were always up for an adventure."

"How did you hear I was with Sandy?"

"Sue."

"Oh."

I wondered if I should ask more just as the waitress came over to give us menus and take our drink orders. When she left, Tim reached across the table and placed his warm hand over mine.

"Are you okay?" he asked, suddenly very serious.

"Yeah. Sandy isn't that reckless a driver."

"I meant about finding Anna."

"I'm okay," I said, nodding. I had planned to work the conversation around to Anna, but here we were talking about her before we even had our sodas.

"I can't believe it," Tim said, pulling his hand away and leaning back.

I stared down at my fork and said, "Tim, I heard the conversation you had with Anna in her backyard." I slowly moved my gaze up to Tim's face.

He looked away, silent for an excruciating moment. He turned back, met my stare for a moment, and then looked down at the table.

"We had a very brief relationship. The last few months have been hard. I know Anna can be very harsh, but she also has her charm."

I interrupted Tim. "You don't need to explain the attraction."

He smiled in appreciation. "It was a weak moment and it felt good that someone found me attractive. I knew it would never be serious, but she stuck the knife in an open wound when she ended the relationship."

The waitress returned with our drinks. Without having taken a glance at the menu, Tim and I ordered cheeseburgers.

I took a deep breath. "Tim, where were you yesterday morning?"

He gave me a blank look and then shook his head. "You think I killed Anna, don't you?"

I blushed. "I saw that look on your face when we overheard Jason and Anna. You were hurt."

"I was angry," Tim corrected. "I didn't much like being replaced by a guy half my age."

"I get that," I said.

Tim picked up his glass and saluted me. "Cheers," he said.

Surprised by the behavioral non sequitur, I touched my glass against his and we sipped our sodas.

Tim put his down and said, "I was with Sue."

I swallowed hard. "Sue?"

"Yes. I thought about Anna and Jason on the way home from

your house. I was angry, very angry with Anna. Jason could have her, for all I cared. And I realized that as hurt and angry as I was over Anna's betrayal, I was over Sue's betrayal. I didn't want Anna back. I wanted Sue, no matter what she had done, and what I had done." Tim stopped for a moment and straightened his silverware. "So I called her when I got home and we talked for more than an hour. We met for breakfast, right at that table over there." He pointed across the dining room to a table by the window. "We talked for a long while. Really sorted things out."

His smile cheered me. "That's great," I said, meaning it.

"And we reconciled. We're back together."

"Wonderful." I could have blown the cloth off our table with my sigh of relief.

Tim beamed. "It is. I didn't have any urgent work for the day, so I decided to take it off. We went over to Lake George and took a long boat ride. We had dinner at The Sagamore, and almost spent the night." He shyly smiled. "But we came home."

"I'm so happy for you, Tim." I reached over and touched his hand for a moment. "That's really great news."

"Thank you, Veronica."

I held up my glass of ginger ale. "Now that deserves a real toast. To you and Sue."

"So you really thought I killed Anna?" Tim asked with a grin across his face.

"Well, I . . ." I shrugged and waved my hands. Tim stared at me. "I thought, with that look on your face when Anna and the mayor started kissing . . ." Tim continued to stare. He wasn't going to let me off the hook. "Well, you know, I have an active imagination." I fiddled with my knife and fork.

He laughed at my embarrassment. "You were in pretend land far too long, Veronica."

I acted all affronted. "I'll have you know Walden, Pennsylvania, was a wonderful place to live. I had six husbands. Only four men, really, because I was married to one man three times. I had delightful children. A nympho daughter and a son who slept with my sworn enemy. And I was the founder and CEO of a major gourmet food company. I built my empire one mail-order gift basket at a time."

"Very impressive. Please accept my profuse apologies."

"I miss that place terribly."

"I'm sorry. But you know, Barton is a wonderful place, too. You can start a food company here."

"Perhaps."

Our waitress arrived with the burgers. I had no appetite a few minutes earlier, so stressed was I about Tim and Anna. Now I was ravenous.

"So, Tim," I said as I squirted some ketchup on my burger and fries, "do you have any thoughts on who might have killed Anna?"

Tim shook his head. "I don't know. It wasn't premeditated. Someone got very angry at Anna and grabbed the closest thing and struck her."

I winced at the image of the skillet striking Anna's head. "That's true. A person planning murder wouldn't come armed with a skillet. It's not something you can hide in a pocket or purse." I swallowed a bite of fry and asked, "How well do you know Jason? We're not much more than acquaintances."

"He's a good guy, Veronica," Tim said sternly.

"I'm just asking. Do you know Vic Thompson, the developer?"

"By reputation only. He's a shrewd businessman. What are you up to?"

I shrugged. "I'm just thinking. Would your business with Anna have anything to do—"

Tim cut me off with a curt "No. That was routine business."

"I suppose you won't tell—"

"Attorney/client privilege."

"Okay."

"Let the police handle this, Veronica."

"Mmm-hmm," I hummed as I took a bite of my burger.

"Don't get involved, Veronica. Like I said, you're not in pretend land anymore." He tapped the table for emphasis.

I purposely bit off a huge mouthful of burger and said, "Mmm-mm."

I hurried to the flower shop after lunch to tell Carol the good news that Tim was not a murderer. I wanted to burst into the shop and shout, "Tim's not a murderer," but Amy's presence thwarted my plan.

"Hi, ladies," I said instead when I entered. I waved over to the refrigerator where the two stood discussing something of great floral importance.

"Hi, Veronica," they said in unison.

They chatted for a few more minutes before Amy picked up a large bucket of tulips and went into the back room.

I scampered over to Carol. "Tim didn't do it," I whispered.

Carol, nonplussed, said, "Of course not."

"Can't you just be a little happy?" I groused.

"I'm absolutely thrilled."

"I'm so convinced," I sarcastically said. "You would have had a wonderful acting career."

"Thank you." Carol bowed and asked, "So how did you discover Tim's innocence?"

"He was with Sue at the time. They're back together."

Carol clapped and beamed with delight. "Yeah! Now that's a nice surprise."

The phone rang as I murmured, "It is."

While Carol took the call, I browsed around, ending up back at the refrigerator. The relief of knowing Tim had nothing to do with Anna's death suddenly overwhelmed me. Tears welled in my eyes.

How could I have ever thought he'd be involved in Anna's death? Had I really spent so much time acting on a TV show where every time a character was murdered everyone was a suspect that I couldn't separate fiction from reality?

A hand on my shoulder startled me and the tears slipped down my cheeks. Carol stood beside me.

"Are you okay?" she asked.

"Yeah." I nodded and smiled as I swiped my finger across my cheek.

"Are you upset that Tim and Sue are back together?"

"Oh, no." I insisted. "Not at all. I'm thrilled."

"Really?" Carol asked, her eyes fixed on mine.

"Really."

She patted my arm and said, "Me, too."

"Carol, do you think I'm disconnected from reality?"

"What?"

"Did I spend so much time in a crazy soap opera town that I think Barton is just like it?"

"Of course not. That's silly."

I exhaled. "Good."

Carol walked back to the counter. "How would you like to make a delivery for me?"

"You're putting me to work? How much will you pay me?" I quipped.

"I'm trying to keep you out of trouble. It's for an old friend. Linda Gallagher. Or should I say an old nemesis?"

"Linda Gallagher?" I asked. The day was getting to be like a class reunion. First Sandy, then Tim, and now Linda.

Carol nodded. "She's Linda McNamara now. It's her birthday. Why don't you take the flowers and go see her. It will do you good."

I considered for a moment and then agreed. "Sure. Why not. Maybe delivering flowers will turn into a whole new career."

"I'm not paying you," Carol teased as she wrote down Linda's address.

"I know. But maybe Linda will give me a tip." I winked and took the paper from Carol.

CHAPTER TWELVE

Nominated six times for an Emmy, I've won twice. Each time I faced strong competition, vying against talented women who excelled in their roles. Every nomination always brought a wonderful sense of fulfillment, but also a case of the nerves. I would spend many sleepless nights wondering what I would wear and what I would say if I won. I can still tap into the emotional high of hearing my name announced, and the low of hearing someone else's name read.

None of this compares to the rivalry I shared with Linda Gallagher through eight years of grammar school and four of high school. I guess that's why they're called the formative years. Linda and I vied for every leading role, from the Virgin Mary in our second-grade Christmas pageant to Nellie Forbush in our senior-year production of *South Pacific*. Though other girls would audition for the roles, it was always Linda and I who were most adept at performing, most comfortable on stage. I would not call Linda an enemy, but our twin competitive natures kept us at arm's length. It didn't help that my friends, led by Carol, would playfully hex and throw the evil eye on Linda during her auditions, while Linda's friends would try to rattle me by muttering, "You're going to forget your lines" or "Don't break a leg," in the halls before my audition.

It was on this past that my thoughts dwelled as I walked up the front path to Linda's door, hauling the heavy vase of flowers someone had sent to celebrate Linda's birth. I rang the doorbell and waited. Butterflies began to flutter in my stomach.

After a few moments, the door opened and there stood Linda. I had no trouble recognizing her. Her nose was still dotted with the freckles she meticulously covered with Max Factor every day in the school bathroom.

Linda's expression changed from the blank questioning look of "Who's at the door?" to a smile at the sight of the flowers, through a moment of "Is that really you?" to a final laugh and grin as she said, "Veronica Walsh! Now *this* is a surprise."

"Happy birthday, Linda!"

She looked first at the flowers, and then at me.

"They're not from me." I hastily added, "Not that I don't wish you a happy birthday. Because I do. I wish you a very happy day."

Linda pushed open the screen door. "Get in here, Veronica."

I stepped into her front hall and held out the flowers. Linda took them, thanked me, and set them on the hall table. She turned back and opened her arms wide to enfold me in an embrace.

"It's so good to see you, Veronica."

"Same here," I said. "It's been a while."

"A very long while," Linda said as we released each other. "I missed the last reunion, and you missed the one before that."

"And you the one before that."

"I was literally in labor."

"I guess I'll accept that excuse."

"Do you have time for a glass of lemonade, or do you have more deliveries to make?"

"This isn't my job," I said with haste. "Carol just thought it would be nice if I delivered them."

"I'm just teasing you. I know exactly what you've been up to," she said as she led me down the hall. "Let's go out to the deck."

"You look great, Linda."

"Thanks. So do you." She stopped and said, "I read about your neighbor. I can't believe you found the poor woman's body."

"It was a big shock, yeah."

Linda shook her head and frowned. "I hope they find the person soon. You're being careful?"

I followed her into the sun-lit kitchen. "I am. But the police don't think it was random. I'm embarrassed to say that makes me feel a bit better."

She took a serving tray from one cabinet and set on it two glasses from another cabinet. "That's understandable and nothing to be embarrassed about." She stopped and gave me a sympathetic smile. "I was sorry to read about your show ending." She pressed her hand against my arm as she went to the refrigerator. She pulled out a pitcher of lemonade and set it on the tray.

"Thanks."

She completed her preparation by arranging Pepperidge Farm cookies on a plate and setting it and two cake plates on the tray. "Can you get the door?" she asked, nodding to the door that led out to the deck.

"Sure." I hurried over and pushed open the screen door, stepping outside and holding the door wide for Linda.

"You must be heartbroken. Thirty years. That was your life." She set the tray on the umbrella-shaded table and gestured for me to sit.

"It was, but I'm okay. You have a beautiful yard," I said, admiring the trim lawn, blooming azaleas and rhododendrons, and a gorgeous row of rose bushes.

"Thanks. My husband and I spend our weekends out here, breaking our backs to keep it nice. My youngest has also taken an interest in gardening." Linda filled a glass with lemonade and set it at my place. She poured a glass for herself and sat.

"How many children do you have?"

She placed a cake plate in front of me. "Three girls. Katie, Emily, and Julia. Katie married in April. Emily will be a senior at Syracuse in September and Julia is starting her freshman year at Villanova. Have some cookies." She pushed the plate toward me.

"Very impressive."

Linda flashed a proud smile. "They're great girls. But now my nest is empty."

I selected two cookies and put them on my plate. "Don't be so sure. These days, kids are moving back with the folks after college."

Linda took a cookie and bit into it. "True," she said. "I'm looking forward to the quiet, in a way. It will be nice to come home to a calm house and have dinner with Dave. But then again, with my work, it's nice to come home to the activity and noise."

"What do you do?"

"I'm a grief and depression counselor."

I felt humbled. Though my work is challenging, it is also great fun. Here I was sitting on the deck of someone who did something hard and meaningful, while I played. "That must be very difficult work."

Linda nodded and took a sip of lemonade. "It is. But helping people through a rough time is rewarding."

"I bet it is."

"You did a good job when your character's daughter died," Linda said.

That was a very emotional storyline, from 1992. My thirteen-year-old daughter died of leukemia, sending Rachel into a deep well of grief. "Thanks," I said. "I talked with a counselor and some mothers who lost children to make sure I got it right."

"I was proud of you when you won the Emmy for that storyline. I was studying for my master's at the time, and appreciated that your work related to my work. I meant to write you a letter, but my kids were young, and I was busy with school and home . . ."

Now I was extremely humbled. "There was no need for that. But thank you. It means more than you know."

We were quiet for a few moments and then she asked, "Did you ever marry, Veronica?"

I shook my head. "No. It just never happened. I was too busy with my career. My work was my marriage, I guess."

She sat back and studied me with an intent gaze. I guessed it was her "counselor stare." "Then it must be so hard, losing your identity."

"What do you mean?" I asked, taking a sip of the pleasantly tart lemonade.

"Well, you just said you were married to your career. And the character you portrayed. She was a very big part of you, of your life. It's like she died. And it all happened so suddenly."

"Not so suddenly," I said. "There had been rumors for a while. We had a good year of warnings before they finally pulled the plug."

I regretted the choice of words, likening the show's end to a death.

"Still. That was your life's work. You surely have grieved its loss. I've counseled a number of people who have lost their jobs. The loss of employment can be just as painful as the loss of a loved one. You've lost your livelihood, and you've lost all the relationships you had at the job."

I felt tears coming, so I bit my tongue with the hope of stopping them. I didn't think a therapy session would come with delivering Linda's birthday flowers. "You shouldn't have to work on your birthday," I said, trying to smile.

"I can't help myself. I don't have an on-off switch. I enjoy helping people. And I want to help a friend when she's hurting." At my startled look, she said, "Yes, I consider you a friend."

"I guess we are, though we competed so hard against each other back in school."

"That was fun, wasn't it? I think we brought out the best in each other. And I like to think I had a part in making you a great actress. I made you push yourself to be the best."

I grinned. "I suppose you did."

"It's good for my ego to think so." Linda wagged her finger and said, "You should have thanked me when you won those Emmys!" She pushed the plate of cookies toward me. "Have another. And tell me how you really feel."

I took a cookie, and advantage of the free counseling. "I feel left behind."

Linda nodded. "Yes. That's a common feeling."

"When the rumors were swirling, we were under siege together. And when we were canceled, we were in the same boat, for a while. I guess that's really why I didn't come back here for my regular visits. I didn't want to come ashore alone."

"You felt safe in the boat. You wanted to stay with the people who understood what you were going through."

I nodded. "But then my castmates started making plans. To retire. Travel. Some got new roles. I hate to say it but I was jealous. I wondered why younger castmates got new parts so quickly when I had so much more experience. And then my agent retired and I couldn't find a new one. I couldn't find work on my own. And I probably won't because I'm considered too old."

I wiped a tear that trickled down my cheek. Linda handed me a paper napkin.

"Thanks. So I finally came home. I feel like I'm regressing." I began to sob.

"It's okay to take a break. It's okay to come home."

"I had something to do every day for thirty-two years. Now I feel like I'm just watching everyone else go about their lives and I'm not moving."

"You feel like you're on the sideline. But this will pass. This is your time to experiment and find something new. There are so many things you can do, Veronica. You can have a second career in a totally different field, if you want. You can find another acting job, too. You're not too old." She reached over and put her hand over mine.

"Thanks," I said. "Are you going to charge me for this counseling?"

Linda leaned back and gave me what I guessed was her professional, assessing look. "Next time. We'll consider this your delivery tip."

CHAPTER THIRTEEN

My thoughts moved from Linda's words to Anna's murder as I drove home. I wanted to talk with Gary Pierce. I knew he would not kill the person about to pay him one and a half million dollars. I thought perhaps something happened after the meeting, between Anna and Vic Thompson, or Vic and Gary. Gary could have a clue.

I decided to stop at The Caffs for a cup of coffee. I pulled into an empty parking space right in front of the shop and got out of the car just as Haley Anderson from All Things was coming out with four cups of coffee perched in a carton carrier.

"Veronica!" She gave me a loose hug as she balanced the carrier in her hand.

"It's good to see you, Haley," I said. "How are you doing with all this?"

She shrugged and put on a smile. "I'm holding up. We're busy as usual, so that's good. Walk with me back to the shop?"

"Sure."

As we headed down the sidewalk, Haley asked, "So, are you going to buy All Things?"

"What?" I asked, almost tripping myself as I stopped.

"Are you going to buy the shop? Anna didn't say anything?"

So that's what Anna was going to discuss at breakfast.

"She wanted to talk with me about something at breakfast. But . . ." I faltered.

"Oh," she said, grimacing.

96

We resumed our slow stroll. "Are you sure that's what Anna was going to ask me?"

"I think so." She sounded hesitant.

"How do you know?"

Haley hesitated and then said, "I overheard Anna telling Claire. I stayed late last Friday to clean up and the two of them were in Anna's office. Anna said she was thinking of selling the store, and she was going to talk with you specifically. She didn't think you'd have anything else to do and that you'd have the money to buy it. She wanted a fast deal."

"Huh. Why would she want to sell it? Did she say?"

"She was tired of it. It was always just an investment to her. That's what I think, not what she said. Anna did put a lot of energy into the business after Mr. Frazer died. I guess once she got it to where she wanted it, it stopped being a challenge." We stopped in front of All Things. "Claire wasn't happy," Haley said.

"Why not?"

"She wants to buy the store. But Anna laughed. She said she knew Claire didn't have the money to buy it and wouldn't be able to get a loan for it. Claire said they had a deal, but Anna said the deal was with Mr. Frazer. Anna didn't want the payment plan Mr. Frazer said he'd accept, she wanted all the money upfront."

"Hmm."

"I feel bad for Claire. She worked hard to build the shop for Mr. Frazer and she developed great relationships with our artists. She loves All Things and it hurt when Anna changed what it was all about. I'm sure if Claire could buy the shop, she would change things back."

"Claire must be very upset."

"She's tightlipped about it, so if she's disappointed, she's not showing it. I don't know where things stand now, obviously.

Maybe I shouldn't have said anything to you."

"No, that's okay. Now I know why Anna wanted to meet me."

She held up the coffee, saying, "I better get this in to everyone."

"You go. It's good to see you, Haley."

Haley hurried into All Things as I digested the news that Anna was going to try to sell me her business.

I glanced into the shop's window. Claire stood on the other side, with another of the shop's employees, Molly. They appeared to be discussing the window display. Molly waved and smiled when she saw me. Claire looked right past me.

I gave a cheerful wave and then hurried back to my car, forgetting all about getting coffee.

With Linda, I had just made amends with an enemy, of sorts. Did I just make a new enemy?

Chapter Fourteen

As I drove by the lush cornfields and towering apple orchards of Pierce Farm, I marveled at how Gary could even consider selling the land to someone who would cover it with concrete and steel. Thinking of selling the bookstore brings tears to my eyes. The place supported my family materially and emotionally for decades. I would want to pass it on to someone who would love it and care for it as much as Mom, Dad, and I had. How could Gary not want to do the same with his family's lifeblood?

I cut him some slack as I turned into the gravel parking lot. I assumed he had made a greedy decision, and I was wrong to do that. Maybe it had been a gut-wrenching decision made because he'd been on the brink of financial ruin. Proceed with an open mind, I decided.

I parked and slid from the car, heading for the small building where the Pierces sold the produce they grew. There's also a bakery section, with a terrific selection of fresh baked cookies, cider doughnuts, and pies.

As I crossed the lot, I thought of the many visits I had made to the farm stand with one or both of my parents. Every summer Saturday to pick up fresh corn, tomatoes, and cucumbers. Stops in the fall to select Halloween pumpkins, tri-corn decorations for Thanksgiving, and a wreath and tree for Christmas.

"Veronica!"

I turned around just as Mark pulled into the spot next to my car. He waved through his open window as he unbuckled his seat belt.

"Hi, Mark," I said, walking back across the lot. "Fancy meeting you here."

When we met, Mark touched my arm, asking, "How are you?"

"I'm okay."

"Good. I haven't heard of any developments in the case."

"There aren't any. Soon, I hope." We began to walk toward the farm stand. "I thought I'd come by, see what Gary's now planning to do with the farm."

"You're not thinking he's involved in Anna's death?" Mark asked in a low voice.

"No. Oh, no. But I want to know what happened with Anna after that open meeting."

Mark held the door open for me. "Are you thinking the developer has something to do with the murder?"

"Yes."

Mark nodded. "I agree. I'd like to know if the deal is back on."

With one sweeping glance we saw that Gary was not there. We approached the checkout, where a teenage girl assisted a customer. We waited patiently until she finished.

"Hi. May I help you?"

"Could you tell us where Gary is?" I asked.

The girl thumbed her finger to the back wall. "He's out in the cornfield."

"Thanks," Mark and I said in unison.

We headed out the back door and across a smaller gravel lot. We walked along the edge of the field, looking along each row for Gary. We finally found him a few yards down a row. He looked up and waved to us.

"Hi, Gary," I called. "Can we talk with you for a minute?"

"All right," he said. He picked up a barrel laden with stalks and came to us. Balancing the barrel on his shoulder, he shook hands with Mark and led us back through the lot.

"I suppose you want to talk about Anna," he said. "I'm sorry you had to be the one to find her, Veronica."

My heart skipped a beat. In the world of soaps, or what Tim referred to as *pretend land,* a killer uttered those words when confronted by the person who had solved the case. Usually the killer had a gun pointed at the person and the action took place on a foggy pier, or in a dark mansion, or in a car as the innocent person drove toward a cliff.

Silly imagination. You're not in pretend land anymore.

"Thanks," I said. "May I ask what you and Anna talked about after the meeting? And did Vic Thompson say anything to you two?"

"Anna and I set up a meeting to hammer out the details. Vic stopped on his way out and the three of us talked for a few minutes. Would you believe Anna actually flirted with him?" Gary shook his head. "Vic flirted right back and said he wasn't going to give up. Anna said 'Bring it on.' She was a tough lady."

"She certainly was," I agreed. "What did Thompson say?"

"He said he would do just that. He told me he was going to think about it overnight and call me in the morning with a new offer."

"Did he?" Mark asked. He held the back door open for Gary and me.

"Yes. He called just before noon with an offer of two million. I told him about Anna."

I asked, "How did he react?"

"He was shocked," Gary said as he led us to a long counter lined with barrels loaded with fruits and vegetables. "And sorry. He admired Anna's move Monday night. He's a businessman. It's not the first deal he's lost. He was looking forward to duking it out with Anna for the land."

"Did you accept his offer?" I asked.

Gary shook his head. "I told him I wanted to put it off for a while." He set the barrel next to one with just a few ears of corn on the bottom.

"Really?" I asked.

Gary nodded and began moving the corn from the nearly empty barrel to the full one. "I've been thinking about what Anna said, about not destroying something so beautiful. I owe it to my parents to keep going. I'm tired, but I can hang in there. This is my home as much as it is the family business. Maybe I'll try again in three or four years, when the economy is better. See if someone will want to keep it going as a farm."

"What did Thompson say?" I asked.

"He was disappointed, but agreed it wasn't appropriate at this time. He said he'd call me in a few months to see if I've changed my mind." Gary chuckled and added, "I don't think I will, but it's nice to be courted by millionaires."

"Stay strong," Mark said.

"I don't know how happy Jason Quisenberry will be with my decision," Gary said. "He was really excited about a mall coming to the village. Like he said Monday night, it would bring jobs and revenue to Barton. I think with him pushing it, the Village Council would have approved the deal."

"Even with residents against it?" I asked.

"I don't think many were against it. A lot of folks would like some variety, something new. I think the business folks were the most disturbed, understandably."

He grabbed a brown bag from a stack beside the barrels and dropped a half dozen stalks of corn into it. He handed it to me, saying, "A welcome-home present."

"Thanks, Gary. I could never get corn as good as yours down in the big city."

"Of course not." He laughed as he headed back outside.

"That's a lot of corn for one person to eat," Mark said. "What do you say I buy some steaks, you bring the corn and I'll cook us a great dinner at my place?"

"I say I like my steak medium rare."

I had just walked into my house when the phone rang.

"Hey, pal," a very familiar voice chirped when I answered.

"Melanie!" I headed for my couch to get comfortable for a good long chat with my dear friend. "How was the trip?"

"Absolutely wonderful. Peter and I had a fabulous time. It was a second honeymoon."

"That's great."

"So what have you been up to? Where are you?"

"I've been in Barton since Monday."

"Great."

"You won't believe this, Melanie. My next-door neighbor was murdered Tuesday morning."

Melanie was speechless for a very long moment. "Murdered? Are you joking?"

"No. And I found her."

Melanie caught her breath and was silent for another stretch. "You *found* her?"

"Yes. I was supposed to have breakfast with her."

"That is awful. How was she killed? Please say they've caught the person."

"She was hit with a cast-iron skillet."

"The poor woman."

"And they haven't found the person."

"Veronica, you must be scared witless."

"I'm fine. The police don't think it was random."

"Do they have any idea who did it?"

"No." I then filled her in on my "investigation."

"Veronica, stay out of it," Melanie warned.

"I am. I'm just asking questions."

"You ask the wrong question of the wrong person and you'll be the next to meet the skillet."

"Yes, ma'am. Now let's talk about something more pleasant."

"Well, I have two bits of news," Melanie said.

"Tell."

"Alison is pregnant!"

"Melanie, that's wonderful. You're going to be a grandmother."

"For years I've cringed at the thought of being called Grandma. Now I can't wait."

"Congratulations." We talked for a few minutes about her daughter's pregnancy. "What's the other news?" I asked.

Melanie hesitated, and then said, "I was offered a role on *Bright Lights.*"

"Wow!" I exclaimed. "That's terrific." *Bright Lights,* a popular cable show set in New York, tells the story of four young actresses struggling to make it.

"It's a recurring part as one of the women's mothers. A small role."

Suddenly restless, I got up and began pacing my living room.

"No small roles," I said, my voice hollow.

"I know. I'm excited."

"Congratulations. I'm really happy for you."

"I miss you, V." She sighed.

"I miss you, M."

"We'll have to get together when you're back in New City."

"Absolutely," I said, wondering when that would be. *If* that would be.

"I've got to go. We'll talk again soon. And, Veronica, please be careful."

"Of course. You're as demanding and bossy as Diana."

Melanie laughed at the reminder of her domineering

character. "I really miss you."

I pushed "End" on my phone and tossed it on the couch.

I deserved an Emmy for that phone call. Not that I wasn't happy for Melanie. I was sincerely thrilled for her joy and good fortune. But my enthusiasm was rather shallow at the moment. While she was thinking about baby onesies and *Bright Lights*, my mind was on Anna's bloody face and the murderer in Barton's midst. I prayed that the thrice Emmy-winning Melanie didn't see through my act.

I began to cry. Sob, actually. The shoulder shaking, flood of tears, gasping kind. I did what Linda wanted me to do. Grieve.

I allowed myself a few minutes of self-pity and then shook myself from it. Didn't I have dinner plans with a handsome, wonderful college professor? And a free bag of corn. I considered calling Melanie back and telling her that. Instead, I wiped my eyes with my knuckles and went upstairs to take a long bath before dinner.

CHAPTER FIFTEEN

I arrived at Mark's stone Craftsman-style home refreshed and hauling the bag of corn. I trotted up his slate path to the front door, admiring the marigolds blooming around the two lampposts and the beautiful, trimmed azalea bushes lined across the front of the porch.

"Welcome," Mark said as he held the door for me.

"Your lawn is beautifully tended," I said. "Do you do it yourself?"

"Yes. It's hard work and relaxing, all at the same time."

I handed him the bag of corn. "I picked it myself."

He grinned and said, "I believe you."

We headed out back after Mark made me a Seven & Seven and a gin and tonic for himself. He gave me a tour of his abundant garden, proudly pointing out the luscious tomato plants, cucumbers, pole beans, broccoli, basil, and peppermint. We settled in Adirondack chairs (when in the Adirondacks, sit in the chair) and toasted each other.

"Are you teaching any classes this summer?" I asked.

"No," Mark said. "I'm working on a biography of Martin Van Buren."

"You mean you're writing a biography?"

Mark smiled sheepishly and nodded. "Yeah."

"I'm very impressed."

"Thanks."

"Martin Van Buren. Eighth president and a governor of New York."

"That's right. Most people give me a blank stare when I mention Van Buren. It's particularly disturbing when I get the look from my students."

"I remember Sister Grace telling us about him in seventh-grade history."

"Great memory."

"It helped me when I had pages of lines to learn every night."

"Let me return the compliment. Your two Emmy awards are impressive," Mark said.

"Thank you. I learned the power of drama from Sister Jacqueline. Remember her?"

"Our second-grade teacher who went berserk over poor penmanship."

"Exactly."

Mark and I went back and forth like that for a while, talking about the good old days of growing up in Barton.

When we finished our cocktails, Mark put water on the stove to boil for the corn. We each peeled a stalk over his picnic table, agreeing to keep two apiece for future meals.

"How long do you plan on staying in Barton?" Mark asked, wrapping up the newspaper we used to catch the corn silk and leaves.

"That is yet to be determined."

"Good."

I looked up and found him trying to hide a grin.

We talked about the murder case over dinner.

"Apparently, Vic Thompson didn't have anything to do with Anna's murder," Mark said. "I had him as the prime suspect. When I think about it now, he's too obvious a suspect. Like

Gary said, he's a businessman and this isn't his first deal to fall through."

"Well, I'm going to ask Tracey Brody about him tomorrow," I said. "I'm sure the police have talked to him. I want to know if he definitely has an alibi."

"I understand your interest in the case, but you seem to be trying to figure it out on your own, Veronica. Why?"

I didn't want to break Tim's confidence, tell his secrets, so I carefully said, "I have a personal interest in it, yes. There are a few people I've wondered about."

"Really? Who?"

I set down my fork, surprised Mark wasn't telling me to stay out of the case. "You're not going to tell me to keep my nose out of the matter?" I asked to confirm my conclusion.

"I love a good mystery. Look at who's on my bookshelves. Agatha Christie. Conan Doyle. Dashiell Hammett. Raymond Chandler." He waved a gesture toward his house.

"I'll take your word for it."

"So, who are your suspects?"

"This stays between us?"

Mark nodded. "Of course."

"I hate to think this, but Pauline. She's been having trouble paying the rent on time every month. The day before she was killed, I heard Anna telling Pauline she'd evict her if Pauline didn't pay her by the next morning."

"Pauline?" Mark asked. He shook his head in disbelief.

"I know. I can't fathom it, either. She's been struggling to pay her rent. She really looks like she's at her wit's end. And maybe Anna carried through on her promise and evicted Pauline. Shut down her family's business on the spot. That could be enough to make Pauline pick up that skillet."

"Okay," Mark said. "I'm not so sure, but we have to consider the possibility. Who else?"

I considered for a long moment and then uttered, "Mayor Quisenberry."

Mark's forehead creased and then his eyebrow arched. "Jason Quisenberry?"

"Apparently he and Anna were a couple." I filled him in on the details, without mentioning Tim.

"That's something," he said, leaning his chin on his fist. "Gary said Jason was in strong favor of the mall. I can't picture him hurting anyone over it. But we don't know." He stood, saying, "I'll be right back."

I ate a last bite of steak as Mark went into the house. He was back in a minute with a pad of paper and pen.

"Let's make a list," he said, pushing his plate aside and setting the pad on the table. "Pauline. The mayor. Vic Thompson, for the time being. Anyone else?"

Without hesitation I said, "Claire Camden."

"Claire?"

I nodded. "Listen to this. Anna was going to ask me to buy All Things."

"This keeps getting better." Mark wrote down Claire's name in the neat penmanship honed by Sister Jacqueline.

"That's why she wanted to meet with me. I think she was going to ask me if I wanted to buy All Things over breakfast."

"How did you find this out?"

"Haley spilled the beans. She overheard Anna telling Claire. She also told me that Claire and Mr. Frazer had some sort of a deal about Claire buying the store, and Anna was not going to honor it."

Mark tapped the pen on the paper. "That's a possible motive."

"I spoke with Claire this morning and she said she had no idea why Anna wanted to meet with me. And she was at Anna's yesterday to drop off the pastries for our breakfast. Claire said she handed Anna the box and left. She claims she never went in the house."

"So Claire told you at least one lie, about the purpose of your meeting with Anna."

"So it would be quite easy for her to tell a second lie."

Mark nodded. "Okay. We have a list." He wrote something on the pad.

"Who are you adding?"

He held up the paper for me to read his addition.

"Wild card?"

"We have to leave room for the possibility that someone we don't know killed Anna. Or that someone we do know killed her for a reason we don't know. Her murder may have nothing to do with the mall. Or a lover's quarrel. Or career ambition. Anna could have been killed over a business deal entirely different from the mall deal or the sale of All Things."

"This is getting complicated," I said.

"Are you still interested in trying to solve it? Or do you want to leave it for the police?"

I thought for a moment and then said, "I'm in. I care about the people on that list. I want to prove myself wrong."

"All right. We'll go to the police station tomorrow morning to check on Thompson's alibi."

I smiled, happy to have a partner. "Sounds good."

Over Pierce's apple pie, we chatted about Mark's fall semester classes, the Van Buren bio, and my visit with Linda (except for the therapy session part of it—doctor/patient confidentiality, of course). Mark then brought the conversation back to All Things.

"So, are you interested in taking over All Things?" He took a sip of his coffee, studying me over the mug's rim.

"I really don't know. It's so out of the blue."

"Do you have any acting roles lined up?"

I shook my head. "Nothing, unless you consider being a pharmaceutical spokesperson an acting role."

Mark grimaced. "You mean doing commercials for prescription drugs?"

"Yep."

"Please don't do that," he pleaded.

"I won't. It's horrifying to me, too. I just don't know what I'm going to do. I know Mom would be deliriously happy if I worked with her and took over the bookstore someday. But I only know how to operate the cash register and to stock shelves. I have no idea how to run a business."

"You know more than you think," Mark assured me. "You grew up in that store. You know about customer service. You know the business side."

"It's been a long time since I've been involved. Things have changed. I've been pretending to be someone else for thirty-two years."

"Stop being negative," Mark demanded, frowning at me. "Veronica, you have the knowledge. Believe in yourself."

"It sounds like you want me to buy All Things." I took a forkful of pie and waited for Mark's answer. I felt like I was in my second therapy session of the day. Linda told me to grieve and go on; Mark was now working on my confidence.

"I want you to find something to do because you won't be happy otherwise. Something that will fulfill you. And Anna's store might just be the thing to do that."

I shrugged. "Maybe."

"I'm just saying you should consider it."

"I will. But please, don't mention this to anyone. I want to think about it without pressure."

"I promise. And I won't pressure you. Though let me say this. I hope your family's bookstore continues forever. Or as long as you want it to continue. But independent bookstores are a dying breed. Your mom knows that. All Things is a strong business and it might be a great thing to add to the family."

"A dynasty," I cracked.

"A fiefdom," Mark retorted.

Despite the quips, my spirit flickered with a glimmer of excitement at the possibility.

I got home around nine-thirty and called Mark, as he made me promise. We talked for a few minutes, commiserating over how we suddenly had to worry about our safety in one of the safest places to live in the country. After I hung up, I went upstairs to my room to change.

I crossed the dark room to turn on the lamp on the night table. Just as I flipped the switch, I glanced out the window and noticed a beam of light in one of Anna's upstairs windows. I turned off the lamp, moved closer to the window, and stared over at Anna's, doubting my eyesight. Within moments, I saw the faint light again.

Someone was in Anna's house.

I moved aside, pulling the curtain a bit to hide myself.

I watched as I considered my options. I could call Mark, my new partner in crime-solving. I could call the police, the safe option. Or I could sneak around the hedge and see who was creeping around the crime scene.

I reasoned that whoever was there would be gone before the police or Mark arrived.

I shoved my feet into sneakers and hustled down the stairs and out to my backyard.

I said a quick prayer as I went down the porch steps and across the yard to the edge of the driveway. I glanced up to the window where I had seen the light, half expecting to see someone staring down at me. The room was now dark.

I crept over to the space between my garage and the hedge. I slipped through and dashed across Anna's driveway to hide behind a lilac bush in her yard. After a moment, I bent over and scurried from the lilac bush and along the side of the house until I was outside the living room window. I moved closer to the window as a surge of adrenaline emboldened me. It didn't help, as closed drapes blocked my sight. I moved along to the dining room window and met with the same obstruction.

A car drove by; I instinctively ducked behind an azalea bush.

A rustling in the bushes a few feet from where I crouched startled me. I froze and held my breath as the sound continued. An animal emerged and slinked across the lawn. A cat, I assumed. Then I noticed the telltale white stripe down its back at the same moment I caught a whiff of its trademark scent. I concentrated even harder on remaining still, watching as the skunk ambled toward the front of the house. As soon as it was out of sight, I straightened and made my way to the back of the house.

I stepped lightly on the porch steps and over to the window—now infamous for my embarrassing encounter with Tracey Brody. I remained still for a moment and then put my knee on the chair under the window. I pressed my hands against the glass and peered into the kitchen. I stood frozen for a minute or two, certain someone would step into the kitchen and sweep it with the light beam. Instead, the room remained in darkness.

I began to think I had imagined seeing the light. Again, I was turning this into a soap plot with ridiculous twists and turns. Or maybe I was creating excitement in my life since it was so devoid of anything interesting.

I sighed and walked back to the hedge. Just as I reached it, I heard the kitchen door open. I dashed around to my side of the hedge and crouched between it and my garbage can for a good look. The door clicked shut and footsteps clunked across the porch.

"What are you doing?"
I screamed and fell against the garbage can.

CHAPTER SIXTEEN

"Are you okay?"

Firm hands slid under my arms and lifted me to my feet. I took several steps back, right into the side of my garage.

"Ronnie? Are you hurt?"

I looked up into Alex's face.

"Alex?"

"What are you doing?"

"What am *I* doing? What are *you* doing here?"

"Veronica! Are you all right?"

I looked down the driveway to see Ellen, clad in her bathrobe, standing on her front door's threshold.

"I'm okay, Ellen! Thank you! I just tripped on the garbage can."

"Are you sure you're all right?" I could hear hesitancy in Ellen's voice. I gave silent thanks for a neighbor looking out for me.

"Yes. This is my friend, Alex."

"Hi, Ellen," Alex called.

"Hello. All right. Good night, Veronica."

"Good night. Thank you." The cheery smile I had wrenched my face into drooped into a frown. "What are you doing here?" I hissed.

"I'm playing in a charity tournament in Queensbury on Saturday. I thought I'd come up a few days early and visit. Surprise." Alex opened his arms wide for a hug.

115

I gave him a dirty look.

"What?" he asked.

I softened, remembering he had no idea why I was sneaking around the hedge. I glanced over to Anna's yard and sighed. Whoever came out was gone, and probably knew that I was aware of his or her presence.

"Whew," Alex said, waving his hand in front of his face.

My companion in the azalea bushes, Skunky, had let loose his calling card.

I clutched Alex's elbow. "Let's go inside," I said.

I led him across to my porch and into my kitchen. The room's brightness startled me after my expedition on the dark side of the hedge.

"What's going on?" Alex asked.

"Let's go sit in the living room." I waved him through into the hall. "Would you like a drink? I think I have some Scotch, though I don't know how fresh it is."

"I don't care. I'll take it."

I went over to the dry sink in the dining room as Alex settled on the couch. I pulled bottles of Scotch and rye from the cabinet, feeling like my lovely dinner with Mark had happened an eon ago.

"So, I repeat, what's going on?" Alex asked as I handed him a glass and the Scotch bottle.

"I'll tell you in a minute." I went back to the kitchen for a can of ginger ale from the refrigerator. I went back through the dining room, grabbed a glass and the rye, and returned to the living room.

I sat on the couch with Alex, poured a couple of fingers' worth of rye into the glass, and topped it off with ginger ale. He watched me with a bemused grin.

I took a sip and said, "My next-door neighbor was murdered yesterday morning."

"Is this comedy night?" he asked. "Are you rehearsing some improv thing? Because that's not funny."

"I'm serious."

"And why were you crouching by the hedge?"

"I saw a light in her upstairs window. I thought someone was in the house. So I went over and looked in the window."

Alex leaned forward and asked, "Did you see anyone?"

"No. Just as I was coming back, I heard the kitchen door open and close. That's when you came along." I punched him in the arm. "And because of you, I didn't see who the murderer is!"

"I'm sorry," Alex groaned, rubbing his arm.

"I'm sorry, too." I caressed his arm as an act of contrition.

"So what exactly happened to your neighbor?" After I told him, he asked, "Why didn't you call the police tonight?"

"I'm trying to solve the case," I said.

He swallowed hard and cleared his throat. "Now why would you be doing that?"

"Because people I care about may be involved. And because I'm bored and need intellectual stimulation."

Alex grinned and took another sip. "I miss our conversations. I miss you."

"Me, too." We sat in silence for a moment. "I talked with Melanie today. She's going to be a grandmother."

"Good for her."

"And she got a role on *Bright Lights*."

"Fabulous. Time marches on."

"And what have you been up to?" I asked.

"Oh, just moseying around. Playing golf."

"And now you're here for a tournament."

"Yes. For a children's hospital."

"A worthwhile cause." I wondered where he was sleeping. Was part of his surprise a stay at my house?

"I'm staying at your lovely village inn."

"Great. It'll be good to spend some time together." I smiled and rubbed his arm again.

"I can help you solve the case," Alex said.

"Yeah," I said. Oddly, I didn't particularly care for the idea. Mark and I formed a strong team and I didn't want Alex getting into the middle of it. But he could be of use. He had great charm. We could use him as a distraction if necessary.

Alex finished his drink in two gulps. "I should get going." He leaned over and kissed my cheek. "Let's have breakfast tomorrow. At the inn." He stood and offered his hand.

"I'd like that. But early. I'm meeting my friend Mark at nine-thirty." I clutched his hand and stood.

"Who's Mark?"

"My friend," I repeated. "We're going to talk about the case."

"Well then, I should be at this meeting," Alex teased with a mischievous grin and twinkle in his eye. "So, let's say breakfast at eight-thirty?"

I agreed and led him to the front door.

"You're okay by yourself?" he asked.

"I'm fine."

He kissed me on the cheek again. "Call me if you're not. You have my cell number."

I watched him until he got to his car and then shut the door.

"I was so close," I groaned as I turned the deadbolt. Why couldn't Alex have shown up two minutes later?

I considered calling Mark to tell him about the intruder. It was late, though, and I was too tired to have a long conversation. I'd tell him when we met at The Caffs in the morning.

I checked the windows and kitchen door and then went upstairs. After the creepiness of looking into Anna's dark house, I left on all my lights.

CHAPTER SEVENTEEN

Alex and I walked up Orchard Street after breakfast the next morning. I gave him the "grand tour," appreciating his enthusiasm and genuine admiration of my hometown's beauty and charm.

From a distance I spotted Mark waiting in front of the coffee shop. His wide grin when he first saw me slowly drooped into a quizzical look as Alex and I neared.

"Hi," Mark said, glancing from Alex to me.

"Mark, this is Alex Shelby, my co-star from *Days and Nights*."

"Husband, actually," Alex said. He winked and gave me a sly smile.

A bewildered Mark stared at me.

"For about fifty minutes, on the show," I said. "Alex, this is Professor Mark Burke."

"Professor!" Alex declared as he shook Mark's hand. "What subject?"

"History."

"Mark teaches at Arden College. And he's writing a biography of Martin Van Buren."

"Terrific," Alex said. I could tell by his tight-lipped smile he had no idea who Martin Van Buren was. "I could use a second cup of coffee. Ronnie, a second cup of straight black?"

Mark's bewilderment returned.

"Sure. Thanks."

"Professor?"

Mark reached for his wallet. "Black, too. But here, let me pay—"

Alex held up his hand. "I'm paying. I'll be back in a minute."

Mark questioned Alex's presence as we settled at a table.

"He showed up last night after I got home from dinner. He's playing in a golf tournament on Saturday in Queensbury and thought he'd surprise me. And he's staying at the inn."

"All right." Mark did not look or sound very amused. "He calls you Ronnie? You didn't like to be called that in high school."

"Yeah. That's Alex. I got used to it." I've never liked people calling me by the diminutive of my name, but it was kind of sweet the way Alex said it. "Listen to this." I leaned in a bit and whispered, "Someone was in Anna's house last night. I saw the beam of a flashlight in one of the upstairs rooms."

"Did you call the police?"

"No. I went over and looked in the windows." I described in detail every moment, up to, but not including, falling against the garbage can.

"You should have called the police, Veronica," Mark said.

"I thought we were going to solve this case."

"Not by putting our lives in danger. You shouldn't have gone over there alone. Especially at night."

"I won't do it again," I said like a chastened child.

Dana and a young woman came out of the shop. The woman, in her early thirties, had a pensive look on her face.

"I wonder what will happen to the café?" she asked Dana.

Dana shrugged. "I don't know. I haven't heard anything."

"Will you let me know as soon as you do? Maybe if I move fast, I can still get it."

"I certainly will."

"Thanks, D." The woman gave Dana a quick hug and left.

"Hi, folks," Dana said to us as she came to where we sat. She took a cloth from her apron pocket and began wiping our table.

"Hi, Dana," I said.

"You haven't heard anything about what will happen with Anna's properties, have you?" She looked directly at me. "Maybe your mother knows something?"

I shrugged. "I haven't heard anything. Are you still worried about your lease?"

Dana finished her cleaning and sat next to me. "Yeah. And something else. That was Connie D'Amato. Do you know her?" After I shook my head, Dana said, "She's a chef at Sheridan's. Near the college. You must know it, Mark."

"I do. Excellent food."

"Connie's fabulous. She's got a small catering business on the side. The restaurant lets her use the kitchen during off hours, but her client list is growing and she really needs a place of her own."

"Good for her," Mark said.

"Yeah. She thought she had a deal with Anna to take over the vacant space where the café was. She was just about ready to take over when Anna said she couldn't have the lease."

I thought of the vacant space across from the bank. The café had closed two months earlier when the proprietors retired and moved to Florida.

"Really?"

"Really. Anna told her Monday afternoon. Connie was ticked."

"I'm sure," I said, imagining Connie's frustration. And her motive for murder. If anyone knew how to expertly wield an iron skillet, it would be a chef.

"Her business is really going to be hurt if she doesn't find a place soon." Her eyes moved to the door and widened. "Oh, my gosh."

I turned. Claire stood just outside the door, talking with

Alex. She had quite a smile on her face as she listened to Alex.

"It was very nice to meet you, Miss Camden," Alex said in what I easily identified as his soap character's suave manner.

"Claire. I hope to see you again during your visit," Claire said. "Be sure to visit us at All Things. We're just a few doors down." She shook Alex's hand and left, never glancing in my direction.

"I will," Alex said as his eyes followed Claire. He returned to the table and handed Mark and me our coffees. Dana stood, running her fingers through her ponytail and across her apron.

"Dana, this is Alex Shel—"

"I know," Dana said, her face suddenly radiant. She extended her hand across the table. "It's a great pleasure to meet you, Mr. Shelby."

"Please, Dana, call me Alex. It's wonderful to meet you."

"I'm a big fan of *Days and Nights*," Dana gushed.

"Thank you," Alex said. He walked around the table and gave Dana a hug. "It's always an honor to meet a fan."

As Alex and Dana chatted and flirted, Mark leaned over and whispered, "Connie has an excellent motive. She could be the wild card."

"It's possible. It sounds like Anna put her in a bind."

"It's a pleasure to meet you, Dana," Alex said as he shook Dana's hand a second time, holding her hand in both of his.

"And you," Dana said, blushing. She waved and returned to the shop.

"You have the most delightful women here in Barton," Alex said. "Starting with you, Ronnie, of course."

"Gee, thanks."

"So," he said, pulling out a chair and sitting. "What are our crime-solving plans for today?"

Mark looked at me, baffled.

"Shh," I said to Alex. "Not so loud."

"Sorry." Alex took a long sip of his coffee.

"We might be able to use him as a distraction," I whispered to Mark.

Mark looked disappointed. "Oh."

"Mark and I are going to the police station to check on the developer's alibi."

"Sounds like fun. I'll come, too."

"I'll drive," Mark offered.

"Great," I said. "But let's stop by and see my mother first. She'll want to say hi to Alex."

Alex grabbed his coffee and stood. "Let's go."

"I'll wait here," Mark said.

I put on a cheerful smile. "We won't be long."

I left my coffee on the table and walked away with Alex.

"Don't say anything to my mother about me sneaking around my neighbor's house last night. And don't say anything about me trying to solve the murder. She'll freak out."

"My lips are sealed."

Just as we reached the bookstore, Pauline's husband Glen called to me. He was crossing the street from the stationery store.

"Veronica!" He charged onto the sidewalk and threw his arms around me. "I finally get to see you. We didn't get a chance to talk at the meeting the other night."

"Glen," I said as I pulled back the breath he had squeezed from me. "This is Alex Shelby. Alex, this is Glen Weber."

The two shook hands and exchanged pleasantries. I noted the contrast between the two: Alex, tall and tanned in ironed khakis and a blue knit polo and Glen, not so tall, pale, and dressed in rumpled clothes.

After a minute, Alex excused himself. "You two chat while I go say hello to your mother."

He headed into the shop while Glen and I exchanged the

standard "How are you," "You look great," and "Sorry about your job, Veronica."

"I heard you sold a house. Congratulations." I gave a cheerful smile to the man I had babysat decades earlier.

"Thanks," Glen said with playful exuberance as he pumped his fists. His smile couldn't disguise his tiredness.

We talked for several minutes and then Glen excused himself, saying he had a house to show.

"Good luck," I said as he walked to his car parked in front of All Things.

Glen waved and got into the faded midnight blue, turn-of-the-century Hyundai. I stood and watched, reminiscing about taking care of him and his sister when they were kids. I remembered how he would plead with me to read to him from one of his L. Frank Baum Oz books.

As Glen pulled away from the curb, the car backfired. The sound jolted my body and I became rigid, staring slack-jawed as he drove up Orchard.

A chill raced up my arms. The boy who loved Oz had been at Anna's the morning of her murder.

CHAPTER EIGHTEEN

"Veronica?"

Mark stood beside me, holding our coffee cups. He looked at me with great concern and asked, "What's wrong? You look like you've seen . . . Well, I won't use the cliché."

"I may have just seen the person who made the ghost," I said.

"What? Are you okay?"

"Did you hear Glen's car backfire?"

"Yeah. Poor guy probably doesn't have the money to get it fixed."

"A car backfired the morning Anna was murdered. Right outside my window. At seven-thirty, exactly."

Mark and I stared at each other, absorbing the fact. Just as he was about to say something, my mother swept from the shop, trailed by Alex.

"Veronica, you and Alex are coming for dinner tonight," she said, beaming with delight. When she saw Mark, she added, "And you as well, Mark. I'm so excited. I have a reason to turn on the grill!"

"Don't make a fuss, Nancy," Alex said. He threw his coffee cup in the trashcan.

"What may I bring?" Mark asked.

"Nothing but your wonderful self," my mother said. "Alex's visit is a nice surprise," she added, grabbing my hand and patting it.

"Yes. It is." I said nothing about the black and blue mark I noticed on my thigh this morning, from my tumble upon Alex's surprise arrival at the hedge the previous night. "May I bring anything?"

"Absolutely nothing. I just want you all at my house at six-thirty with hearty appetites."

"Yes, ma'am," Alex said.

Mom walked over to him and patted his cheek. "I'm happy Veronica still has her friends from the show."

I rolled my eyes and said, "Mom, I didn't lose my friends when I lost my job."

"I know, Veronica. But people lose touch after a while when they're not seeing each other every day."

"It's been barely a month."

She came over to me and touched my shoulder. "I know. I'm just saying, it's nice that Alex is here. I'll see everyone at six-thirty." She rubbed her palms together, a sign that she was already on stage three of her plans for the evening, and breezed back into the shop.

"What a charming mother you have, Ronnie," Alex said.

"Yes," I agreed. I clapped my hands, my own plan to enact. "The fun's over. Let's get to the police station."

The three of us marched into Barton's police station five minutes later. A male officer sitting at the front desk greeted us as we entered the main room. Tracey sat at her desk, conducting a phone conversation as she ate yogurt from a cup. Ron Nicholstone sat at his desk, busy with work.

"May I help you?" he asked.

"We'd like to speak with Officer Brody, please," I said.

"She's on the phone. She'll be with you in a moment."

"Thank you."

We backed away from the desk and patiently waited.

Mark leaned over to me and whispered, "Now this is a flash from the past. Remember that class trip?"

I nodded, recalling our seventh-grade class field trip. "Remember the horrible green paint on the walls?" I snickered.

"Oh, yeah. The beige is so much better."

Alex glanced around, absorbing the scene. "It's funny. For all the time I spent on that police station set on the show, I've never been in a real stationhouse."

"Really? I thought you had gotten into a drunken fight with a co-star and were hauled off," Mark said, grinning wickedly.

"Nope. That was Roger Blanche," Alex said.

"Wow. I forgot about that," I said. "It happened years ago. The late eighties. He was off the show within the week."

"I think he's doing dinner theater in Canada now," Alex added.

"Tough break," Mark whispered.

Alex snickered. Ron Nicholstone looked up from his work and nodded to us.

"I understand, Mrs. Jenkins," Tracey said as she swallowed a spoonful of yogurt. "I know you have your job to do, but we can't allow you in Ms. Langdon's house just yet. Tomorrow." She paused for a few moments, surely getting a stern lecture from Sandy. "Tomorrow, Mrs. Jenkins. And I promise I'll let you know when." Tracey hung up the phone, shaking her head with amusement.

"Officer Brody," the officer at the front desk said. "These folks would like to speak with you."

Tracey looked up and smiled when she saw us. She was probably relieved we weren't people who would harangue her as Sandy Jenkins had just done.

"Good morning, Veronica," she said as she approached us.

"Good morning, Tracey. This is Alex Shelby and Professor Mark Burke."

She shook hands with my companions, saying to Mark, "I see you often around the village. It's nice to finally know your name."

"Likewise, Officer," Mark replied.

"Do you have a few minutes?" I asked.

"Sure." She gestured for us to follow her.

We traipsed behind her down a hallway. As we passed Chief Price's office, I glanced in to see him at his desk, talking on the phone.

Tracey led us into a small conference room. "Please, sit."

There were six chairs around the table. Mark and I sat on one side, with Alex across from us. Tracey took the chair at the head of the table.

"What would you like to discuss?" she asked, as if she didn't already know.

I had rehearsed the conversation, my first script to learn in a month, a dozen times. "Have you talked with Vic Thompson, the gentleman who was going to buy Pierce Farms before Anna Langdon made a better offer? We have a citizen's concern that he may be involved in Anna's murder in some way."

Alex said, "You certainly understand Ms. Walsh has more than a passing interest in this case. She is the person who found the poor woman's broken body."

Tracey got up, closed the door to the room, and sat down. "We have talked with Mr. Thompson and are confident he was not involved in Ms. Langdon's murder."

"He has an alibi?" I asked.

She nodded. "Yes. He was in his office in Albany at the time."

Alex said, "He could have hired someone. A hit man."

"Anna was struck on the head with an iron skillet. I think a professional hit man would kill with more finesse."

"That's true."

Tracey and I exchanged glances. She bit back a smirk.

"We are confident Mr. Thompson was not involved," she said.

"Is there anyone else you've eliminated?" I asked.

There was a hard knock on the door before it swung open. Chief Price stepped into the room.

"Ms. Walsh, did you remember something?" he asked. "Officer Brody, you should have called me."

The chief's glower scared me. I didn't want to get into trouble, or to cause trouble for Tracey.

Startled, I forgot my script. "I was just telling Officer Brody that I think I saw someone in Anna's house last night."

Neither Mark nor Alex uttered a word. Tracey, her face blank, asked, "And at what time was that, Ms. Walsh?"

"Around nine-thirty."

"And did you see who it was?" Chief Price asked, moving to where I sat so that he towered over me.

"No. The house was completely dark. I couldn't see anything from my window."

"Thank you for sharing this information. Why didn't you call us last night to report it?"

I sighed. "Well, Mr. Shelby arrived at my house at that time. I wasn't expecting him—"

"Sorry about that," Alex muttered.

"And by the time I got over the surprise, I think the person was gone. And then I just—" I stopped abruptly.

Chief Price looked down on me for a very long moment. Of course, I wanted to run, but he blocked my path to the door. "Perhaps, if this happens again, Ms. Walsh, you can give us the courtesy of a phone call," the chief scolded. He turned and stalked from the room.

I felt my face glowing red.

"It's all my fault," Alex lamented. He leaned his head against his fist. It reminded me of a scene from a few years back, when

I caught his character in bed with another woman.

"Is this true, Veronica, or did you just make it up?" Tracey asked.

"It's true," I said, too embarrassed to make eye contact with her. "There was someone in the house. I saw a light beam in an upstairs window. And I really didn't see who it was. I'm sorry I didn't call." I slowly raised my eyes. Though her expression was unreadable, Tracey didn't seem to want to lock me in a cell and throw away the key.

"Thank you for telling us now. We'll take a look around this morning." She pushed her chair back and stood. "Is there anything else?"

"No," I said as the three of us stood.

"Okay. Thank you for coming."

She walked to the door and opened it. As I passed her, I murmured, "I hope I didn't get you into trouble—"

"Not at all," she replied. "Chief's under a lot of pressure to solve the case. Don't worry."

"You're so cool," I said. "If I ever play a cop, I'm going to use you for inspiration."

The officer blushed and gave a shy smile. "Thanks."

Mark, Alex, and I walked through the station and out to the car in silence. I let loose as soon as Mark slammed his car door.

"I haven't felt like I was four years old since I was nine!" I shouted. "That man made me feel like a child."

"It's all my fault!" Alex wailed. "Had I not shown up when I did, you would have seen the person. You'd be getting a medal right now for solving the case. I should have called. I should have waited until morning."

Mark, quiet, drove from the parking lot. He harrumphed as he turned onto the street.

"Do you have something to say, Professor?" Alex asked.

"You two really chose the right profession," he said. Then he chuckled. "You're quite dramatic."

"Excuse me," Alex said, offended. "I'm not familiar with local ways. You think that scene was funny?"

"No. I think you two are a little overly sensitive. What would you have done if Chief Price had arrested you for obstruction? Or withholding evidence?"

"Could he have done that?" I asked, wide-eyed.

"I would have called my lawyer and sued," Alex said.

Mark laughed harder. After a moment, I joined him. Alex looked across at Mark, and then turned his head to look at me in the back seat.

"Well, he would have been severely overstepping his authority to arrest an innocent person simply for not reporting a supposed beam of light."

"Supposed!"

"All right. A confirmed beam of light."

"I also heard footsteps."

"I'm really sorry I came over to your house last night," Alex griped. "Had I known what trouble it would cause, I would have stayed at the inn. Maybe I shouldn't have come here at all."

Mark acted as appeaser. "But if you hadn't gone over to Veronica's, she might have come face to face with the intruder, who might have then harmed her."

"You're my hero, Alex," I said. I patted his shoulder to convey my sincerity while thinking how ridiculous it all was.

He was quiet for a few moments. "I am," he finally said.

Mark, unable to stop himself, laughed again. Alex looked at him, and then at me. He shook his head and grinned. Relieved, I did as well.

We approached the florist shop just as we all got over ourselves.

"Let's stop at Carol's," I said.

"Who's Carol?" Alex asked as Mark pulled to the curb.

"My best friend. You've met her many times," I said, irritated, as I got out of the car.

"I'm sorry. I'm all out of sorts." Alex slammed his car door.

I glanced across the car to Mark. He was still grinning. I guessed he felt better about Alex the tagalong.

When we entered the shop, Carol was at the refrigerator assisting a customer. At the jingle of the bell they both turned. The customer was Connie!

Carol smiled at our trio. Connie gaped when she saw Alex and me. Then her eyes began to sparkle.

"Oh, my gosh!" she exclaimed. "Alex Shelby!"

Her exuberant attention pleased Alex. He gave a smug glance to Mark. Mark smiled in return. For a moment I thought it was a "Yes, you have the attention of this one young woman, but every semester I have dozens of coeds fawning over me," look. And then I remembered this was Mark. Kind, sweet, gentlemanly Mark. He was just being polite.

And then I felt a strange tug in my belly. I hoped he didn't have dozens of coeds fawning over him.

Connie and Alex walked toward each other, their handshake taking place over a bucket of red roses.

"What a thrill it is to meet you, Mr. Shelby," Connie gushed.

"Please, it's Alex. My father is Mr. Shelby. And your name?"

I inwardly groaned at the old trope, "My father is" blah blah blah.

"Connie. Connie D'Amato."

"Beautiful name. And you must know my co-star, lifelong Bartonian Veronica Walsh?" Alex made a dramatic gesture in my direction.

"Not personally, of course. But I've seen you around the village. And in church. But I never wanted to intrude on your personal time. It's such a pleasure to finally meet you."

I walked over and shook hands with Connie. "Hi, Connie. This is my friend, Professor Mark Burke."

Connie politely nodded at Mark, saying, "It's nice to meet you, Professor. I think I've seen you at Sheridan's. I'm one of their chefs."

"I've been there often. I can honestly say everything on your menu is superb."

"Thank you." Connie blushed and turned back to me. "I'm so sorry about your neighbor, Anna Langdon. How gruesome you found her."

"It was a shock."

Mark joined Carol by the refrigerator. He watched as she pulled flowers from various buckets, sizing up the bouquet she apparently was making for Connie.

Connie then smiled and I saw the faint outline of an illuminated light bulb over her head. "Are you two doing anything this afternoon?" she asked.

"Well—" I began.

"Because it's my grandmother's ninetieth birthday. She has watched *Days and Nights* since it began. She got me hooked when I was seven."

"Wow," Alex said.

"We're both in mourning over its end."

"That's a comfort to us," Alex said.

"We're having a party for her this afternoon. And it would be a big thrill for her if you came. We're serving lunch. And cake, of course. It's going to be fun. And you wishing her a happy birthday would be the best gift for Grandma."

I glanced over Connie's shoulder and saw Mark mouthing something to me.

Wild card.

"We certainly can." Alex accepted before I could say a word.

Connie bounced up and down, her face radiant with delight. Casey looked in from the workroom, observed the scene for a moment, and then disappeared.

"This is so exciting! Grandma is going to flip!"

"She won't get too excited and have a heart attack or a stroke?" I asked. I was concerned for our longtime fan's health.

"Oh, no. She'll love it."

While Carol put together a bouquet for Connie's grandmother, Connie gave us directions to the assisted-living facility where her grandmother lived. She was so happy about our attendance, I'm certain she floated from Carol's shop.

As soon as the bell jingled her departure, I turned to Mark and asked, "Now I'm not so sure that sweet lady murdered Anna."

"What!" Carol shouted. "You promised you'd get out of it once you found out Tim wasn't involved."

"Tim?" Mark and Alex simultaneously inquired.

"I'll explain later," I said. "Carol, it's . . ." I hesitated for a moment. "It's nothing."

"I'm sure Connie had nothing to do with it," Mark said. "But let's be sure. And it's a party. You need a diversion."

"You're in on this, too?" Carol huffed as she glared at Mark.

He shrugged. "I need a break from Van Buren."

Carol threw her hands up and sighed with exasperation. "I give up."

"Before you do, can you please put together a bouquet for Mrs. Walsh?" Mark asked. When Carol looked at him for explanation, he added, "She kindly invited me to dinner this evening."

"Me, too," Alex said.

"I'll be there, as well." I said.

"That's good," Carol said. "You can't get into trouble at your mother's."

I walked over to the refrigerator and picked out a small basket of flowers. I held it up for Carol to see, asking, "May I take this? We should bring something for the birthday girl."

Carol nodded, saying, "It's about time you bought something in this shop, all the times you've been in here."

"I'm a browser." I handed her money for the basket, teasing, "Do I get the family discount?"

Carol passed me a single and a handful of change. "Enjoy the party. And do come again."

"I'll think about it. Let's go, fellas," I said, clutching the basket.

Carol set a time for Mark to pick up the flowers and the three of us left the shop.

"I'm going to pop into the liquor store," Alex said.

I knew why. "Mom likes white wine."

"Thanks. I'll see you later, Professor." Alex nodded to Mark and jogged across the street.

"He's something," Mark said.

"On and off screen, yes." I turned to him. "So how am I supposed to get Connie's alibi at her grandmother's birthday party?"

Mark nodded toward the liquor store. "Get Alex to do it. He can charm it out of her while you're eating cake."

"I like that plan. So what will you do this afternoon? I hope you won't go sleuthing without me."

He smiled. "No, I promise. I think I'll do some fall course-work and try to get some writing done. So what's this about Tim?"

"Please don't tell anyone this," I began, and then told him everything about Tim, Anna, and Sue.

When I finished, all Mark said was, "I'm happy Tim and Sue are back together. They never belonged apart. And I've already forgotten everything else you just told me."

"You are a gentleman and a scholar. You're the only person I can honestly say that to," I told him. "And thanks for being patient with Alex. He really is a mature, stable adult. He's just a bit lost without the show. Like me."

"I understand."

We stood quietly for a moment, staring at the liquor store. "I'm really worried about Glen and Pauline," I finally said.

Mark put his arm on my shoulder. "I'm sure there's a simple explanation. We can work on that tomorrow."

"All right."

"Have fun at the party."

"Have fun doing real work."

I said goodbye to Mark and headed over to the liquor store. Alex came out a few minutes later and we walked down Orchard together, formulating a plan for the party. Alex eagerly took on the role of detective after I told him about our suspicions of Connie.

"I'll be smooth as silk," he promised.

CHAPTER NINETEEN

Tracey was leaving Anna's house when I got home. She waved and walked over to my yard.

"Hello again, Veronica."

"Hi, Tracey." I nodded toward Anna's. "Did you find anything?"

"No," she replied, shaking her head. "Everything is in order."

"Very odd."

She took a step closer. "Veronica, are you sure you saw a light in Ms. Langdon's house? It couldn't have been a reflection from the street, or your own house?"

"Yes, I'm certain of it."

"I understand you're under stress. You're recently unemployed and your neighbor was murdered. Stress can cause people to see or hear things, or think things, that aren't real."

I remained calm at her attempt to put me in the bin marked "Loony." I smiled and said, "I'm really not stressed, Tracey. And I'm okay, though I do not currently have an acting job. There are no financial worries, if that's what you're implying."

"I'm not implying that. And I don't mean to upset you. I'm just saying, the case is very much in your thoughts, so maybe your mind is just imagining things that aren't happening."

"I didn't imagine it," I firmly answered. "I saw a light beam moving around in one of those upstairs rooms. And I heard someone on the porch outside the kitchen."

"You what? You didn't mention that before."

I sighed; I'd have to tell her everything. "Can we sit down?"

"Sure."

Once we settled on the porch chairs, she asked, "So you heard someone come out of the house?"

"Yes." I spilled the beans—seeing the light from my bedroom window, sneaking around looking in the windows, hearing the kitchen door open and the footsteps, Alex startling me, me falling and getting a lovely bruise on my thigh.

I braced myself for a scolding. Instead, Tracey laughed. "I'm sorry. This really isn't funny. And I should be furious with you. But this is like a scene from a movie. Or, I should say, a soap opera."

I thought about it for a moment. "Yeah, it does sound like a soap plot."

"I know you're trying to help, Veronica. And no harm came of this. But if there's a next time, please stay in your house and call us."

"I will," I said.

"Thank you."

"Okay." I paused and then asked, "What's it like, working a murder case?"

She was quiet for a moment. I studied her face, but couldn't detect anything from her impassive look.

"It's quite a responsibility," she finally said. "So much greater than finding a thief or vandal. Not only is it our job to protect the community from the killer, but it's also our duty to bring justice to the victim and her family. It's been hard leaving work every day. I feel like I should work around the clock until we find the person who took Ms. Langdon's life."

"I'm thankful to have such a dedicated person protecting Barton," I said.

"Thank you. Now please, let me do my job."

"So, I have to find out where Connie was Tuesday morning, between seven-thirty and nine?"

"Correct."

Alex and I were on our way to the assisted-living home in Bolton Landing. My basket of flowers sat in a box on the back seat, right next to a large box of chocolates Alex had purchased.

"You know, Maura would set this scene at a corner, candlelit table in a romantic restaurant. Soft music, dim lights. A bottle of wine." Alex spoke of Maura O'Loughlin, head writer of *Days and Nights*.

"If you happen to spot such a setting at the retirement home, feel free to take advantage of it. Otherwise, we have to improvise with what we've got."

"An assisted-living home."

"Yes."

"Who's Tim?" Alex suddenly blurted.

"My high school boyfriend."

"And you thought he was somehow involved with your neighbor's murder?"

"Yes. He had a brief fling with her while separated from his wife. But they reconciled the morning of Anna's murder."

"Succinctly put. Maura would stretch that for six months."

"And I got the answer in twenty-four hours," I teased as I turned into Belle Park's lot.

"This looks nice," Alex said. "They have turrets. Maybe you should put your name on the waiting list while we're here."

"Perhaps I will."

We parked and walked into the building. This was my first time in an assisted-living home. My last experience with a facility for the elderly was in 1977, when my maternal grandmother spent her last year in a nursing home. That facility, with its linoleum floors, harsh fluorescent lights, institutional beige walls, and antiseptic smell, was on my mind when I entered Belle Park Assisted Living.

It was like walking into a five-star hotel. Plush carpeting covered the floor. The soft glow of the pale yellow walls welcomed and soothed. Arranged for small groups to gather and have private conversations were couches and chairs you could sink into for a good nap. And the aroma? Not the nose-wrinkling kind from 1977. Rather, I detected a faint vanilla scent.

"This is like a mansion," I said. "Maybe I will move in."

Connie lurched from one of the couches and charged toward us. "Veronica. Alex! You came."

"Of course we did," Alex said. He greeted her like an old friend, giving her a kiss on each cheek. I felt obliged to do the same.

"Oh, you brought Grandma flowers," she said when she saw my basket.

Alex held up his box. "And chocolates. I hope she likes them."

"She loves them. Can you believe she still has all her own teeth?" She took a firm hold of my elbow, linked her arm through Alex's, and led us through the great room to a hallway. She chattered about how excited her grandmother would be, how excited she was, how excited her mother would be, until we arrived in a room decorated with balloons, several flower arrangements, and a banner reading *Happy 90th Birthday Rose*. A large sheet cake sat on one table. Laid out on another table were platters of sandwiches and salads.

There were about twenty-five people in the room, standing in small groups, gripping plastic cups and making small talk. Myrtle Evans and Ella and Madeline Griffin were among the celebrants, as well as their friend, Dotsie Beattie.

Connie led us to a group of four standing by the cake. "Grandma, I have a surprise for you."

A small woman with a face full of wisdom lines (my mother's term for wrinkles) turned and looked at us. It took one second for a smile to reach her clear blue eyes.

"Well I'll be darned. Rachel and Cal." Her eyes twinkled as she looked from me to Alex. I recognized the woman, but couldn't put my finger on how.

"Veronica and Alex, actually," Connie said. "I met them in the flower shop this morning. Grandma, remember Ms. Walsh grew up in Barton."

"Oh, I know. I've seen you in church over the years," Rose said, looking at me.

"I knew I recognized you," I said. "Happy birthday!" I handed her the basket of flowers.

"Happy birthday," Alex echoed as he presented his chocolates.

Rose seemed thrilled by our gifts. "Thank you. I'm stunned to have two TV stars at my party."

I said, "Connie told us you've been watching the show since the first day. It's our pleasure to celebrate a loyal fan's special day."

Rose handed off the basket and chocolates, pressed my face between her cool hands, and kissed my cheek. She then did the same to Alex, except she kissed him on the lips.

"You can't leave until you tell me how you two end up on the show."

Connie beamed with delight. "Can you stay a while?" she asked us.

"Absolutely," Alex answered.

We posed for pictures with Rose, Connie, and several others. Alex and I served ourselves sandwiches, salad, and soda, and sat at an empty table. Soon Connie's family members stopped by to greet us, as well as a number of Belle Park's female residents. They were all very sweet and wanted details of the show's ending, which they'd have to wait two more weeks to watch.

After a while someone put on a Frank Sinatra CD. Connie's father began to dance with Rose. Connie's mom danced with her son and Connie began to dance with one of her young nephews.

I leaned over to Alex and said, "You need to get a move on with Connie. Dance with her when the next song starts."

"Aye-aye, boss lady."

I watched Alex walk over to Connie and give her a courtly bow. I bit my lip to keep from laughing. The man was forever performing. Like a gentleman, he held out his hand and spoke a few words. Connie accepted and took his hand just as "Fly Me To The Moon" began.

"Veronica."

I turned; Dotsie Beattie had summoned me and was now waving me to the table where she sat with Myrtle and the Griffins.

"So this is what I'm reduced to now," I mumbled as I walked over to their table. "The old ladies' table."

"How wonderful you're joining us," Madeline said. Madeline, the middle child of three Griffin daughters, always had a smile on her face and a kind word for everyone. I can personally attest to her patience; I tested it twice a week from ages seven to thirteen as she attempted to teach me how to play the piano. My fingers didn't exactly move gracefully across the keys.

"It's my pleasure," I said, sitting in the empty chair between Dotsie and Myrtle. Myrtle held an unlit cigarette between her thumb and index finger, as if she was smoking it.

"I quit three months ago," she explained. "But I haven't quite cut the cord."

"I understand," I said, wondering if I should recommend a

session with Linda. "It's very difficult to quit. I give you a lot of credit."

"And it's kept me from replacing smoking with eating."

"It's a security blanket," Ella said, frowning with disapproval. Ella always had a bit of a grumpy attitude.

"It's a better habit than the smoking," Madeline said, her smile the opposite of her sister's expression.

"Enough about me," Myrtle said. She swiveled ninety degrees in her seat and eyed me, squinting despite her glasses. "Your neighbor is the talk of the village."

"It's horrifying," Madeline exclaimed.

"She was the worm of Orchard," Dotsie declared.

I looked at her, stunned by the statement. A tall, broad-shouldered woman, the seventy-something Dotsie is a local legend for providing the entertainment for Barton's children on their birthdays. She and her late husband, Lou, had a stable on their property where they housed three beautiful horses. For free the Beatties would bring one of their horses to a child's party and give rides to all the kids. Dotsie, Lou, and a handsome chestnut brown horse named Chester attended a series of my birthday parties.

"The worm?" I repeated.

"Anna Langdon wasn't a well-loved woman," Myrtle said. She was the junior in the group, being only in her sixties.

"Except by the men she dallied with," Dotsie said.

Ella harrumphed. "This is an unpleasant conversation."

Dotsie said, "About an unpleasant woman."

"People must be happy she stopped the mall deal."

Myrtle snorted. "She did that for purely selfish reasons."

"Selfish or not, I'm glad she did," Madeline said.

I glanced at Dotsie and delicately asked, "She dated many men?"

Myrtle and Dotsie snickered while Ella made another har-

143

rumphing sound. Madeline turned her attention to the few couples dancing.

"I think she went through every eligible man in Barton," Dotsie said. "And some of the ineligible ones. One of them might have killed her. Or one of their wives." Dotsie took a forkful of cake and ate it.

"She had problems with many people," Ella said.

Myrtle said, "She certainly got your goat when she wanted to buy your house and turn it into a spa."

"She did?" I asked.

Ella nodded. "She told Madeline and me we were too old to be living alone and that we should be in a facility. Graceless woman."

Dotsie nodded. "She certainly ticked off all the artists who used to do business with the shop. A number of local folks made good money selling their goods in that shop when Edward was in charge. My neighbor, Paul Baldwin, was one of them. And Anna just cut them off at the knees. Paul has three shelves about to snap from the weight of birdhouses he can't get rid of because she wouldn't sell them."

"He should stop making them," Ella said, verbalizing my thought exactly.

"Does he have an alibi?" Myrtle asked, turning the cigarette in her fingers.

Dotsie shrugged. "I'll find out."

"Dotsie Beattie," Madeline said. "You'll do no such thing."

"I'll ask without him even suspecting I'm asking."

"Because you're known for your subtlety and finesse," Myrtle said.

Ella gave me a stern look. "How is it that you heard nothing, Veronica? You were right next door."

"Anna's windows were closed," I said.

"And you saw nothing?"

"I . . . I didn't look out the window." I swallowed hard. Ella's interrogation was just as intimidating as Chief Price's. I dared not tell her I had been in bed, still asleep.

Madeline came to my rescue. "Veronica, do you play canasta?"

The strange change of subject left me speechless. Dotsie filled in my silence by saying, "A wonderful idea, Madeline." She twisted in her chair and asked me, "Well, do you?"

"I haven't in a while. A very long while."

"It's like riding a bicycle," Madeline said. "You can take Ingrid's place, God rest her soul."

"Ingrid?"

"Ingrid Stevenson," Myrtle said. "She passed away last month."

"I'm sorry to hear that."

"She was in our canasta club for twelve years," Dotsie said. "We meet every week, for lunch or dinner, and play cards. We take turns hosting. It's Ella and Madeline, Myrtle and Sandy Jenkins, and me. Ingrid was my partner."

"Well, I—"

"Sandy would love to have someone her own age in the club," Madeline said.

"Are you staying in Barton?" Ella asked. "It would make no sense to join if you'll only abandon us in a month or two."

"Well, I—"

I thought Madeline had saved me from Ella's spotlight, only to put me in one of her own. Did this complete my retirement? Admission into a ladies' canasta club?

A gentleman spared me from making a commitment. Not Alex, but a man with wisps of white hair combed across his head. Leaning heavily on a cane, he walked to my chair and asked, "May I have this dance, young lady?"

"Hello, Edgar," Dotsie said.

"Hi, Dotsie." He looked at me and said, "I'm Edgar Munson." He peered at me intently from behind his dark-framed, round eyeglasses.

"Veronica Walsh."

"It's a pleasure to meet you, Veronica. Would you care for a dance?"

I wondered how he'd manage without his cane, or with it, but I was sure I could support him just fine. "That would be nice."

I stood and pushed in my chair. He hooked his cane over the chair's back and then linked his arm through mine.

"I think I'll cut in on Connie and that handsome actor friend of yours," Dotsie said, getting up.

Dotsie walked ahead of us, snapping her fingers to the music. With Edgar leaning on me, we slowly made our way to the side of the room where people were dancing. It took us half of "Send In the Clowns" to get there.

Dotsie tapped Connie on the shoulder and loudly said, "I'm cutting in, dear. I'm older. You'll have plenty of time to dance with handsome television stars."

Connie laughed and said, "Just be gentle, Mrs. Beattie."

"I'm Dotsie," Dotsie said to Alex as Connie left.

I turned my attention away from the unlikely pair and put my hand on Edgar's shoulder. He put his hand on my back and we joined hands.

"I understand you're an actress?" he asked.

"Yes, I am."

"On one of those soap operas."

"Yes. Though the show I was on was just canceled."

"What a shame. I've never seen one episode of any of those shows. Not one. But what a shame."

"Thank you. And do you live here, Edgar?" I thought it would be polite not to assume him a resident.

"Yes. I live two doors down from the birthday girl. I'm the only man on the floor. The ladies spoil me."

"Lucky man."

His hand gripped mine. "How long have you lived here?"

"Three years," he said. "I moved in two years after my wife, Louise, died."

"I'm sorry."

"I didn't enjoy living by myself in our house. And I couldn't mow the lawn anymore. Or shovel the blasted snow."

"It's good to be around people."

"Are you married, Veronica?"

"No."

"Divorced?"

"No, sir. I've never been married." I wondered if he was thinking of setting me up with a bachelor son. Or of proposing to me. It could be my ticket into Belle Park.

"A career gal, then."

"Yes. But I was married six times on the soap opera."

His laugh tickled me. "Fabulous. All the fun, none of the work."

"That man over there"—I pointed to Alex—"was my last husband."

"He looks like a keeper. But I think Dotsie has her eye on him."

Alex caught us looking at him. He gave me a wink and a grin.

"Do you have any children, Edgar?"

"Louise and I have one son. Alan. He's a doctor in Saratoga. He calls me every day and visits every weekend."

"A good son."

"Always has been."

We shifted back and forth for a few moments without talking.

Edgar said, "You're a wonderful dancer."

"Thank you. I learned on my show."

"So what are you going to do now that your show's been canceled?"

"I really have no idea, Edgar."

"You'll figure it out. I have every confidence in you."

"Thanks. I do, too."

The song ended. "I enjoyed that very much," Edgar said.

"So did I. Thank you for asking me."

Edgar linked his arm through mine again and we began our snail's pace back to the table.

"I used to be able to dance for hours," he said. "Louise and I would go dancing every Saturday night. Even after Alan came along, we'd still go out. That was our date night."

"That's sweet," I murmured.

Myrtle sat at our table talking with an elderly woman. Ella and Madeline had moved to the next table to talk with Rose. When Myrtle and the woman saw us, the woman stood and said to Edgar, "You owe me a dance."

"Okay, Ethel." Edgar shouted.

"You're in high demand," I said to him as I handed him his cane.

"Ethel lives next door." Edgar lowered his voice and said, "I think she has her eye on me."

"As well she should."

"It was a pleasure, Veronica. I'll be the talk of the place, dancing with a big television star."

"Not so big." I gave him a kiss on the cheek and watched as he escorted the woman to the dance floor.

I took my seat next to Myrtle. "How's your husband?" I asked.

"He's having a hip replacement next month."

"I'm sorry to hear that. I hope it goes well."

"It's not fun getting old," Myrtle said. "Try not to do it."

"I won't," I told her, amused. We sat quietly for a couple of minutes and then I asked, "Do you really think Dotsie's neighbor might have killed Anna?"

Myrtle snorted. "It's not in Paul Baldwin's constitution to kill. Anything. He was in my office once and a spider crawled across the desk. I was about to squash it, but he wouldn't allow it. He picked it up in his bare hand and walked it outside."

"That was kind of him."

"One day I was at Dotsie's and I saw a family of squirrels, not just a nuclear family, but the whole extended family, going into his attic, suitcases in paws."

"Did he have a neon vacancy sign on his roof?"

Myrtle smiled. "Maybe there's some signal only squirrels can hear and Paul's cracked the code."

Dotsie and Alex returned to the table. "You wore me out, Mrs. Beattie," Alex said, pulling a chair out for Dotsie. "You're quite a dancer." He sat down on Dotsie's other side.

"It comes from years of riding horses," Dotsie said.

Alex slyly said, "Really?"

"Really."

We chatted for a few minutes until Ella, Madeline, and Rose came to the table. Rose thanked us for coming, gave us each a hug, and kissed Alex, on the lips, again. When she left, Connie came over, smiling like the Cheshire cat.

"You were the hit of the party," she said to me. "The best present by far. I hope you weren't too bored."

"I had a wonderful time," I said, and I meant it.

"I enjoyed myself, too," Alex said when Connie looked at him. "And I wish you all the best in your business ventures."

"Thank you," Connie said. "I think I just may get what I want."

★ ★ ★ ★ ★

Alex and I walked with the Griffins, Dotsie, and Myrtle to the parking lot.

"Think about the canasta," Madeline said as we parted.

"I will," I said.

Alex gave me a quizzical look; I responded with a "never mind" glance.

We said goodbye to the women and headed for my car.

"Do you want to know what I found out from Connie?" Alex asked.

I located my keys and pushed the remote to unlock the car. "Of course I do. But now I feel bad, because we had an ulterior motive for coming to the party. Connie and her family are very nice people."

"They are."

After we got in the car and I started the engine, I asked, "So what happened?"

"Connie is a delightful young woman," Alex began as I pulled from the parking spot and we were on our way. "She invited us to the restaurant where she works for a meal on the house."

"Great. So where was she Tuesday morning?"

"Let me tell you everything she said." When I sighed, Alex said, "You feel bad, so listening to the whole story will be your penance."

"All right."

"First let me tell you this. She assumed that we're together." He rubbed his hands together. "Isn't that great?"

"What?"

"She said it was wonderful that you and I were a couple. That she understood, with all the hours we spent together and all our love scenes."

"What did you say?"

"I neither confirmed nor denied her assumption."

"All right. Go on." I was accustomed to fans asking whether I was involved with my leading man, or outright assuming I was.

"So anyway, I asked what she did for a living and she told me all about being a chef and a caterer."

"We know all that."

"I'm just telling you what she told me. I asked what her goals were, and she told me all about wanting to open her own catering business, full time. She said she had a good list of clients, all she needed was a facility to meet her expanding needs."

"Did she mention Anna?"

"Yes. She told me that your neighbor had promised to rent her a space where she'd have a full commercial kitchen. She said it was perfect for her needs and she was close to securing it when Anna changed her mind. Connie said she wanted to rip Anna's lungs out when she told her."

I gasped. "Really? Rip her lungs out?"

"Yep. Connie said she saw red. She was so furious."

"Does she have an alibi?"

"Connie said she was filled with guilt when she heard about Anna. She actually thinks she wished death on her. Poor girl."

"Her alibi?" I asked, impatient.

"She readily, and unwittingly, offered it, because she thought it was so ironic. She was in the kitchen at the restaurant, making two hundred meatballs for a party. Anna had recommended Connie to the client. Connie actually said she was in the kitchen pounding and slapping the meat, pretending it to be Anna's face. It was a real catharsis. And then she felt guilty when she got the phone call that Anna was dead." Alex snapped his finger and slapped his forehead. "She mentioned her sister was helping her with the meatballs. I should have danced with her to corroborate Connie's alibi. What kind of a detective am I?"

"Don't beat yourself up," I said.

"I really should have talked with the sister."

I knew his remorse was more about how pretty Connie's college-age sister, Francesca, was, than about her potential in clearing Connie. "Don't worry, Alex. I believe Connie."

Really. Who could make up such a tale while dancing with a soap star at a senior citizen's birthday party?

"I'm glad. I really like Connie," I said. "Thanks for helping me." I looked over at Alex, reaching for his hand to pat it.

"It was my pleasure." He clasped my hand. In a moment, he was gently stroking my thumb.

I said nothing and let him hold my hand for a few minutes, until I had to merge onto the highway. We drove the rest of the way in silence. By the time we reached Barton, the sky had become overcast and a few rain drops splattered across the windshield.

I pulled in front of the inn and put the gear in park.

"So I'll pick you up at six-fifteen?" I asked.

"All right. You don't want me to drive?"

"No. You might want to get smackered on that white wine you bought my mother."

"A fine cap to the day," Alex said.

"Thanks again for your help," I said as he got out.

Alex leaned into the car, gave me the gleaming smile he gave me so many times as the cameras rolled, and said, "I'd do anything for you, Ronnie."

CHAPTER TWENTY

Alex and I bickered as we headed to Mom's. The afternoon rain shower had given way to early evening streaks of sun cast across the grass.

"Remember, don't say anything about me and Anna's murder to my mother."

"Ronnie, you told me this morning. You don't need to remind me twice."

I turned onto Mom's street. "I was just saying. You can be very chatty."

"I know when to be quiet."

"All right."

I pulled into Mom's driveway. She and Mark stood on the front lawn, Mom gesturing at an azalea bush as Mark nodded attentively.

"You forget I'm working with you on this. Who got Connie's alibi?" Alex asked.

I gave a final warning before opening my door. "And don't say anything about last night."

"I won't."

"Hi, Mom," I said, the admonishing tone I used with Alex gone.

"Nancy!" Alex exclaimed. He too flipped his mood switch to exuberant. We actors are exquisitely adept at it.

Mom gave us each a kiss on the cheek and asked, "So what did you two do today?"

"We took a lovely drive through the countryside," Alex responded, shooting a glance at Mark. "How did your writing go, Professor?"

"Very productive. Thank you."

Alex presented his bottle of wine to Mom. "To your good health, Nancy."

"Thank you, Alex." Mom looked at me, empty-handed.

"I just brought my wonderful self," I said.

"That's all I ever need," Mom said with a grin. She gave me a second kiss on the cheek and led us inside.

Alex was like a fly to honey when he saw the family photos scattered around the living room. He shot into the room, grabbed one picture, and declared, "Ronnie, look at you in your school uniform."

Mom dashed after him, confirming my cuteness. I took this opportunity to grab Mark's elbow and pull him into the kitchen and out to the patio.

"So how was the birthday party?" he asked, chuckling at my grab and go.

"Connie's no longer a wild card," I answered as we took seats at the picnic table. I told him about the party and my conversation with the elder ladies.

"I know Paul Baldwin a bit. I second what Myrtle said."

"Yeah," I said. "It doesn't make sense that he would choose Tuesday morning to settle a long-time grudge."

"So we crossed someone off the list."

I rubbed my hands against my cheeks, saying, "I really dread what we may find out about Glen and Pauline. And then there's Claire. I forgot all about her."

"Tomorrow. Just enjoy dinner."

Mom came outside, followed by Alex carrying a tray of drinks and snacks. Alex set the tray on the table and handed me a glass of Seven & Seven.

"I added some pizzazz," Mom said, using her code word for booze. "I assumed."

"Correctly," I said. "Thanks."

After she and Alex sat, Mom raised her glass and said, "To good friends and family."

We echoed her toast and touched glasses.

"Alex, what are you doing now that the soap is over?" Mark asked.

"There are a few possibilities out there," Alex said vaguely. "My agent's hard at work."

"And what about your agent, Veronica?" Mark asked.

I cleared my throat. "She took the cancellation hard and retired. She's recovering on a golf course in South Carolina."

"You can certainly find a new agent."

"That's not so easy as it sounds, for a woman of a certain age," I said.

"That's not fair," Mark said.

My mother said, "It certainly isn't. No one minds seeing a middle-age man, or an old man, romancing a younger woman, but a woman of the same age with a younger man is *verboten*."

"It's the way of the world," I said.

"Ronnie, you should have told me you were having trouble. I can talk to my agent," Alex said.

"And all he could get me would be menopause commercials."

"Perhaps not."

"Well, maybe a spot as a spokeswoman for cholesterol pills."

"Don't be so defeatist," Alex said.

Mark took pity on me and changed the subject. "How's business, Mrs. Walsh?"

We talked for a while about the struggles of an independent bookstore. Finally, Mom excused herself and went into the kitchen.

"Did Ronnie tell you what an excellent job I did getting Connie's alibi?" Alex asked Mark.

"Yes."

"Ronnie, you should really think about my offer," Alex said. "I'm sure Larry would scoop you up in a minute."

"I'll think about it," I said. The truth was, I had already talked with Alex's agent and been told that his client list was full. A polite way of saying, "Sorry, I don't want you." I sure as heck wasn't going to tell Alex that, or admit it in front of Mark.

Mom returned, not a second too soon, with a platter of chicken cutlets. "Mark, are you still willing to grill the chicken?" she asked, setting the platter on the table. "The grill's already warm."

"Absolutely," Mark said. He rose and took the platter over to the grill. Alex remained seated, swirling the ice in his drink.

"Veronica, could you help me with the salad?" Mom asked.

"Sure." I jumped to my feet and followed her back into the house.

"Are you really going to talk with Alex's agent?" she asked as soon as we stepped into the kitchen.

"No."

"Good. I have a business proposition for you." She handed me a knife and tomato. "Anna's brother is here to collect Anna's body."

"Have you met him?" I asked as I sliced the tomato.

"Yes. He's a very kind man. Very unlike Anna. I know that's not nice to say, God forgive me. Anyway, I had a short chat with him. He says the family is going to auction off the properties Anna owned. But he's going to give the tenants an opportunity first to make an offer on their own lots."

"That's good of him."

"It's a terrific opportunity for all of us. I talked it over with Anita, Nick, and Charlie and we all think we'll be able to buy our spaces and stop being renters after all these years."

I set the knife down and looked at Mom. She was busy check-ing the potatoes baking in the oven. "That's fabulous, Mom."

She crossed her fingers. "I think I can swing it." Giving me a sly look, she asked, "How would you like to go in with me on the bookstore lot?"

I looked down at the cutting board and was quiet for a mo-ment. "Did Anna's brother say anything about selling All Things?" I asked.

From the corner of my eye I saw Mom shake her head. "No. I'm sure he'll have no problem there, it's such a hot property."

I took a deep breath. It was time to tell Mom what I knew. "I've heard that Anna was going to ask me to buy the shop."

My mother spun on her heels, mouth agape, and clasped her hands together. "Veronica, what an opportunity that would be."

"I haven't really thought about it."

"But what an opportunity it would be," she repeated.

"Yeah, but I don't know." I went back to slicing the tomato.

Mom walked over to me and laid her hand on my shoulder. "Veronica, you need to make a decision about what you're go-ing to do. You're too young to hide out and shelve books at the shop. I'm afraid that, after a while, those menopause com-mercials are going to become attractive to you. And you know you won't be happy doing that. And it would be a big step down for me, going from saying, 'My daughter is an actress on the best daytime drama on television,' to 'Yes, that's my daughter talking about hot flashes.' Think of your old mother's self-esteem, dear."

I finished slicing the tomato. I pulled the salad bowl over and arranged the slices over the lettuce. A tear slid down my cheek. "I know. But acting is all I've ever done. It's hard to say it's over."

Mom turned me toward her and embraced me. "I know, honey. I know. This doesn't mean it's over. All the great actresses don't just act. They have perfume lines and jewelry collections and restaurants. And you do have a degree in business. Dad and I really pushed you to take that on as a second major, just so you could have something just in case acting didn't work out. And acting worked out so well, you now have the money for the business." She clapped her hands together, as if that settled everything.

"I'm thinking about it," I said.

"That's good enough for me."

We didn't talk about business, agents, or murder during dinner. Instead, we talked about the weather, politics, and religion. The phone rang halfway through dessert, sending Mom dashing into the kitchen. She returned within minutes with her purse in her hand, a peeved look on her face.

"I'm sorry, everyone. I need to get down to the police station."

"What's wrong, Mom?" I asked, standing.

"The mayor's been arrested!"

Chapter Twenty-One

Mark and I traded knowing glances. Alex continued to eat dessert.

"You stay here and finish your coffee and cheesecake. I'm sorry to rush out like this," Mom said as she rummaged through her purse for her car keys. Finding them, she crossed the backyard to the gate that led to the driveway.

"We'll meet you there," I called. I grabbed my coffee cup and dessert plate and headed into the kitchen.

"I'll drive," Mark said, grabbing his cup and plate.

"Shotgun!" Alex said.

The three of us hurried to the kitchen and placed our dishes in the sink. I locked the back door and windows. As I led the way to the front door, Alex said, "I thought this was a quiet village you lived in, Ronnie."

"Used to be," I muttered.

We piled in Mark's car and headed for the station. We were silent for a few minutes, catching our collective breath from the sudden rush from the house.

"I don't understand why your mother is going to the police station," Mark finally said.

"Neither do I," I said. "We'll know soon."

"Maybe this means the end to your sleuthing days," Alex said.

"Just when I was starting to enjoy it," I cracked.

Mark said, "Maybe that should be your new career. Private detective."

"Excellent idea," Alex said. "I'd like to be a silent partner," he said, turning in his seat to look at me. "An investor. Let's see. You'll need a large magnifying glass. A trench coat. Surveillance equipment. Handcuffs."

"Handcuffs!" I exclaimed.

"For making citizen's arrests," Mark said, chuckling.

"Wonderful," I said. "Look. The police station." Despite the not so wonderful scene at the station that morning, I couldn't wait to get away from the needling conversation.

Mark parked and we hustled into the police station. There was a different officer at the front desk than was there that morning. He jumped to his feet when he saw us, three slightly out of breath, middle-age adults. Maybe he thought there was a fire somewhere. Or that we needed an escort to the hospital.

"Good evening, Officer," I said. "My mother, Nancy Walsh, was called down here." I glanced over to the deserted desk area. I wondered if Tracey was still on duty.

"Yes, Mrs. Walsh is here," the officer said. "She's with the chief. You'll have to wait until they're finished." He pointed to the hall. "You can have a seat in the hall."

"Could you tell me why my mother was called? She said the mayor—"

The officer's expression hardened. "I'm sorry, ma'am, you'll have to wait."

"Okay. Thank you."

The three of us went back out into the hall and sat on a long wooden bench beside the door. I was impatient after thirty seconds and began to fidget.

"What does my mother have to do with the mayor?" I whispered to Mark.

"I have no idea."

I rose and slowly walked past the doorway, casually looking in to see if Tracey was at her desk. She wasn't. I walked down to the water cooler at the end of the hall, took a drink, and then walked back to the bench.

Alex looked up and asked, "Do you want me to cause a distraction? Throw a stink bomb or something so you can run in and find out what's going on?"

I said, "Yes, let's cause a scene in the police station so we can be arrested." I crossed my arms over my chest and paced back to the water cooler.

"You're going to need an office when you become a P.I.," Mark said.

I let my head fall back and closed my eyes. Mark's and Alex's teasing was stretching my worn nerves thin. "I'll just work out of my house," I retorted. "Private detectives need their privacy." I resumed pacing.

"Of course," Alex said.

I stopped in front of the bench and got sassy. "Since your funding this endeavor, I'll also need DVDs of all the seasons of *Prime Suspect*." When Mark snickered, I said, "I've always admired Helen Mirren's acting talent, now I can learn from her detecting skills. And *Murder She Wrote*."

"Excellent," Alex said. "You should also get copies of *Police Woman*."

"Pepper," Mark said with great reverence.

Alex nodded. "And then there's *Charlie's Angels*."

"Okay, new subject," I said.

"All right. Professor, you've known Ronnie most of her life. What was she like as a young girl?"

"Disruptive. Disheveled. Impertinent."

I touched Mark's ear and gave it a playful tug. "I was sweet, brilliant, and the cleanest, neatest girl in the class."

"So what's the truth?" Alex asked, grinning.

"In the middle somewhere," Mark answered.

I smiled and walked to the exit door, stopping to look out at the Barton night.

"So what's it like to work with the adult Veronica?" Mark asked.

"Delightful. Best twenty-eight years of my life."

"Hmm," Mark said.

They were quiet for a moment, and then Alex asked, "So, Professor, have you always lived in Barton?"

"No," Mark said, and then he went on to explain his educational travels, from undergraduate at Arden to graduate studies at Duke and early career work at three universities until he earned a position at Arden.

"That's very impressive," Alex said with genuine admiration.

"Thank you."

I paced the hallway as the two talked about Mark's fall classes. On one of my passes, I spotted Tracey at her desk. She looked up and saw me; I wiggled my fingers a bit and tilted my head to indicate I wanted to see her in the hall.

"Who is it?" Mark said, his voice low.

I stepped away from the door and whispered back, "Tracey."

I sat down between the two, expecting Tracey to join us in a moment. When she didn't, I mumbled, "Where is she?" and got back up, moving to the doorway. I got there just in time to collide with Jason.

"Jason!" I exclaimed as I took two hurried steps backward.

"I'm sorry," he said, reaching out to balance me. "I didn't expect to see you here."

"Well, we were having dinner with my mother—"

"I'm sorry I interrupted it," he said.

"Is everything . . . all right?" I asked.

Jason looked at me, opened his mouth, and then looked over at Mark and Alex. "It's fine. Everything's fine."

Just then Mom came out and said, "You three didn't have to come."

"We were concerned," I said.

"Thank you, dear. All is well."

We all stared at each other for a long moment. "Thank you again, Mrs. Walsh," Jason finally said.

"I'm happy I could help."

"Good night, everyone." Jason nodded to us and hurried out of the station.

"What was that all about?" I asked, my impatience at its breaking point.

"The mayor was brought in for questioning about Anna's murder."

"And what does that have to do with you?"

"I was with him that morning," Mom said with a nonplussed expression.

"You're the mayor's alibi?" I gaped at her. Alex gently pushed my chin up; Mark suppressed a laugh.

"He's my accountant, dear. We meet every month to go over the shop's books."

"Since when is he your accountant?"

"Since Bert Hoover retired last year. You knew that, Veronica." Mom clicked her tongue with disapproval.

"I apologize profusely," I said. So there went another suspect from my list. "Why did the police think Jason was involved?"

Tracey stepped into the hall. "We got an anonymous tip," she said.

"Huh," I said.

"Yes." Tracey turned to my mother. "Thank you for your help, Mrs. Walsh. We really appreciate it."

"I was glad to do it. I'd love to know who sent that tip," Mom said with a scowl.

"It happens," Tracey said. "Sometimes people are grinding an axe, or just pulling a prank. Sometimes they're simply mistaken."

"Well the person should be arrested for making a false report. Accusing the mayor of murder! It's beyond slanderous."

Tracey put her hand on Mom's shoulder. "We're going to investigate it, Mrs. Walsh. Thank you again for coming down here so quickly. I'm sorry we interrupted your evening."

"I'm just doing my civic duty," Mom said, her temper calming.

"You all drive safely," Tracey said as she stepped back into the main room.

"I can't believe someone would accuse Jason of murder," Mom said as we walked to the exit. I kept my mouth shut, guessing she did not know of Jason and Anna's relationship.

"Mark, Alex, thank you for coming to dinner. I'm sorry I had to leave so suddenly."

"We understand, Mrs. Walsh," Mark said as he held the door open for her.

"All's well that ends well," Alex mused.

Raindrops plunked on our heads as we walked toward the parking lot. "Who drove?" Mom asked.

"Mark," I answered.

"So you'll ride back with me to get your car. What about you, Alex?"

"I'll give Alex a ride to the inn," Mark offered.

"I'll go with—" Alex began.

"Thanks, Mark," I said. I was tired; I didn't want Alex asking to prolong the evening by coming back to my house or inviting me for a drink at the inn.

"I'll see you in the morning then." Alex kissed me on the cheek, and then gave Mom a kiss, thanking her for the delicious meal.

"Let's all meet for coffee in the morning," I said in response to Mark's quizzical look. "Ten o'clock?"

"All right," Mark nodded. He copied Alex's farewell, kissing first my mother and then me.

I watched as the two men walked silently to Mark's car. "Don't talk about me," I jokingly called after them.

Mark grinned and Alex shouted, "We make no promises."

The gentle raindrops became a steady rain as I drove home. A nerve-rattling boom of thunder chased me across the yard to my back porch. I quickly unlocked my kitchen door and rushed into my home's dry, soothing confines. I thanked myself for turning a few lights on before I left for dinner; these weren't days for walking into a pitch-black house. I brushed my hands up and down my arms, rubbing away the goose bumps caused by the storm. Another bang of thunder sent me hurrying to the drawer where I kept emergency candles and matches. I turned toward the window just as a flash of lightning illuminated my backyard. I quickly pulled the curtains across the window.

The light on my answering machine was blinking. I pressed the button and listened as Madeline Griffin's serene voice filled my kitchen.

"Hello, Veronica. This is Madeline Griffin. It was wonderful to see you at Rose's party today. What a pleasant surprise that was. I'm calling you about our canasta group. We are meeting on Saturday for lunch and a game and would love to have you join us. You don't have to make a firm commitment to join us permanently, but it would be lovely if you would give it a try. We would enjoy your company, even if just for one afternoon. Please call me and let me know if you can join us."

I jotted down her phone number. All I remembered about canasta was that it required two sets of cards. A real handful, so to speak. I'd give it a try, I decided, if only to spend an afternoon with Dotsie, who would give me a good laugh or two. There was also the free lunch.

165

The doorbell rang as a crack of thunder shook the house. Taking a candle and the box of matches, I grabbed the flashlight I kept on the counter and headed down the hallway.

I stopped and listened to the swirling rain and thunder. Had I really heard the doorbell? It was almost nine-thirty. Who would be out at this time, and in this storm?

The doorbell rang a second time. I started and dropped the matches. My heart beginning to beat a little too fast for my liking, I stooped and picked up the box. Three hard knocks against the door reverberated in the hallway.

Clutching my flashlight, candle, and matches to my chest, I crept to the front door.

I pulled back the lace curtain that covered the sidelights just as a flash of lightning lit my porch. I could see the bulk of a person, but could not tell who it was.

"Who is it?" I called as thunder boomed.

"Glen Weber!"

Chapter Twenty-Two

I stood motionless for a moment, wondering if I should open the door. In the soap world, foreboding music would accompany my every move and foreshadow something sinister. I was in the real world, however. I shook myself and opened the door.

"What are you doing out in this storm, Glen?"

"I'm sorry, Veronica, but I really need to talk to you." Glen's hair and shirt were damp from the rain; droplets covered his eyeglasses and dripped from the frame.

"Come in," I said, stepping aside so he could enter.

"Thanks." Glen crossed the threshold and took two steps inside before stopping. He took off his glasses and wiped them against his shirt. "It's nasty out there."

"Let's sit in the living room," I said, pointing at the room with the flashlight. I let him go first, gripping the flashlight in case I needed to use it in self-defense.

He sat on the couch. I took the chair across from him, setting the candle on the coffee table. I struck a match and held it to the wick.

"Good idea," Glen said.

"So what do you need to talk about?" I sat back, clutching the flashlight in my lap.

Glen moved forward so that he was on the cushion's edge. "I know you know I was at Anna's Tuesday morning."

"How do you know that?"

"I saw that look on your face when my car backfired. You

weren't just startled by the sound."

"Yes," I admitted. "I heard the backfire that morning and I told the police about it."

Another clap of thunder, the loudest yet, preceded a blackout by seconds. I suddenly found myself staring at Glen through the eerie glow of the candle.

"Perfect," I muttered.

"Remember when we used to play with the Ouija board? It always freaked me out how the planchette moved around. It was years before I realized you were doing it."

"That wasn't me." When Glen raised his eyebrows, a look he probably gave his children when they fibbed, I said, "Okay, it was."

The humor helped us both relax. "I was dropping off Pauline's rent check," Glen continued. He was quiet for a moment and then said, "Pauline said you might have overheard her fight with Anna about it. She was really embarrassed."

"It's nothing to be ashamed of. Many people are having a hard time right now."

"I told Pauline you'd be cool about it. Anyway, I didn't even go in the house. Anna didn't invite me in. She just took the check and told me she expected the rent on time, every month. She wasn't going to give Pauline any more grace periods on the grace period." Glen stared at me. I could tell he was desperate for me to believe him.

"Why did you drop off the check and not Pauline?"

"She was running late getting the kids ready to take to her mother's. And she really dreaded going to Anna's. Anna had a way of making Pauline feel really small because the stationery store didn't make as much as Anna's store. Pauline avoided Anna as much as she could."

"Pauline should be proud of the way she runs the store."

"I'll tell her that." Glen and I were silent for a minute. I didn't know what else to say, and I guess he didn't either. Finally, he said, "So that's it. I dropped off the check and left. Anna was very much alive. You can ask Claire. I passed her on Sycamore. She was walking to Anna's." Sycamore Road links my street, Willow Lane, to Orchard Street. "I bet Anna gave her the check to put right in the bank."

"Huh," I said, thinking hard.

"You believe me, right?" Worry lines wrinkled his forehead.

I said I did. His shoulders drooped in relief and he leaned back against the couch. "I hear Anna's family is going to auction off the buildings she owned," I said.

"Yeah, I know. There's no way we can make a bid. I'm not selling houses, Pauline's not selling cards. Everyone's buying them in the supermarket these days, or sending those electronic, cutesy cards."

"I'm sorry you and Pauline are having such a hard time. Things will get better."

"You can help. Want to buy a house?" Glen chuckled and smiled.

"You sound like a six-year-old boy I used to babysit. Always trying to talk me into something. Staying up later. Two more scoops of ice cream. Just fifteen more minutes of TV."

"That kid hasn't changed. His requests have only gotten more expensive."

"I didn't offer you anything. Would you like something to drink?"

"No, thank you. It sounds like the storm has let up. I should be going." He rose and said, "Thanks, Veronica. I'm sorry to come so late, but I really had to explain this to you."

I stood, turned on the flashlight and used it to guide us to the front door. "I'm glad you came. I knew in my heart you weren't involved. But it's right next door, and my imagination went a little wild."

Glen placed his hand on my shoulder and said, "I completely understand. I'd think the same." With his hand on the doorknob, he asked, "Are you going to be okay here in the dark?"

I told him I would, that the lights would probably come back on soon. "Drive carefully," I said as he stepped onto the porch.

The rain had stopped and the thunder and lightning had moved on to harass another town. I watched as Glen trotted to his car and then shut the door.

"Two suspects off the list in an hour's time," I said as I went back to the living room and sat on the couch. I gazed at the glimmering candle, wondering why Claire had acted as though Pauline still owed Anna the rent.

Just as I was about to nod off from the mesmerizing effect of the single flame, power returned and the two lamps in the living room made the candle unnecessary.

I blew on the candle just as an idea came to me. I believed Glen, but I needed to prove it.

I went into the kitchen and used the landline to make two phone calls.

"I'm changing our plans. Meet me in front of All Things at nine-thirty."

On the second call I said, "Change of plans. We're meeting at Carol's at ten. I'll bring the coffee."

CHAPTER TWENTY-THREE

Alex stood outside All Things, looking very eager to start the day.

"Good morning," he said.

"Hi."

"So why the new meeting place? Where's the professor?"

"Mark will meet us at Carol's. I need to do something here, and I thought I needed a backup who has a master's in flirting."

Alex flashed a pleased grin. "How can I be of service?"

"I need to talk to Claire Camden about the morning her boss was murdered. Remember Claire? You met her yesterday at the coffee shop."

"I remember. Lovely woman. A beautiful smile. You're not telling me you think she murdered your neighbor?"

"I don't know. I need to ask her about a tenant's check. She's a bit cool, and I thought—"

Alex interrupted me with, "You think if she's a bit frosty to you, I could warm her up with my charm."

"Yes," I said.

"Lead the way," he said as he opened All Things' door for me.

Walking into All Things is like walking into another world. For all her toughness and no-nonsense attitude, and her arrogance at dropping Adirondack from the store's name, Anna really knew how to create a warm, inviting environment that made one want to drop a bundle of cash. A mixture of vanilla, cinnamon, and apple scented the air. The soft overhead lighting, complemented by charming table and floor lamps, soothed shoppers traipsing from store to store. The only two-story shop on Orchard, Anna stocked the space with a plethora of items that would turn a home into a showcase, from scented candles and one of a kind clocks to colorful glassware and beautiful linens.

"It's about time you brought yourself in here," one of Anna's employees, Molly McDonald, said.

"I saved the best for last," I responded as we hugged.

Molly's creative flair served Anna's business vision very well. She designed the window displays and arranged settings around the store that enticed shoppers to drop in and buy. My favorite part of the shop was her Christmas corner. Year-round she maintained a selection of ornaments hung on three fake spruces strung with garland and lights with nearby tables displaying other holiday decorations. "There's no better way to say you loved your Adirondack vacation than a trinket to hang on your tree," was Molly's saying.

"Anna's brother will be here shortly," Molly whispered as she held the embrace. "You two should talk."

"About?"

"Haley told me. I'd love to have you as a boss," she said before releasing me.

"Well, thank you. Actually, though, I'm here to talk with Claire. Is she in?"

"Yes. She's up in Anna's office." Molly fingered her hair, tousled by the morning's work. Looking at Alex, she gave me a glance and a grin to convey she wanted an introduction.

"This is Alex Shelby. Alex, this is Molly McDonald. She's the genius behind the store's displays."

The two shook hands, Alex saying, "You'd make a fine set decorator."

Molly blushed and beamed. "Thank you."

I led Alex up the stairs to the second floor, where shelves of linens and quilts surrounded racks of women's clothing and accessories. As I headed across the floor to the narrow hall that led to Anna's office, a fantasy of breezing through every morning on the way to *my* office flashed through my mind.

"Hi, Claire," I said, tapping on the office door.

Claire, seated and leaning over an open file cabinet, started at the sound of my voice. "Veronica!" she said too loudly, as if caught with her hand in the cash register.

"I'm sorry to startle you," I said, taking a step into the office. "You remember Alex Shelby?"

Alex stepped in behind me, turning on the charm. "Good morning, Miss Camden." He reached over and offered his hand to Claire.

Claire pushed shut the drawer and took Alex's hand. "Of course. Good morning, Mr. Shelby."

"Alex, please. You're looking lovely this morning, Claire."

She blushed. "Thank you. How may I help you?" she asked, looking at Alex.

"I wanted to ask you something about the morning Anna was killed," I said. Gesturing at the two chairs in front of the desk, I asked, "May we?"

"Yes. I'm sorry, I should have offered," Claire said, flustered. She folded her hands over a file on the desk.

Alex pulled the chair out for me, waited a moment while I settled, and then sat beside me.

"Glen Weber mentioned that he dropped off Pauline's rent check at Anna's Tuesday morning," I began, studying Claire's expression. Her eyes widened ever so slightly. "Did Anna give it to you? Glen's concerned because it hasn't been cashed. He worries that whoever killed Anna stole the check." I mentally patted myself on the back, pleased with the story I had thought up the night before while trying to fall asleep.

Claire looked from me to Alex and back. "Anna didn't give me the check," she replied and shifted her gaze to her hands, which she gripped tightly on the desk.

"It must have been stolen, then," Alex said.

"Perhaps the police found it," I said. "Did they say anything to you, Claire?"

"No."

"Glen said he saw you walking on Sycamore, heading toward Anna's, when he left."

"I didn't see him," Claire said quickly but calmly. "Maybe he was mistaken."

"Maybe," I said, still staring at her.

"He must have come after me. If he had dropped off the check before I got there, Anna certainly would have given it to me to deposit the second the bank opened."

"My father was like that," Alex said. "He used to say, 'Put the money in the bank where it will gain interest.' Wise advice."

"So you have no idea about the check?" I asked.

"I just said no."

Claire and I stared at each other as Alex shifted in his chair.

"You have beautiful eyes, Claire," he said.

It was good to see that Alex had taken his role in my plan so seriously.

"Thank you, Alex," Claire said, flashing him a smile. She looked at me and coolly asked, "Is that all you wanted, Veronica? To ask about Pauline's rent check?"

I thought for a moment, and then decided to ask about the shop, just to see her reaction. "I heard Anna's brother is going to auction off the buildings. Has he said anything about selling All Things?"

"Brian," Claire said, looking over my shoulder.

I turned to find a man clad in jeans and a navy blue polo

standing in the doorway. In his mid-forties and with the same dark eyes as Anna, I guessed immediately that he was her brother.

"I'm sorry. I didn't know you were in a meeting. I'll wait downstairs," he said.

Claire rose, saying, "No, stay. We're done."

Alex and I stood. Since Claire was slow on the introductions, I said, "I'm Veronica Walsh, Anna's neighbor."

We shook hands. "I'm Brian, Anna's brother. I hear you found my sister."

"Yes. I'm so sorry," I said. Gesturing to Alex, I said, "This is Alex Shelby."

"I'm very sorry for your loss," Alex said as he shook Brian's hand.

"Thank you." Brian turned back to me and asked, "I understand you may be interested in buying Anna's shop?"

I heard Claire lightly gasp as Alex's stunned look bore into me.

"Possibly," I answered.

"I'm leaving this afternoon. Can we meet later this morning to talk about it?"

I said that would be fine and we agreed to meet at The Hearth for coffee at eleven-thirty.

Claire gave me a very wide, stiff smile and said, "Thank you for dropping by, Veronica. I appreciate your support in this difficult time."

She turned to Alex, her grin genuine. "And it was a pleasure to see you again, Alex." She held out her hand.

Alex took her hand in both of his and held it. "Likewise."

He and I walked downstairs in silence. Molly stood at the foot of the stairs, eagerly watching our descent.

"Well?" she asked when we touched down beside her. "Did you meet Brian?"

I nodded. "Yes. A very nice man."

"And? Did you make an offer?"

"Patience," I replied. "How did he know I might be interested in the shop?"

Molly grinned. "I told him."

"Instigator. Interloper."

"I try my best," she said. "Just think, if you buy All Things, you won't have a commute at all. And you don't have to get up early to get to some studio. We open at the very reasonable nine a.m. And you won't even have to be here then."

"You're quite good at sales."

"Well, I'm in the biz."

"I'll see you later, Molly."

"Okay, boss."

"Get back to work," I snapped. I smiled and added, "I like being bossy. Have a good day, Molly."

"Bye."

"Are you serious?" Alex asked when we were out of the store. "You're thinking of buying that place?"

I shrugged. "Possibly."

"Why? What about your career?"

Before I could answer, Pauline's shout of my name beckoned me. I turned and saw her standing in her shop's entry, waving at me. She wore an anxious expression.

"I'll meet you at the coffee shop," I said to Alex. "Order three black cups and whatever you want."

I trotted across the street, ignoring his bewildered, "Veronica!"

Pauline disappeared into the store before I reached the curb. I entered and found her pacing the birthday card aisle.

"I am so horrified," she wailed as I came up to her. "I can't bear to think that you would think that Glen murdered Anna."

I reached out to touch her flailing hands. "It's okay," I said.

"I'm just horrified!" Pauline's eyes welled.

"Pauline, it's okay. I really didn't suspect him. I was just startled by the sound of his car backfiring. This whole thing has me on edge and I'm overanalyzing everything."

"Really?" Pauline asked as she wiped her eye.

"Really. I never truly thought Glen would do such a thing."

Pauline exhaled and smiled. "I freaked when Glen told me you heard the car backfire. I know you heard Anna telling me she'd evict me if I didn't pay up. It's easy to put two and two together and make me the prime suspect."

She made me feel like a rat the more she talked. How could I ever suspect this sweet woman of murder?

"You're being silly. Now that it's all straightened out, let's not talk about it anymore."

Pauline threw her arms around me. "You're the best, Veronica," she said.

"Back at you."

She pulled back, putting on a smile. "Was that Alex Shelby with you? I heard he was visiting you."

"Yes. He's playing in a charity golf tournament on Saturday and came up a few days early to visit."

"Interesting," Pauline said with a suggestive wiggle of her eyebrows.

"We're just friends, Pauline."

"Uh-huh." She continued with her implying smile. I liked it better when she was frantic I thought her husband a murderer.

I looked around the store. "Do you run this store all by yourself? Don't you have any help?"

"Sure. I have a couple of part-time people. I can't hire anyone full time right now."

"I'm sorry."

"Thanks," Pauline sighed. "Sometimes I think of just closing the business. Mom's been talking about it a lot lately."

"That would be a sad end of an era," I said.

"Yeah. But it's too much. And it's hard to watch others do so well, and nobody comes in here."

"I'm sorry to hear that. But you should do what will make you happy and give you peace of mind."

The bell over the door jingled; we turned to find a woman and a young girl entering.

"Good morning, Shelley," Pauline said. "Hi, Amanda."

"Hey, Pauline. I need two birthday balloons," Shelley said.

"Coming right up." Pauline directed her to a book by the counter that showed what balloons she sold.

"I'll see you later, Pauline," I said, heading for the door.

"Off to meet Alex?" she teased.

As I opened the door, I turned back and said, "It's good to see you smiling, Pauline."

I called Madeline on my way to the coffee shop. After exchanging pleasantries, I accepted her invitation to lunch and canasta.

"I'm thrilled," she chirped.

I caught up with Alex at The Caffs. He stood at the counter, chatting with Chloe as she filled our order. One of their employees, Nate, was helping another customer.

I said hello to both and was immediately greeted by Chloe with the exclamation, "You're thinking of buying All Things?"

I gave Alex a disapproving look.

"She already knew," he said.

"You must," Chloe continued. "How cool would that be!"

"Totally cool. Mom told me last night Anna's family is going to auction her properties. Can you and Dana buy your space?"

"Dana and I are discussing it. We're not sure if we can afford it. I hope we can."

"I hope so, too."

"So how are you doing, Veronica?" Chloe asked. "Are you

still staying with your mom until the murderer is caught?"

"No, I'm back at my house."

"You're so brave," Chloe said. "I'm having nightmares about it."

"I'm sorry to hear that."

"I slept at Dana's last night because I just don't want to be alone. Dana's not nervous at all. She figures the person is far from Barton by now."

Just then Dana came through a swinging door that separated the service area from the back room. She carried a tray loaded with three carafes of milk, tall cups, and a stack of napkins.

"Hey," she said as she walked behind Chloe.

Just as she was passing Nate, he turned and bumped into Dana. Everything on the tray slid onto the floor.

Chloe started and screamed. Dana uttered an expletive, followed by an angry, "Watch where you're going, Nate!"

Nate turned bright red. "I'm sorry, Dana." He knelt and began picking up the clutter.

"That scared me half to death," said Chloe, her hand pressed against her heart.

Dana ran her fingers through her hair, grasping the strands for a moment as if she were going to pull them out.

"It's okay," she finally said. "I'm sorry I yelled, Nate." She leaned over, picked up the napkins, and tossed them in a garbage can.

"I'll be more careful," Nate said as he placed the carafes on the counter.

"Nothing broken, nothing spilled. All is well," Alex said.

Dana forced a weary smile as she placed the carafes in a refrigerator under the counter. "That's right. No spilled milk to cry over." She took the tray and returned to the back room.

Chloe set a carry-carton holding four cups on the counter.

Alex waved me off as I reached into my purse for money.

"I've got it, Ronnie."

He pulled a few bills from his wallet and handed them to Chloe.

"Are you enjoying your visit?" she asked Alex.

"I'm loving it. Bartonians have been very welcoming." When Chloe tried to hand him his change, Alex waved it off, saying, "My contribution to the building fund."

Chloe's face beamed and she said, "Thank you so much, Alex."

"You're very welcome. This is a really great establishment you have here. I wish you continued great success."

Chloe sighed. "From your lips." She rubbed her fingers together and said, "It's all about the dough."

"Isn't everything?" Alex said.

Chloe smiled, just for Alex, and said, "I really hope to see you again before you leave."

"I'll make a point of it."

We said goodbye to Chloe and Nate and left.

"This village has the most remarkable women," Alex gushed as we headed for Carol's. "And you, my dear, are the most remarkable of them all."

"You can stop flirting now. Your mission has been accomplished."

"How'd I do?"

"You passed."

Alex took a gulp from his cup. "So what *is* this about you buying that shop? How come you haven't told me?"

"Because I just found out a couple of days ago and I'm not sure if I'm going to do it."

"It would be a good investment. And Claire could run it, so you wouldn't even have to be there. Have you thought about what I said last night? I could talk to Larry."

We reached Carol's. I stopped in front of the window and

took a deep breath. "I've already talked with Larry. And a number of other agents. No one's interested in representing me. No one wants me. Okay? Let's not talk about it anymore."

Alex stared at me for a moment and then pulled me in for a hug. He held me tightly with one arm as he held the carry-carton. Through the window I could see Mark and Carol watching us.

"Everything's going to be okay," he murmured as he kissed my cheek.

"I know. Let's go inside."

Amy came out just as Alex reached for the door.

"Hi, you two," she said. She carried a large binder in her arms.

"Where are you off to?" I asked.

"A meeting with a bride."

"About cake?" Alex asked, grinning.

Amy laughed, which made his grin widen. "Amy Reynolds," she said, offering her hand.

Alex took it, saying, "Alex Shelby."

"It's nice to meet you." I noticed a faint blush spreading across her cheek. "I have to go. See you later," she said. She walked away, glancing over her shoulder at Alex.

"Yet another beautiful Barton lass," Alex said.

I shook my head and pulled open the door.

"Good morning," Carol said as we entered.

"It's a beautiful one," Alex said.

Mark said nothing, just looked from me to Alex.

"I have a lot to tell you," I said. I took the carry-carton from Alex and set it on the counter. "Help yourselves."

"Mark told me about last night," Carol said. "I can't believe they pulled the mayor in for questioning."

I took a sip of coffee and said, "I'd love to know what the tipster said. I mean, did they mention the mayor's relationship with Anna? Did they know about it?"

"It could have been a prank," Carol said.

"So what do you have to tell us?" Mark asked.

"Glen Weber came to my house last night after I got home from the police station. Remember when his car backfired yesterday morning, Mark?"

"Yes. And you heard a car backfire before Anna was murdered. What did he say?"

"That he had gone by Anna's that morning to drop off Pauline's rent check."

Mark's eyebrows lifted. "He dropped it off?"

"Yes. He said Pauline dreaded being around Anna. So he dropped off the check and left. He didn't even go inside. And Glen mentioned seeing Claire on her way to the house as he was leaving."

"That's interesting."

"You two don't seriously believe Claire did it?" Carol asked.

"We have to consider everyone who was at the house that morning," Mark responded.

"Claire wanted to buy All Things and Anna just laughed at her," I said. "Maybe they had a heated conversation about it that morning. Claire could have made another offer and been rejected again."

"But she's so lovely," Alex moaned.

I ignored him and told Mark, "We talked with Claire this morning. The other day she implied that Pauline had more time to pay her rent. But you'd think Anna would have given her the check Glen had just given her for Claire to deposit. But Claire said Anna didn't give it to her, and that she didn't see Glen on the way to Anna's."

Mark nodded. "So one of them is lying. Either Glen is lying and he didn't see Claire. Or Claire is lying. They both want you to believe that someone saw Anna alive after they did."

I sank onto the stool beside Mark. I didn't want to believe Glen or Claire to be a liar. Or a murderer.

"So are you saying it's definitely either Glen or Claire who murdered Anna?" I asked.

"I don't know. I don't want to guess at that. We need proof."

Alex said, "Ronnie, if Claire killed Anna because she didn't want her to sell the shop to you, maybe you shouldn't buy it. You would be making yourself a target."

Carol looked at me, her mouth open and her expression blank. "Veronica, Anna wanted to sell you the shop?" Carol asked.

Oops. I had slouched in my best friend duties by not telling said best friend the important news first.

"Yes," I confessed. "I found out that's what Anna wanted to talk with me about."

"Were you going to tell me?"

"Yes, of course. But Alex showed up, and I fell into the garbage can, and then Connie D'Amato was in here buying flowers, and then the mayor was hauled in, and then my lights went out when Glen was trying to convince me he wasn't a murderer."

"Will you at least let me know before the ink is dry on the sale?" Carol asked, giving me a stern look.

"Of course I will. If it happens. I'm meeting with Anna's brother at eleven-thirty. Let's see what he says. For now, let's get back to the case. How do we figure out who's telling the truth?"

"Find the check," Mark said.

"Great. I'll just rummage through Claire's purse," I complained.

"You can always just stop," Carol said. "Like I keep telling you. Leave it to the police."

"The voice of reason speaks again," I said.

A customer entered the store, smiling in surprise when she saw the four of us clustered around the counter.

"Good morning, Cheryl," Carol said as she rounded the counter.

Cheryl greeted Carol and began to explain what she wanted. Mark, Alex, and I grabbed our coffee cups, waved goodbye to Carol, and left.

"Same time, same place tomorrow," Carol called after us.

"So where to next?" Alex asked as we strolled down the sidewalk.

I looked at my watch. "I'm just going to hang out at the bookstore until I have to meet Brian Langdon."

"I'll hang with you."

I needed a break from Alex. "Why don't you go back to the inn. Or do something fun."

"But I'm going to the meeting with you."

"That's not necessary," I said as politely as I could.

Alex eyed me. "Maybe you need some backup. This is a big deal you're considering."

I gave him a cross look. "I can handle this on my own, Alex."

Mark's grin straightened to a sober look when Alex looked to him for male support.

"Veronica's quite a capable wheeler and dealer," he said.

"All right," Alex said, discouraged.

"Thank you for offering," I said to appease him. "Why don't you go practice your golf swing or your putting?"

"Perhaps."

I asked Mark, "What are you doing today?"

"I have to run over to campus for a meeting. It will be good for all of us to take a break from our investigation, such as it is."

"Yeah," I said, still wondering about the missing check.

We stopped at the corner and tentatively looked at each other.

"Well, see you later, then," Alex said. He wandered across

Orchard, looking a bit forlorn.

"Poor guy," Mark said.

"He'll get over it."

"No impulse buying," Mark warned me with a grin.

"Don't worry, I won't be bringing my checkbook. And I doubt Brian accepts credit cards."

CHAPTER TWENTY-FOUR

I arrived at The Hearth to find Brian seated in the dining room. He stood to greet me, shaking my hand and waiting until I sat before taking his seat.

"I hope you don't mind, I ordered our coffee when I arrived."

"Not at all. I know you don't have much time. I want to say again how sorry I am about your sister's death," I said.

"Thank you. I'm not quite over the shock of it yet. Our mother is devastated."

"Please pass my condolences on to her."

Our waitress came, tray in hand. She gave us each a cup and saucer and then filled the cups with coffee poured from a silver pot. After she placed a small pitcher of milk and bowl of sugar packets on the table and left, I said, "It's a shame that your family lived so far apart from each other."

Brian said, "It was better that way. Anna and our mother had a difficult relationship. They were very much the same—stubborn, perfectionist, demanding of others. They got along better with Mom in Florida and Anna up here. And it was easier for me, not having Anna hovering around me all the time, dominating and telling me how to do everything. She did enough of that from Barton."

"What is your work?" I asked.

"I teach science at a private high school in Philadelphia."

I glanced at his wedding ring. "And you're married. Do you

have children?"

"A son and daughter. Both teenagers." Brian sipped his coffee and then asked, "And you? I understand you're an actress." After I gave him a very brief account of my career, he nodded and said, "Then All Things is a perfect opportunity for you."

"Maybe," I said.

The sound of breaking glass pulled our attention to the bar area, just a few feet beyond our table in the dining room.

"Sorry," a young man behind the bar said.

A man was sitting at the bar, halfway turned in his seat so he could see into the dining room. He wore thick-framed glasses beneath slicked-back hair. He spun quickly on his stool when our eyes met.

Good grief. It was Alex.

I clenched my teeth and smiled at Brian. "It might be a very good opportunity. I'm not sure how much . . ." I said, treading carefully into the subject of the sale price.

"Anna's lawyer and accountant are going to work with Claire to come up with a number," Brian said.

I glanced over his shoulder. Alex was once again turned on the stool and watching us as he sipped a drink from a tall glass. I wanted to clobber him, or at least give him a wicked look.

"Has Claire expressed interest in the shop?" I asked.

"Yes. But she'd have trouble getting a bank loan. She proposed a payment plan, but my mother and I would rather just sell the shop and be done with it."

"That's understandable."

"So as soon as I get that number, I'll get it to you so you can go over it with your lawyer and accountant."

"Sounds good." I didn't have a business card to hand him, so I wrote my phone number on a scrap of paper from my purse and handed it to him.

When he put the paper in his pocket, he pulled out a key. He placed it on the table and slid it over to me. "This is to Anna's front door. I hate to ask you to keep an eye on her house, but just in case something happens, I don't know what—"

"I'd be happy to keep an eye on it." I took the key and dropped it in my purse.

We sat quietly for a minute or two, drinking our coffee. I took a few darting glances at Alex, who appeared to be in deep conversation with the young man who dropped the tray.

Brian set his cup down and ran his hand up and down his cheek. "I just can't get over Anna being murdered. It's surreal. Who would do that to her?"

I put down my cup. "I've been trying to figure that out myself. What have the police told you?"

"They're working on it. They've asked me more questions than they've answered." Brian regarded me for a moment and then asked, "Did Anna have any problems with anyone?"

I shook my head. "I wasn't around enough to know."

"I'm worried that they'll never find her killer. That there will never be justice."

The little comfort I could give him was a softly spoken, "They'll find the person."

Brian drained his cup and looked at his watch. From behind him I could see Alex lean over in his chair, peering around Brian to look at me.

"I have to get to the funeral home," Brian said, gesturing to our waitress. He reached into his back pocket for his wallet. "Thank you so much for meeting with me, Veronica. I'm sorry to rush out."

"I understand completely. Thank you for taking the time to talk with me."

The waitress came over and handed Brian the check. He gave it a quick glance and handed her a few bills. They thanked each other before the waitress headed into the bar.

Brian and I stood and shook hands. "I'll be in touch," he said.

I trailed him as he dashed through the bar and into the hallway. Without a word I walked up to Alex, crossing my arms across my chest and giving him my best stern look.

"That seemed to go well," he said, gulping down the last mouthful of his drink.

"Nice glasses."

"Thank you." Alex took them off and turned them in his hand, regarding them with pride. "I picked them up at the drugstore."

"Why the disguise?"

He put the glasses back on, saying, "I thought it would be better to go incognito, as they say."

"Who says that?"

"Everyone."

"This isn't a soap plot, you know."

"I know."

"So why did you follow me? I can handle this myself."

"I know. But I feel protective of you. I don't want you to be taken advantage of."

I softened a bit. "Thank you. But my lawyer and accountant will see that I'm not."

"So what's he asking for the shop?"

"The number is being worked up, as they say."

"So what are we doing next?"

I sighed. "I'm going home and having a peanut butter and jelly sandwich."

"May I come? Or am I still in the doghouse for having your best interests at heart?"

I let him squirm for a moment and then said, "Please join me. But take off those glasses. They don't suit you at all."

Alex whipped them off, flashing his soap star smile. I had to laugh.

"Come on," I said, tilting my head toward the exit.

"So you didn't make an offer? I saw you write something down and give it to him."

"My phone number," I said as we crossed the restaurant's narrow entry hall.

Alex opened and held the door for me. "And then he gave you something. It was all very interesting."

"Sharp observational skills, Alex. He gave me Anna's house key, in case of an emergency."

An idea came to me as I stepped into the parking lot and turned toward Orchard. Alex's babbling about the delights of an Adirondack summer day became a distant hum as the idea became a plan.

CHAPTER TWENTY-FIVE

"Am I betraying Brian's trust?" I asked before taking a bite of my sandwich.

"I don't think so," Alex said.

"I do," said Mark.

"This could be considered an emergency," I said.

"You are trying to solve his sister's murder," Alex said.

"That's my sole reason. I'm snooping for a cause." I swallowed and looked across my yard to Anna's house.

"Why not ask the police? They may have the check," Mark said.

"I don't want to implicate Glen if he's innocent. And wouldn't they have questioned Glen, or at least told him they had the check?"

"But finding it, or not finding it, won't necessarily prove anything."

"But we'll know if Glen's telling the truth about the check. If he delivered the check, Anna would have no cause to evict Pauline. And Glen would have no reason to kill Anna. If I don't find the check, I'll figure out some way to ask Tracey."

Mark sighed; he knew I was set on my plan no matter what he said. "Be careful, Veronica. Very careful," he urged.

"I promise I will."

"I have to go. I'll see you later."

"Thanks, Mark." I shut my cell phone and put it in my pocket.

"You didn't really need to call him," Alex said.

"He's my partner in this."

"So am I," Alex said, a bit hurt.

"You're right. I'm sorry."

"I should really be the one to go in," Alex said. "Let me take the heat if someone comes."

"No, I'm going. It's my idea and I can move faster. And I'm the neighbor, so if I'm caught, I have an excuse. You're my lookout."

"All right."

This was my plan—gain access to Anna's via the key Brian gave me and search for Pauline's rent check. Alex would "stand guard," alerting me if anyone tried to enter the house. I'd have my cell phone in my pocket, set to vibrate. If someone, like the police, approached, he'd dial my number to alert me. Then he would distract the person, giving me time to sneak out the back door and slip around the hedge.

The nervousness I usually felt as stage fright intensified as I gobbled the rest of my sandwich. I wiped my mouth and hands with a napkin, grabbed my paper plate, and went inside, saying to Alex, "I'm going to make a pit stop before we execute the plan."

I paid my visit to the bathroom, brushing my teeth as well. I had to burn off some of my excess nervous energy, plus I wanted fresh breath, just in case the plan went awry.

"Ready?" I asked Alex when I returned to the backyard.

"Yes," he said. "Now where do you want me positioned?"

"Sit on the front porch."

"Will do." He put his hands on my shoulders and said with great seriousness, "Good luck, Ronnie."

"Thanks," I said.

We walked down the driveway together, separating when we got to the front. Alex, whistling, turned right and dashed up the porch steps. I turned left and crossed my driveway and Anna's.

Clutching her house key, I hurried up her front walk and porch steps. I unlocked the door and slipped into the front hall.

I didn't expect an instantaneous creepy feeling to hit me. The house's eerie silence, accentuated by the dimness of the curtained rooms, stopped me right inside the door. My concern over unwanted discovery suddenly became a fear of something far more sinister happening.

"Don't be silly. It's not a haunted house," I whispered.

Anna's office was to the right. I figured she would have put the check on her desk, so I headed in there. I realized that, while on a mission to find the missing check, I might also discover other clues as to who murdered Anna. I hastened my pace.

My eagerness plunged immediately. There was no appointment book or calendar I could thumb through. There were several unopened envelopes of junk mail soliciting business for gutter cleaning, high-speed Internet access, and a spa a few miles from Barton. Our local newspaper, *The Chronicle,* lay unfolded on the center of the desk. It was from the day Anna died. I lifted it, hoping to find the elusive check. How easy would that be!

What I found was a copy of the *New York Times.* Peeling that back, I found a sheet of paper with a handwritten list of national retail stores. On the list were Glenda's Brew, Pip's Books, and Lamb's Greetings and Gifts. It read like a list of enemies; the shops that would end Orchard Street as we knew it.

There was nothing more of note on the desk. I pulled open the center drawer, only to find it filled with plain white paper and a box of fancy stationery. Just as I was pushing the drawer closed, I heard a key turn in the front door.

I shoved the drawer closed and ducked beside the desk. I patted my pants pocket to check for my cell phone. It was there. Why hadn't Alex sent the signal?

The door opened and closed. Keys jangled. I held my breath, not daring to move. I heard footsteps move into the living room and then a drawn-out sigh.

I leaned forward a few inches, enough to see Claire start up the stairs to the second floor

The doorbell chimed several times.

Claire impatiently said, "Oh, hold on!"

I pressed myself into the corner created by the desk and wall as Claire opened the door.

"What the hell is going on?" she asked.

"I don't have long," Pauline said. "Mindy is alone."

Claire shut the door and asked, "Why did Glen say he was here Tuesday morning? And why is he telling Veronica he saw me on Sycamore?"

Just as I was about to lose my balance, my muscles tightened at her words. My phone remained still in my pocket. Where was Alex?

The two remained in the hall. "He's protecting me," Pauline said in a defensive tone. "Glen doesn't want the police to know I was here."

"*I* protected you! The police questioned *me*, of course, because I worked for Anna."

"They talked to me, too," Pauline said. "They talked to all of Anna's tenants."

"But they know I was the one who dropped off the pastries. I could have told them you were here, too, but I didn't. I could have told them Anna wasn't going to renew your lease. There's a motive. Eviction! And then Glen implies to Veronica that I was the last to see Anna alive."

Just as Mark said.

"You probably were," Pauline said. She hastily added, "I mean, before whoever killed her."

"What if she tells the police what Glen told her?"

"Veronica won't do that."

"You don't know that. Veronica's being very inquisitive. She asked me this morning about the check *Glen* supposedly dropped off. What if she tells the police what he told her? They just might go after him."

"Veronica won't," Pauline said. "Glen convinced her he dropped off the check and left. She's probably just bored. She has nothing to do. And being on the soap for thirty years, she probably has a very active imagination. Veronica's nice. She won't say anything."

"She needs to stop snooping. She might get hurt."

I tucked Claire's words away for future interpretation. At the moment I was solely interested in remaining undetected.

"I didn't tell the police you were here. But if I'm pushed, I will. I'll tell them everything."

"I can tell the police some things too, Claire."

"Don't threaten me."

"You were very upset about Anna wanting to sell the store to Veronica. The two of you had a deal. Actually, you and Mr. Frazer had a deal and Anna squelched it."

"Shut up about that."

"I'd just have to tell the police the truth. I left first."

"That wouldn't prove anything."

One of them started up the stairs.

"Where are you going?" Pauline asked.

"Anna's brother is coming for her burial clothes. He'll be here any minute."

"Do you still have my check?" Pauline asked, her voice moving away as she followed Claire up the stairs. If Claire gave an answer, I didn't hear it.

I crouched beside the desk until I could no longer hear Claire and Pauline. I considered my options. I could relocate to a safer hiding place and hope the pair said more when they returned.

Or I could get out of there when I had the opportunity. If found, I wouldn't be surprised if Claire called the police and turned me in as a suspect.

Mark's warning rang in my ears. "Be very careful."

I went with my better judgment and hastily tiptoed across the study to the front door. Just as I reached it, a key turned in the lock.

Brian!

In my haste to get out, I had forgotten what Claire had just said. Senior moment!

I raced through the living room and into the dining room. In a flash I was under the table, praying that the chairs and overhanging tablecloth would provide me ample cover.

"Hello," Brian called out as he closed the door. "Claire, are you here?"

"I'll be right there!" I heard Claire call from above the dining room.

Brian took a couple of steps into the living room and stopped. With his hands in his pockets, he just stood there. I couldn't see his face, so I filled in his expression with a tired, forlorn look of grief and disbelief over how his week started out normal and ended with the difficult task of burying his sister.

Claire's and Pauline's footsteps on the stairs put me on alert.

"Hi, Brian," Claire said as she came into my view. "This is Pauline Weber. She runs the stationery store across from All Things. Pauline, this is Brian Langdon, Anna's brother."

I watched as Pauline stepped into the living room and shook Brian's hand.

"I'm so sorry for your loss," she said.

"Thank you."

I heard the clash of clothes hangers and saw Claire hold up a navy blue outfit and one in lavender. "I thought one of these would be nice."

Brian sighed, taking the garments from Claire. "Thank you, Claire. I'll take them both and let my mother and wife decide."

Pauline hummed in sympathy.

Claire then handed him a box. "Her valuable jewelry is in here. I left the rest upstairs. Would you like me to get them for you?"

That was an interesting point. What if the night intruder was not involved in Anna's murder, but a common thief taking advantage of the situation? Would Claire know if jewelry was missing? What if she was the night visitor?

"No, that's fine. Thank you. I appreciate all your help, Claire. You've really been a comfort."

"Anna was a friend."

"She was my landlady," Pauline said. "She always treated me fairly."

Hmm. Did Pauline fib out of sympathy, or was she rewriting history to cover herself?

Brian chuckled. "I'm sure she was also very tough if you were even a minute late with the rent."

"Not at all," Pauline said.

"I have to get going. I have to pick up my family at the airport."

Claire reached over and touched Brian's arm. "Take care. I'll see you on Sunday."

"When are the wake and funeral for Anna? I'd like to attend," Pauline said.

"The wake is Sunday and Monday in Saratoga," Brian answered. "We'll bury her on Tuesday."

"I have the details," Claire said.

The three walked into the hallway, disappearing from my sight.

"Thank you again, Claire," Brian said. "It was nice meeting you, Pauline."

"Likewise," Pauline said, "though I wish under better circumstances."

Brian left and Claire shut the door.

"Nice comment about Anna being fair," Claire snorted. "I think Brian saw right through it."

"What should I have said? She was the wicked witch of the Adirondacks?"

The back door closed and a loud thump sounded in the kitchen.

"Who's that?" Pauline whispered.

"Hello?" Claire shouted with unmistakable annoyance.

"Hi back. It's Sandy Jenkins." I heard Sandy hurry through the kitchen and into the hall. "Who's here?" she demanded.

"It's Claire and Pauline, Sandy. Why are *you* here?"

"To clean my employer's house," Sandy responded sharply. "Why are *you* here?"

Way to go, Sandy! Someone who could go toe to toe with Claire.

"I have to get back to the store," Pauline said. Within seconds the front door opened and closed.

"Anna's brother needed a few of her things," Claire said in a none-of-your-business tone.

"Poor man," Sandy clucked.

"I have to go, too. I left my purse in Anna's bedroom," Claire said.

As Claire hurried upstairs, Sandy stepped into the dining room and knelt beside the table. "What are you doing under there?" she whispered.

"Eavesdropping," I hissed.

"Okay."

She stood just as Claire came down the stairs. "Happy cleaning," she trilled as she headed for the door.

"Good seeing you, Claire," Sandy called as the door slammed shut. She bent over and said, "All's clear."

I crawled from under the table. Sandy held out her hand; I gratefully grabbed it and smiled my thanks as I stood.

"So, what'd you hear?" she asked.

Already flushed from my crawl, I was glad Sandy couldn't detect my embarrassed blush.

"Oh, just a conversation about burial clothes and the service."

"You can hop a ride to Saratoga with me on Sunday, if you'd like."

I hadn't even thought about attending the wake or funeral. "Thanks. I'll let you know."

Sandy headed back to the kitchen. "So why were you here in the first place?"

I followed and discovered the source of the thumping noise standing on the counter—a large plastic caddie loaded with cleaning supplies. "Well, Brian gave me a key, just in case of emergency."

Sandy twisted the plug in the sink and turned on the faucet. "Was there an emergency?"

"Sort of. I was looking for a certain rent check."

Crossing to the table to retrieve a bottle of Mr. Clean from a plastic bucket on the table, Sandy asked, "Your mother's?"

"Uh-huh," I said. "She's worried it may have been lost in the, you know . . ." I didn't want to dig too deep of a lie.

"Yeah. If it's here, it would be on Anna's desk. But Claire probably has it." She waved her hand at me. "But go, have a look. If Claire or anyone else comes, just tell them you saw my van and came over for a chat, and that I put you to work."

I didn't want to admit that I had already checked the desk, or that I knew the check I was really looking for was in Claire's possession. "No one who knows you will believe that you relinquished even the slightest of cleaning duties to me," I teased.

"Then tell them you're the scout, checking for dirt in advance of my attack."

"I owe you one, Sandy."

"Be a great canasta player and you'll owe me nothing."

"What?"

"You're my new partner. You didn't forget about the canasta game tomorrow, did you?"

"I didn't. We're partners? I thought Dotsie was."

"Yeah. Dotsie was supposed to be your partner because she partnered with Ingrid, God rest her soul. But Dotsie doesn't trust your playing skills, so she insisted on playing with Myrtle. So I'm with you."

"Good."

"It will be fun. Now go look for the check, and let me get to work."

I went to the office and just stood there for a couple of minutes, reviewing what I had learned from Claire and Pauline. I couldn't wait to tell Mark.

I returned to the kitchen and thanked Sandy.

She held up her hands as if I were approaching the edge of a cliff. "Wet floor," she bellowed. "Just walk in a straight line to the door."

"Yes, ma'am," I said.

"Any luck?"

"No. Thanks for letting me look. And for not telling anyone."

"It's our little secret."

I hurried across Anna's backyard and onto my driveway. Alex, his back bent and hands cupped on his knees, stood peering around the far end of the hedge. My irritation swelled as I marched down the driveway. Here was my chance for some retaliatory fun, not only for his poor job of acting as a lookout, but also for the scare he gave me the night of his arrival.

I stopped right behind him. "What are you doing?"

Alex started, shouted, fell against the hedge, and then went down on one knee.

I then remembered he was a man in the age category that suffered heart attacks.

"I'm sorry," I cried as I helped him to his feet. "Are you all right?"

Alex nodded. "Are *you* all right? Whose van is that?"

"Sandy, Anna's housekeeper."

"Did she see you? How did you get out of the house? What happened?"

"That's my question for you. Claire Camden, Pauline Weber, Brian Langdon, and Sandy Jenkins all entered that house and you didn't send me one signal."

"I'm sorry," he said. "I got a call on my cell."

"A call!"

Alex looked at the ground. "Yes. I had to take it."

"Seriously? What was more important than watching my back when I was in the house where a murder was committed?"

"I'm sorry, Ronnie. So sorry. Did they see you?"

"No. I hid under the dining room table."

Alex followed as I walked back up the driveway. "I'll make it up to you. I'll take you to dinner tonight, the fanciest place in town."

I didn't feel much like sitting in the fanciest restaurant in town. "You don't have to," I said. "Why don't I just make dinner? I can tell you and Mark what I found out at Anna's."

"All right. I'll bring the wine. Red and white," he said, as if that was suitable amends.

We reached my back porch. "Fine."

"I'm really very sorry, Ronnie," Alex said.

One glance into his pleading eyes and I took pity on him. "I forgive you."

He exhaled and thanked me, promising I'd have his full attention the next time I entered someone's home uninvited.

"Now I'm going to go get that wine. The most expensive the store has," Alex said with a gleam in his eye. He dashed down the porch steps and through the yard to the driveway.

Despite the peril in which he had placed me (I was in the mood to be a drama queen), I had to laugh at my recent predicament. It reminded me of the time on the show when my character was in a similar situation, but in a closet and wearing high heels and an evening gown. Rachel ended up with a gun in her back.

I hoped reality wouldn't put me in the same circumstance.

Chapter Twenty-Six

I called Mark to invite him to dinner, and then headed off to the Food Mart to buy what I needed for a grilled shrimp and penne dinner. When I returned home, I found the mayor sitting on my front steps, sending text messages. I parked at the top of the driveway and carried my shopping bags to the front of the house.

"Hi, Jason."

He looked up, a bit abashed to be discovered in the act of typing. "Hi, Veronica."

I carried my bags over and set them on the top step. "Are you here because you really needed texting privacy?" I said. Since my mother had proven his innocence the night before, I felt much lighter and unguarded around him.

"Well, no. I'm not as addicted as I look right now," he said, holding up his iPhone before returning it to the clip on his belt. "And I don't normally settle on a neighbor's porch when they're not at home."

"What a relief."

"I'd like to talk with you, if you have the time. I want to explain some things."

"I'd be happy to listen. I have to put this in the fridge first," I said, pointing to my shopping bags. "Would you like a soda, with maybe a little pizzazz in it, as my mother, your client, would say?"

"I'm still on duty. I'll take a straight soda."

He picked up the bags and followed me through the house to the kitchen. I took two glasses from the cabinet and two ginger ales from the refrigerator and handed him one of each. We chatted about the weather as I quickly stashed the food in the refrigerator.

"Shall we sit out back?" I asked as I poured my own glass of soda.

"Sure."

We settled in porch chairs. Jason's expression, so relaxed when we were in the kitchen, had become somber and taut.

He looked me in the eye and said, "Veronica, you know Anna and I had a relationship."

I nodded. "I heard you two Monday night, after the meeting."

"It started two months ago. I can't even explain how. It was just a sudden, crazy attraction. We were both involved with other people, but that didn't stop us. We had a very passionate relationship. Anna wasn't the love of my life, but I cared for her deeply. She was tough and confident and very demanding. She expected excellence from herself and everyone around her. That was very appealing to me because I have the same ethic, though I'm not as harsh as she was when people didn't reach her high bar."

He paused to take a sip of his drink. I remained silent.

"And as you heard, we didn't agree about the mall. Anna thought it would destroy Orchard Street business. I didn't agree. I think the two could peacefully coexist. It would have increased revenues for the village. It would have provided more shopping options for Barton residents and people from nearby towns. And I believe it would have brought new people to the village who would then discover the charms of Orchard."

I had to interrupt. "And if it had a bookstore it would have put my mother out of business."

"I don't think so. Your mother does a good business. People would be loyal to her."

"Maybe," I muttered. I found his assumption to be naive wishful thinking, but I bit my tongue.

"So Anna and I didn't agree on the mall," Jason continued. "We talked about it briefly that night and that was it. I left around midnight. Everything was fine between us. I can't blame you for suspecting me—"

I felt guilty, knowing that he was innocent. "Jason, I—"

"You don't have to apologize or explain," he said. "I would have suspected me, too. But as you know now, I was meeting with your wonderful mother at the time Anna was killed."

"Good," I said. "I'm very glad you didn't do it."

"Thank you," Jason said. "I'm not finished, though."

"Oh?"

"That was me at Anna's house Wednesday night. You were outside—"

"That was you!" I exclaimed. "I saw a light moving around in an upstairs room and came over to check it out. I tried to look in the windows, but the drapes were closed."

"You almost caught me."

"And you almost caught me. But my friend gave me the surprise instead. So why were you there?"

"I wanted to retrieve a bracelet I had given Anna. I know it was foolish and reckless, but I'm sentimental. I wanted something tangible to remember her."

"That's understandable."

"When I was leaving, I heard you scream and a man talking to you. I listened for a few seconds, to make sure you weren't in peril. When I knew you were okay, and figured out it was your friend, I hurried through Anna's yard and over to Sycamore. I practically ran back to the Village Hall where my car was."

We sat in thoughtful silence for a few moments.

"I hear you're considering joining the Barton business community."

"I am. Yes."

"You'd be very welcome."

"That seems to be the word on the street."

"I hope you do buy the shop. It's a great business and it would be great to have a member of the Barton family running it."

Jason picked up his glass and stood. I did as well and shook his hand when he offered it.

"Thank you for explaining things," I said. "You didn't have to. I appreciate that you did."

"Thank you for listening. I'd appreciate it if you didn't talk about this."

"I won't."

"Thanks. I told your mother, too, if you're wondering. I thought she had the right to know after being called down to the station to confirm my alibi."

"You know she'll never speak a word about it."

"I know," he said. "If you see another beam of light in Anna's house, know it's not me and call the police immediately. I don't want you to get hurt."

I thanked him and took his glass. We said goodbye, and I watched him as he bounded down the steps, so much lighter after his confession, of a sort.

I felt much lighter too, knowing I hadn't come close to harm at all that night of creeping around the hedge.

I should have stopped while I was ahead.

CHAPTER TWENTY-SEVEN

"I can't believe you weren't paying attention!"

"I've said I'm sorry a hundred times!"

"Anything could have happened to Veronica."

"But nothing did."

"But something could have happened."

"But it didn't."

"I can't leave you two alone for five minutes!"

Mark and Alex stood at the grill, supposedly keeping an eye on the shrimp. When I heard them yelling, I left the penne boiling on the stove and hurried outside.

"Sorry," Mark said.

"Yeah, sorry," said Alex.

"You're not letting the shrimp burn, are you?"

Mark said, "Of course not. I wouldn't let that happen."

Alex shot him a look, insulted at Mark's insinuation that he would burn the crustaceans. I wondered if he got Mark's deeper implication—that he wouldn't let anything happen to me.

"They're done," Mark said.

"So is the penne."

I returned to the kitchen. After a couple of minutes Mark joined me, carrying the shrimp plate.

I drained the pasta and dumped it in a big bowl. Mark added the shrimp and I followed with the pesto sauce. He tossed the whole thing with a serving spoon while I grabbed the salad.

I could tell Mark was holding his tongue, politely not telling me he told me so. So I said, "Thank you for putting the shrimp, not Alex, on the barbie."

He cracked a smile. "He's lucky. There was room for both."

He picked up the pasta bowl and followed me outside. Alex had poured wine for us and stood by the table.

"Thank you, Alex," I said.

He took the salad bowl from me and placed it on the table. He then pulled out my chair, pushing it in as I sat.

I thanked him again and said, "You're forgiven. Please stop being so obsequious."

"My apologies."

Mark placed the pasta bowl next to my plate. "Now tell me what you learned at Anna's."

I hadn't yet told Mark and Alex about my misadventure inside Anna's house. Mark arrived at my house a few minutes after Alex's arrival. He overheard Alex, holding the promised red and white wine, apologizing again for "not being a proper guard." Explanation followed, leaving Mark with the mission's conclusion and nothing of the preceding incident.

"It's kind of anticlimactic now, isn't it?" I teased as I spooned penne and shrimp on my plate. "You already know how it ends."

Mark gave me an impatient look as I handed him the bowl. "What happened?"

I told them everything. Every time I mentioned my efforts to remain hidden—the crouch by the desk, dash to the dining room, dart under the table—Mark scowled at Alex.

"This Sandy sounds like a wonderful woman," Alex said when I finally finished.

"She is," Mark said. Then, "It worries me that Glen is lying to protect Pauline. Claire's right. Eviction is a strong motive. But why would he lie if Pauline left Anna's first?"

"Maybe Pauline went back to Anna's, to plead her case some more. She's always been a bit of a nervous Nellie," I said. "I can see her being afraid to tell the police she was at Anna's. She would be a wreck trying to defend herself if Claire told them of her eviction."

"I'm having dinner with Claire tomorrow night," Alex said abruptly.

Mark and I looked at him, stunned.

"What?" I asked.

"I met Claire this afternoon after I left here," Alex began. "In front of her shop. I felt so bad about failing in my guard duty, I thought up a plan to get information from Claire. She was very friendly to me, so I thought I'd cozy up to her over dinner. She accepted without hesitation. We'll have some wine, a good meal, I'll work my charm on her. Maybe she'll drop her defenses and tell me something."

Mark and I looked at each other as we considered the proposal.

"I did something similar on the show," Alex said. "Remember, Ronnie? Cal wanted to take over Diana's company, so he wined and dined her assistant to get some insider information."

"I remember," I said.

"And it worked," Alex said.

"And Cal also got slapped in the face when the assistant found out that she had been used. We don't want you to get hurt if Claire finds out what you're doing."

"What can she do to me in a restaurant? She most probably won't have poison in her purse, like Samantha had when she dined with Cal that time."

"I thought you only got slapped in the face," Mark said.

"Different storyline," Alex and I said at once.

"Oh."

"But just in case, I'll keep my eye on my drink the entire time."

"I don't like this," I said.

Alex said, "It's worth a try. Both Claire and Pauline are wary of you. You can't ask them anything now. How else are you going to find out?"

"But what if Claire has an ulterior motive for accepting?"

"We can be his backup," Mark said.

I turned to him. "What do you mean?"

"We'll go to the restaurant and keep an eye on them."

"That won't look obvious," I said with sarcasm. "Are we going to follow them in the car when they leave, too?"

"If necessary."

"I like the idea," Alex said.

"But Claire will see us," I said to Mark, "and know it's a setup."

Mark reflected on that for a moment. "Have you made a reservation?" When Alex said he didn't, Mark said, "Giacinta's."

Barton's fine Italian restaurant. "What about it?"

"Alex and Claire can sit out on the patio, and we can get a table inside, by the window."

"The catbird seat," Alex chortled. "I love this plan."

"I don't know," I said.

"You did something much riskier, going into Anna's house." Mark reminded me. "Alex will be out in public."

He pulled his cell phone from his pocket. "I'll make a reservation for Alex and Claire at six-fifteen. We'll have a reservation for six-thirty. That way we won't run into each other."

I watched as he punched in a number.

"You know the number?" I asked. I imagined Mark dining there every weekend, and with a different woman each time.

"I'm friends with Dominic."

That would be Dominic Abruzzi, the son of the restaurant's namesake. I felt better.

"Hi, Dom," Mark said. Alex and I sat very still, listening. "I'd like to reserve two tables for tomorrow night. Do you have a full

210

house? Terrific. I'd like one out on the patio, for six-fifteen. Under the name Alex Shelby . . . And the second one inside, by the window overlooking the patio. For six-thirty and under my name." Mark listened for a moment. "I'm making the reservation for an out-of-town friend who's visiting. My date and I want to give him some space for his date . . . Wonderful. Thanks, Dom. I'll see you tomorrow."

"Good work," Alex said as Mark slipped his phone back into his pocket.

Mark patted my hand. "It will all work out."

Alex made another suggestion during dessert.

"We need some sort of a signal, in case of emergency. I think we should change our phone ringtones so that you will know when I call, and I will know when you call."

"Why do we need to do that?" I asked. "We'll just answer the phone."

"But I might not answer," Alex said, "and you might not answer. But if I know it's one of you, I'll answer, and if you know it's me, you'll answer."

"You didn't use your phone this afternoon," I reminded him.

"I thought you forgave me."

I sighed and relented. "All right. So how do we do this?"

"I'll program your phone," Alex said.

"Okay. But nothing too crazy."

I went into the house and brought back my phone. Then, while Mark and Alex went about programming our phones, I took the dessert plates inside and put them in the dishwasher. When I went back outside, the two were hunched over the phones.

"All set?" I asked.

"I think so," Alex said. He pushed a button on my phone and then handed it back to me. "Here you go. All the phones are set to bark if we need to talk with each other."

"That's appropriate. Dogs bark when they sense danger. And they're great at guarding things."

Alex frowned.

"I've forgiven you."

"Let's give it a test run," Alex said. He dialed my phone, which barked three seconds later. Then he got the same result after calling Mark's number. "Call mine," he said to me. I did, and again we heard barking. Then Mark called Alex's number. Same result.

"That poor dog is all barked out," I joked.

"Let's give him a rest until tomorrow night," Alex said.

Mark said, "Let's hope we don't need him tomorrow night."

"Alex, please don't call unless you really need help. I don't want to have a heart attack during the main course."

Alex held up his hand, as if taking an oath. "I promise."

"So what are you going to say to Claire?" I asked. I was still concerned about Alex's plan.

"Don't worry, Ronnie," he assured me. "I'll go wherever the conversation takes us. Let's say we meet back here afterward and I'll give you a full report."

We all sat back, relaxed, and looked up at the darkening sky.

After a few moments, Alex broke the silence by asking, "So why is it that none of us is married? Mark, were you ever married?"

Mark shook his head. "I came close twice, with wonderful women who ultimately put their careers first. The first was a fellow grad student at Duke. And the second was an associate professor at Arden. That ended a few years ago."

Alex's gaze rested on me for a long moment. "You got more than your fair share of marriage."

"And then some. I guess the fellas confused my fictional life with my real one and ran."

"That can't be true," Mark said.

Alex said, "That wouldn't scare off every man."

"I don't know if I'd want the man who wasn't scared off by a woman married six times."

"I guess it would depend on what happened to her six husbands," Mark said.

"Rachel really was only married to four men, just to clarify," Alex said.

"I guess I just got too tired acting out all that romance, I didn't have the energy for it after work."

That was true. Between the soap, the television movie roles I got for a time, and the off-Broadway and regional theater plays I did, I really didn't have the time or energy for a relationship. I did have my share of dates in my youth, and a couple of long-term relationships, one with a playwright and another with a stockbroker. But love and marriage just never happened for me and after a while, I gave up even thinking about it.

Alex said, "Well, if you didn't have that policy of not dating co-workers, you might have gotten lucky."

"My mother wisely advised me not to do that," I said. "I'm very glad I followed her advice."

"It's a good policy," Mark agreed.

Alex was quiet for a moment and then said, "It's not as messy as you think. I dated a few co-stars, and we remained friends afterwards."

"A few?" I asked, incredulous. I only knew of two relationships Alex had with actresses in the cast of *Days*.

"Some women wanted to be more discreet than others. Serena Watson and I were together for a year." Alex sounded more sad than proud of the revelation.

"I didn't know that," I said. Serena Watson was about ten years younger than Alex and a rising star when she joined the soap in 1993. She was a supporting player who became very popular with the fans. She left in early 1995 for a big role on Los Angeles–based *Sullivan's Way*, a move that made perfect sense to the cast. *Sullivan's* was the number one soap at the time and it offered Serena, who had played the ingénue on *Days*, a more adult role.

"She might have been the one that got away," Alex said. "But it would have been foolish for her to refuse that offer from *Sullivan's*. Serena's the star of the show now, and married to an investment banker." After a moment of silence, Alex asked Mark, "Have you ever had an affair with a student?"

"Alex!" I scolded.

Mark grinned. "I'm not that kind of professor."

"He's the ethical, mature, professional kind," I said.

"Did you two make one of those pacts where if neither of you is married by age forty, you'll marry each other?" Alex asked.

"Obviously not," I said.

"Maybe we should have," Mark teased.

"Maybe *we* should have," Alex said, not in a teasing tone.

"Maybe *we* should change the subject," I said.

"Does everyone have a will?" Alex asked. When I groaned, he said, "Just in case my plan goes awry tomorrow night."

"Another new subject, please," Mark pleaded.

We chatted for a while about various topics until the cricket-chirping increased in volume.

"Do you have a long drive home, Professor?" Alex asked.

Mark gave him a funny look and said, "No. I live just on the other side of Orchard." He looked at his watch. "Don't you have an early morning? What time does the tournament start?"

"Not too early," Alex said.

Since the two guys wanted to get rid of each other, I decided to get rid of both. "Maybe we should call it a night. We'll need to be rested for tomorrow night's mission."

Mark pushed his chair back and stood while Alex lingered.

"You must be exhausted, Veronica," Mark said. "You've had a long day, what with all that sneaking around and hiding under tables."

I stood and caught his grin in the glow of the citronella candle.

"It was quite an aerobic workout. I'm glad that Alex will be doing all the work tomorrow. I can sit back and enjoy the pasta."

Alex stood. "I just hope I don't have to crawl under the table. I won't fit, and I'll hurt my back."

I blew out the candle and grabbed my coffee mug. Mark and Alex took theirs and we went inside to the kitchen. Mark locked the door behind us and closed all the curtains. His small gestures of kindness touched me.

"Thank you, Mark."

"Thank you for a delicious dinner. I enjoyed it."

Alex set his mug in the sink. "Thanks, Ronnie," he said, enfolding me in a bear hug. "And I apologize again for shirking on my guard duty."

"Accepted, for the hundredth time."

I walked them to the front door. Mark gave me a kiss on the cheek. Alex quickly mimicked him. We said good night and I watched them walk to their cars before closing and locking the door.

I went back to the kitchen to put the coffee mugs in the dishwasher. Just as I added the soap and slammed the washer door shut, the doorbell rang.

I tensed for a minute and then decided it must be Mark or Alex. I hurried to the front door and glanced through the sidelights to check on my caller. Alex stood outside; he smiled when he saw me peeking through the window.

What now?

I flipped back the dead bolt and unlocked the door. "Did you forget something?" I asked when I opened the door.

Alex's grin widened as he said, "I thought he'd never leave. Can we talk?"

"All right."

Alex stepped into the living room as I shut the door. I followed him, amused by how he flopped onto the couch and patted the cushion beside him.

"What's up?" I asked as I settled on the opposite end of the couch.

"There's something I have to tell you." Alex paused and then said, "I've accepted a role on *Passion for Life.*"

I wasn't too surprised, since that was the rumor for a while. I scooted to his end of the couch and gave him a one-armed hug. "Congratulations. That's wonderful."

"Thanks. It means I'll be moving to California."

"Of course," I said. This was bittersweet news. Inevitable, but still it wrenched me. I had worked with Alex for twenty-eight years; it truly was the end of an era.

"That was the call I got while you were snooping around your neighbor's house." Alex leaned back, as if expecting a punch from me.

"So that's why you weren't watching my back. You were taking care of your own."

"It all turned out well," he countered.

"As of now."

"True."

I squeezed his hand and said, "I'm happy for you."

"Thank you, Ronnie." Still holding my hand, he said, "You know, we're no longer co-workers."

"I noticed that."

"So your policy is no longer in effect."

He leaned over and kissed me. It was nice, but it felt no different from the hundreds of kisses we shared on set.

"Come to California with me," he said.

"Alex—"

"There's plenty of work out there. You'll have no problem finding a good role. So many prime-time shows, and they all need guest stars."

"I—"

"We're so compatible, Ronnie. Our chemistry is just as good offstage as it is on. We should give ourselves a shot at romance."

"I love you, Alex, but not—"

"In that way. I know. But why not see what develops? Give it a year. Come to California. Please."

I sighed, lost for words.

"We'll get a house on the beach."

I'm not a big fan of the beach, and I'm definitely not a fan of cohabiting while not married. I'm old-fashioned and proud of it. "I hate the beach," I blurted.

"So we'll live in the Hollywood Hills. Or you can get a place anywhere you want. Are you really going to stay in this small village the rest of your life?"

"Maybe."

Alex looked at me with disbelief. "You're really thinking of staying *here*? Giving up your acting career to go into retail?"

"I'm not giving up my career. But nothing's happening for me on the acting front, and I have to do some kind of work. If I got a call tomorrow with an offer, I'd click my heels and grab it." I put my hand over his and continued. "Alex, I love you. I absolutely adore you. But I'm not *in* love with you. If I ever felt that way about you, I wouldn't let that policy stop me. I can't move across the country to give it a shot. I'm sorry."

Alex kissed my hand. "The good ones always get away."

"Not always," I assured him.

Pushing himself up from the couch, he said, "I hope I didn't ruin things between us. I had to ask." He looked down at me with a worried expression.

I stood up and hugged him. "You could never ruin things. And thanks for asking." We walked to the front door. "Have fun at the tournament."

"I will. Have a nice dinner with Mark." He winked.

"I will."

"Yes, while I'm risking my life, you'll be wining and dining with the professor."

"Good night, Alex," I said as I pushed him out the door.

I waited until he was in his car and then closed the door. No, he certainly hadn't ruined anything with his declaration.

CHAPTER TWENTY-EIGHT

"V!"

I instantly recognized the raspy voice, even with only the one letter uttered. My retired agent, Barbara, had deigned to call me from her South Carolina paradise.

"Hi, Barb. How's life down South?"

"Fabulous," Barbara chirped. "Though I'm still not sold on grits. But you have to come visit."

"Sure," I said.

"So what have you been up to?"

"I'm in Barton—"

"A wonderful place to recharge your battery."

"Yeah," I said. As I considered telling her everything that had happened since my arrival, Barbara changed the conversation.

"I know it's Saturday morning, but this is a business call," she said.

"I thought you were out of business," I cracked.

She laughed. "I thought so, too. But you're pulling me back in."

"I am?"

"Yes, you! I got a call from a Brad Farley from Parker Street Productions. They produce programs for the Internet. Brad is creating a soap and wants you as its leading lady."

"Huh?" I blurted, too stunned to say anything more intelligent. I sank into a chair at my kitchen table, pushing away my cereal bowl and pulling my coffee mug closer.

"The soap is going to be called *Harbor's Light*. He's putting a cast together and you would be the headliner of the group. You would be the star, Veronica."

"Huh. And this would just be on the Internet?"

"Yes. That's the future, hon. There are already two soaps online. I bet in five years there will be no soaps on television. They'll all be on the 'Net. And the money's good. Not what you made on *Days*, but pretty good."

"Okay." My heart began to beat faster. I remembered what I said to Alex the previous night. If I got a call tomorrow with an offer, I'd click my heels and grab it. My prescience tickled me.

And then Barbara dropped an anchor that dragged my heart right down to my toes.

"It will be filmed in California."

"Oh."

"Keep your mind open. You can commute back and forth, Veronica. Don't let that be a deal breaker. We can put it in the contract that you don't work Mondays and Fridays, if you want. You can go home every weekend, or once a month. Whatever you want."

My brain quickly summarized the commute. A five-hour flight from L.A. to New York, plus the drive to Barton. I'd be tired from the lag all weekend, and, just when my energy returned, I'd have to make the reverse trip. And I hated flying.

"This is a great opportunity for you, hon. You're not going to get a better one in soaps. And if you did, it'd be in Los Angeles. You know all this."

"Yeah, I know."

"You're an actress, Veronica. A damn good one. An Emmy winner. Twice! Seize the opportunity!"

"*Carpe diem.*"

"You got it."

"When do I have to decide? How long do I have to think

220

about this?"

"Why don't you think about it this weekend and we'll talk on Monday?"

"Okay. I will."

We chatted for a few more minutes. I didn't mention the murder, or my possible purchase of All Things.

I hung up and walked out to my backyard. I drew in a deep breath, appreciating the wonderful scent of the flowers and trees mixed with the Adirondack air. I've been to California several times, and know full well about the smog. But it's also a beautiful state, and I knew I would find a house as lovely as my Barton one. Did I want to?

This sudden, significant decision I had to make gave me a case of cabin fever. I locked my doors and walked over to Orchard Street. I resolved to tell no one about Barbara's job offer, not even my mother or Carol. I knew what they would want me to do. Stay in Barton, or, at the very least, in New York state.

Orchard was busy with the usual Saturday morning commerce and traffic. I walked past All Things and glanced through the window. They had their fair share of customers, a sight that pleased me. The bookstore had a few as well, and there was not a vacant table outside The Caffs.

I reached the next corner and waited for the light to change so I could cross the street. In my mind, the summer morning changed to a fall day. Barton is a real beauty in autumn, her leaves changing into nature's jewels and her air turning crisp and refreshing.

The picture in my mind flashed to our Adirondack winters. In December, white or multicolored lights would frame Orchard Street windows. Christmas trees and menorahs would be in shop windows. Mom would put a child's train set under her three-foot tree, and the Rizzutos would adorn their window with snowflake decals. The Ingersons would put frost around theirs, and Pauline would place garlands of evergreen in her windows.

My mind finally lingered on the Barton spring. Orchard would sport a green line down its middle for the Saint Patrick's Day parade. Not only would it beckon celebration of the day, but of the soon return of the green of our trees and lawns. Crocuses, hyacinths, tulips, and daffodils would bloom and short-sleeved shirts would regain their place of prominence in closets.

Would Los Angeles have twinkly lights, green lines up Sunset Boulevard and Rodeo Drive? Would its seasons be marked so brilliantly? Even if it did, would it have the same sentimental weight as Barton's?

Of course not.

The light changed and I strolled across Orchard, my mind returning to the warm morning. I hurried along to Carol's, to spend time with my best pal and get some floral therapy.

"Good morning, sunshine," I said as I breezed through the door.

"Good morning," Carol said. "You're in a good mood."

"It's a beautiful day."

"It is. Many times I wish I didn't have to be cooped up in here."

I knelt beside a bucket of roses to admire them. "But look at the beauty you have in here."

"Very true. That's what keeps me cooped up in here."

I went over to a bucket of bouquets ready for sale. I picked a pretty pastel arrangement and brought it to the counter.

"I'm going to the Griffins' to play canasta," I explained as I opened my wallet to pay for the flowers.

Carol smirked. "Have fun."

She took my money and was just handing me my change

when the phone rang. To give her privacy, I walked to the door into the workroom. Amy was there, alone.

"Hi, Amy."

"Hey, Veronica. How's it going?"

"It's going good," I said. I walked over and sat on a stool beside the worktable. I watched as she arranged a colorful array of flowers—pinks, whites, and lavenders—in a basket. "How's it hanging with you?"

She laughed at my attempted hipness. "It's hanging."

"You're very good at that," I said, nodding at the basket. "You have a serious talent for it."

"Thanks." She worked quietly for a few moments and then asked, "So how long are you going to hang around Barton?"

"I'm not sure."

"Well, it's good to have you back. Carol likes having you home."

"I like being home. And seeing my best friend every day." The words rooted in my heart.

"Do you have any work lined up?"

"I have a couple of irons in the fire." I marveled at my turn in fortune. When I arrived in Barton, my future appeared bleak. Now, I really did have two possibilities.

"Good," she murmured. "Do you miss your life as a soap star?"

"Well, I do miss having my hair and makeup done. I picked up a lot of tips in the makeup chair. I miss being on a team. The collaboration."

"Uh-huh."

"I don't miss the long hours. The pages of dialogue to learn every night. That was a real chore sometimes. But I do miss playing with my friends. We were a great team." I pointed at the basket. "That's beautiful."

"Thanks." She set it down and did a bit more work on it. "I

223

hope you find something that gives you as much happiness."

"Thanks, Amy."

In our silence, I wondered if I'd have that same feeling of teamwork with the cast of *Harbor's Light*. It would take time to develop, for sure.

Carol came in, her face somber. "We're going to be getting orders for a wake."

"Who?" Amy asked, frowning.

"Edna Grady. I don't know her. Do you?" After Amy shook her head, Carol said, "She was ninety. Passed away in her sleep."

"God bless her," I said.

"That was her daughter on the phone. She wants a blanket of pink roses for the casket."

"Wakes and funerals must be very sad work," I said.

"I hate them," Amy said.

"Sometimes it's heartbreaking. It's difficult when a child dies, or someone is killed in a horrible accident. But it's balanced by the joy of doing new mom arrangements and weddings, one of which I have to set up for in an hour," Carol said as she glanced at her wristwatch. "I consider it my service to the community."

"Good attitude." I slipped off my stool. "I'll get going so you two can work."

I gave them both a quick hug and left. Carol's view of her job as a service resonated with me as I continued my sentimental journey down Orchard.

I ended up at the bookstore and went in to say hi to Mom. She greeted me with such enthusiasm, two hugs and a kiss on both cheeks, it was as if I had been away for years.

"Where's the fatted calf?" I joked.

Mom pinched my cheeks. "I just love seeing you every day."

"I like it, too," I said. I waved to Todd at the register as I followed Mom to the children's section.

Mom turned her attention to the shelves, always in disarray, thanks to eager little ones. I pitched in and helped her straighten the books.

"Have you ever gotten tired of this, Mom?"

She smiled and stacked a collection of Clifford the Big Red Dog books. "Countless times."

"Do you ever think about selling the place? Getting out of the business?"

"Sometimes. But as tiring as it is, I still love it. I love helping the people of this village. And I like meeting the folks visiting our village. I enjoy going to book conferences and meeting my fellow booksellers and dealing with publishers. And it's still exciting when an author comes to the store for a signing."

We worked quietly for a few minutes and then she said, "I think you'll find the same joy if you buy All Things. Wink wink, nudge nudge." She turned to me, grinning. "Not that I'm pushing you, or anything. Just campaigning." Then she really winked and nudged me.

The bell over the door jingled and several customers entered.

"You don't think we'd slowly drive each other crazy, being in such close proximity?"

"You'll be so busy, and I'll be so busy, that we could go days without seeing each other. We'd have to take up smoking so we could meet in the alley."

"Sounds good to me."

She flashed me one of those stern looks only mothers know how to give, then winked. "Speaking of smoking, can you dash out back and ask Wendy to come in? We're getting busy."

"Sure. Do you want me to help?"

"No, thanks. We can manage. Enjoy the day while you can. Once you're in retail, you'll never have the time." Another wink. Another nudge.

I walked through the stockroom and opened the door that led to the small alley behind the building. Wendy leaned against the building, her arms crossed and a cigarette angled between her fingers.

"Hi," she said.

"You're back to your old spot."

Wendy nodded. "I felt guilty. Anna was barely dead and I kind of danced on her grave. I'll observe the proper mourning period and then maybe go out front."

She bowed her head and swept her foot over the gravel alley.

"Everything okay?" I asked.

Wendy looked up; there were tears in her eyes. "I've been feeling bad about my attitude to Anna. I never liked her and I didn't hide that from anyone, even Anna. I should have been nicer, because you never know."

"Don't beat yourself up about it," I said. "None of us are angels."

She smiled. "I'll try to be nicer, anyway."

"You can start by getting back to work. Mom sent me out here to tell you you're needed inside."

She dropped her cigarette to the ground and stamped it out with her foot. "Are you really considering moving back here for good, Veronica?"

"There's a strong possibility I will."

"You sound like a Magic 8 Ball."

"I could use one."

"I hope you do. It will be fun having you here permanently. And I know it will make Nancy very happy."

"She's made that very clear."

The opening bars of "Born To Run" came from her pocket.

Wendy pulled out her cell phone and checked the screen. "Todd," she said. She held up the phone to flash me a glance of the message. "Get your butt in here."

As she passed me, she said, "You'll be an improvement at All Things." She grimaced. "I just vowed to be nicer."

"New habits take time."

She grinned. "I'll see you, Veronica."

I walked home humming "Born To Run" and considering my options.

Did I want the hard work and glamour of acting, or the hard work and comfort of Barton? The teamwork of acting on a soap opera, or the teamwork of running All Things? Where did I want to make my contribution?

I remembered what I had said to Linda about not wanting to leave my soap boat after we learned of the show's cancellation. Now I was firmly back in the Barton boat. Did I want to disembark?

As I walked up my front path, I looked over to Anna's quiet yard. It had been nice not thinking about *that* for a little while. I wondered how Alex was doing at the golf tournament, and how the evening would go. I worried that something would go awry and there would be trouble.

I sighed and glanced at my watch. It was time to get ready for my canasta audition.

Chapter Twenty-Nine

I arrived early for lunch. As important as it was for me to get to the police station when expected, it was even more imperative to get to Ella Griffin's on time. The woman was a police chief, five-star general, and Catholic school principal all rolled into one.

I stood on the sidewalk for a moment to admire the Griffins' home. I've always considered the house the jewel of Orchard Street, with its wide porch that stretches across the front of the house, screened-in side porches on each side as well as two on the second floor and one on the third, gables that add an air of mystery, and a pristine lawn bordered with beds of marigolds, pansies, and chrysanthemums. On this ground Godfrey Griffin began the family business, opening the original Barton Inn in 1770, five years after the village's founding.

Madeline opened the door and gave me a hero's welcome.

"I'm so happy you could come."

I walked up the porch steps and handed her the bouquet from Carol's.

"How lovely. Thank you."

"Thank you for inviting me, Miss Griffin."

"It's time you start calling me Madeline," she said.

"All right," I said, unsure if I really should call my elder and former piano teacher by her first name. I followed her into the wide front hall that had welcomed so many.

Madeline gave me an unexpected hug and then held me at

arm's length. "I'm so happy you're home."

"Thank you."

"Now we're just waiting for Sandy," she said, leading me into the living room or what Madeline and her sister referred to as the parlor. "Dotsie and Ella are in the kitchen, discussing the seating arrangements."

Myrtle sat on the sofa, in the smoker's pose—elbow leaning on the sofa's arm, cigarette clenched between her fingers. "Ella wants you and Sandy on the ends, so us old gals don't have to reach so far across the table. But Dotsie likes to sit at the head of the table to stretch out those gams of hers."

"I can partner with Dotsie and we'll take the ends," I offered.

"Dotsie's not so sure about your playing ability," Myrtle said.

"Let's not talk about that," Madeline said. "Veronica, please sit. Would you like a drink? We have iced tea and lemonade, both homemade."

"Iced tea, please." I sat in a chair across from Myrtle.

"Do you remember this, dear?" Madeline asked, pointing to the piano.

"Ah, yes. The medieval torture device."

Madeline laughed and said, "It wasn't that awful."

I lied and said she was right, it wasn't too bad.

"You should play for us," Madeline said.

"Only if I don't like canasta and want to be kicked out of the club," I quipped.

"You'll love it. I'll go get your tea," Madeline said.

I swept my gaze across the parlor. Framed photographs of Madeline, Ella, their sister Amelia, and their parents Richard and Eloise sat atop the piano. On the table beside my chair was an amusing shot of Ella, Madeline, Dotsie, and several other women crammed into the drugstore telephone booth at the height of that craze. Above the piano hung a painting of the house with the Griffin family standing on the front porch steps.

"I hear you might be joining our illustrious business community," Myrtle said.

"I might be," I said. "I had a talk with Brian Langdon yesterday about buying All Things."

"I hope you do it."

"Thank you." Myrtle's encouragement pleased me. She was a tough cookie; winning her approval was akin to winning an Emmy. "We'll see how things go," I said, thinking about the call from Barbara.

Dotsie bounded in, carrying a glass of lemonade and one of iced tea. "Here you go," she said, handing me the tea. She settled on the sofa, took a long sip of lemonade, and then set it on the coffee table.

"I'm happy to report Paul Baldwin did not kill Anna Langdon," she said.

"And how did you find that out?" Myrtle asked.

"I asked him."

"You really asked him?" I asked.

"In a roundabout way."

"This should be good," Myrtle dryly said. She set her unlit cigarette on the coffee table and leaned back, crossing her arms across her chest. "Do tell, Dotsie."

Dotsie stretched out her long legs. "Well," she began, "I was outside yesterday putting out some seed for the birds. I saw Paul working in his garage." She looked at me and explained, "His garage is actually his workshop. He's a fantastic carpenter. If you need anything built, he's your man."

"Good to know."

"So I walked over to pay him a visit. He's working on the most divine dining table I've ever seen. It rivals Madeline and Ella's." Dotsie pointed at the Griffins' ten-foot table in the dining room across the hall.

I was unnerved. Was I about to become a furniture sales-woman?

"Is that the kind of thing he wants to sell at All Things?" I asked.

Dotsie and Myrtle guffawed at my naiveté.

"Oh, no, Veronica," Dotsie said, holding her side because my question was so hysterical. "He makes smaller things that you could sell. Birdhouses. Christmas ornaments. Rocking chairs. End tables."

"Oh," I said.

"We talked about the table for a few minutes. It really is a gorgeous piece. It's for some lucky duck in Bolton Landing. So then I mentioned that they hadn't yet found Anna's killer and what did he think about that." She paused to take a long drink of her lemonade.

Myrtle looked at me, exasperated. I shrugged; Dotsie did have a flair for the dramatic.

"Paul said it was a shame she was murdered. He was happy that she had saved the farm from the developer."

"So he wasn't so bitter about his surplus birdhouse inventory," I said.

"Oh, no, he's still ticked," Dotsie said. "But this is the important part." She leaned forward and placed her hands on her knees. "He said that he and Trudi Goetz had set up a breakfast meeting that morning to discuss the mall. He said it would be a violation of nature if they built the thing. They were going to brainstorm with a few others about fighting the deal to save the land."

"So he's an environmentalist, too?" I asked.

Dotsie nodded and Myrtle cracked, "And he loves animals."

I smiled as I remembered what she said about Paul's compassion for spiders and squirrels.

"When they saw the newspaper that morning with the

headline that the land had already been saved, he and Trudi turned it into a celebration breakfast at Trudi's place."

"So that's settled," I said.

Dotsie's head bobbled. "At least as far as Paul is concerned. But Hal Hargrove is another person who was angry with Anna. He does the most beautiful wood carvings of animals and Anna called them kitsch. His work is displayed at the library and in the Village Hall and Anna wouldn't sell them in her shop."

"Dotsie, Hal Hargrove did not kill Anna," Myrtle said. She picked up her cigarette and began rolling it in her fingers.

"Do you know that he has an alibi?"

"No."

"I'll ask."

"No, you won't. You must stop accusing good people simply because they had a business disagreement with Anna two years ago."

"Their bad feelings could have festered until they burst, like a bad boil."

I took a sip of tea, wondering if this was typical conversation for a canasta get-together.

Myrtle narrowed her eyes. "I think Anna was up to something. I think she was about to make a big move."

Dotsie leaned forward, eager to hear more. Also intrigued, I set down my glass and sat up straighter.

"What do you mean?" I asked.

"I got a call from Anna Monday morning. She wanted to know how her premiums would be affected if she made structural changes to her buildings."

"Structural changes?" I asked. "Like an addition?"

"Or a combination," Myrtle replied. "Taking two retail spaces and making it one."

My breathing momentarily stopped. "That would put some people out of business."

"Not a concern to the Worm of Orchard," Dotsie groused.

Myrtle nodded. "Anna never had much respect for the businesses on Orchard. They weren't upscale enough for her. She constantly pestered Edward to rent to what she thought were better stores. But Edward was loyal. He considered his tenants to be partners and friends. Anna didn't."

I remembered the list I found on Anna's desk. What I had assumed to be an enemies list. Perhaps not.

"She didn't have much respect for her husband's own business," Dotsie said. "It's no surprise she didn't care about anyone else's."

The ring of the doorbell startled me.

"I'll get it," Dotsie said. She got up from her chair and hurried into the hallway.

"Perhaps someone found out she had a plot brewing," Myrtle said, "and *stopped* Anna."

"Perhaps."

We stared at each other, listening as Dotsie gave Sandy an exuberant greeting.

Sandy charged into the parlor, carrying a large brown bag in each hand. "Hi, partner," she said as she hustled to my chair. She kissed my cheek and then bounced over to the couch to give the same greeting to Myrtle. "Hello," she said to Madeline and Ella, who stood in the entrance to the parlor.

"We're all here," Madeline said, beaming with delight.

"Hello, Veronica," Ella said.

"Hi, Miss Griffin," I said, taking no chances that Madeline's first-name invitation extended to Ella.

"Lunch will be served in five minutes. I just need to put it out," Sandy said, holding up the bags.

"Do you need help?" I asked.

"That would be lovely," Ella said.

Sandy gave me an apologetic look as I got up and followed

her across the hall and through the dining room.

As we passed through the butler's pantry that connected the dining room to the kitchen, Sandy said, "Ella still acts like she's running an inn and has a staff to command. That or they're talking about you."

"It gives us time to lay out a canasta strategy."

Sandy set the bags on the kitchen counter and we started removing the salads, cold cuts, and rolls.

"Did you ever find out about that check you were looking for?" Sandy asked as she removed the plastic wrap covering the cold-cut platter.

"Yeah, I did."

"Good. Can you put the salads into those bowls?" Sandy asked, nodding to the china bowls on the table.

"Sure," I answered. While Sandy brought the platter to the dining room, I removed the covers from the potato and macaroni salads and spooned them into the bowls. I went over what Myrtle said. Was Anna preparing to evict more businesses from Orchard than just Pauline's? Pip's Books was on the list; was my mother a target? I couldn't wait to talk about this with Mark over dinner.

Sandy returned and asked, "Do you need a quick refresher on canasta?"

"Yes. And maybe we can come up with a system of hand gestures so we can pass information to each other undetected."

"Okay." Sandy made the universal cuckoo sign—the finger circling motion near the side of the head—and said, "This will be our sign for Dotsie."

I clenched my hand and we did a fist bump. "This just might be fun," I said.

I did have a fun afternoon with the canasta club. Sandy and I won, to Madeline's delight and Dotsie's consternation. She tried to "take me back" as her partner, but Sandy would hear nothing of it. Although there was no induction ceremony and I didn't take an oath of office or get a membership card, I think I left the Griffins' an official member of the club.

I drove down Orchard looking at the shops with a fresh perspective. If Myrtle was right about Anna plotting something, and I was right about the list, then the suspect list expanded considerably. Though I doubted Anna had told anyone. But what if someone had found out? Claire would be the most likely person to discover the plot. Everything always went back to Claire.

A nervous twitter went through me, similar to the feeling I had before every opening night back when I was performing in plays. But the upcoming evening did not hold the same promise of fulfillment and fun. Instead, I prepared for it under a growing sense of dread.

Chapter Thirty

Giacinta's, located at the quiet south end of Orchard, is a five-star Italian restaurant that has sated Bartonians' appetites for more than forty years. Besides serving the most delicious meals, the family-owned restaurant has played a role in the most important moments of peoples' lives. The welcoming atmosphere has acted as the backdrop for many marriage proposals, christening parties, and anniversary celebrations.

Mark and I settled at our window table and ordered drinks. As soon as our waiter left, we leaned over and glanced at the patio below us.

I spotted Alex and Claire immediately, seated at a table in the corner of the patio. Claire had her back to us. She sat slightly forward, as if hanging on every word uttered by Alex. Even with the fading sunlight, I could see him making full use of his debonair smile.

"So far so good," Mark said as he turned back to face me.

"Maybe we should have wired Alex," I said, still intent on the pair.

"That would be a bit much. Relax and enjoy dinner."

"I still don't think this was a good idea," I said. "Alex might screw up. Or maybe he'll forget what he's supposed to be doing. Put a pretty woman in front of him—"

Mark reached across the table and put his hand over mine. "Just enjoy dinner, Veronica. The rest will work itself out."

Except for Alex's recent displays of affection, it had been a while since a man had held my hand for real, not as dictated by a script. A long while. It was very nice, and it did the trick of pulling my attention away from Alex and Claire.

"How much trouble can he get into?" I cracked.

"That's the spirit."

Our waiter, Doug, brought our drinks. Mark pulled back his hand as Doug set the glasses on the table.

"Are you ready to order?" Doug asked.

"We need a few more minutes," Mark said.

I said, "Sorry, I was too busy looking at the pretty lights around the patio."

Doug smiled and said, "It is a beautiful evening. I can check if there's an available table on the patio?"

"Oh, no, thank you," I said. "This table is perfect."

"I'll give you a few minutes," Doug said and left.

"You almost spoiled the whole plot," Mark said.

"That's so like me."

We studied the menu for a few minutes, making the typical comments about the pasta, chicken, and fish choices. After Doug returned and took our order, I raised my glass to Mark.

"Cheers," I said.

We touched glasses and then took long sips. I glanced out the window; a waiter had just brought Alex and Claire their salads.

"I have a second theory," I said.

"You do?"

"Yes. When I was at Anna's, I found a list on her desk of the stores that would have opened shop at the mall. At first I thought it was a sort of enemies list, all the stores that would have competed against Orchard Street businesses."

"Uh-huh."

"But Myrtle Evans told me something today when I went to the Griffins' to play canasta."

"Canasta?" Mark asked, amused.

"They have a group that plays every week. They want me to replace someone who passed away."

"I'm sorry to hear that. About the deceased, not the card game."

"Myrtle thinks Anna was up to something. She said that Anna never had much regard for Barton's businesses. She always pushed Mr. Frazer to rent to upscale stores."

"So they could charge higher rent, I'm sure."

"Yeah. But Mr. Frazer wouldn't sell out, or rather, kick out, his friends."

"He was a gentleman."

Doug carried over our salads and placed them on the table. I thanked him as he wished us *bon appétit* and left.

"Myrtle thinks Anna was going to make some sort of a change. Anna called her Monday and asked what would happen with her insurance premiums if she made a structural change to a building."

"That's interesting."

"It is. So this is my theory, what if the enemies list is actually a friends list? What if Anna was going to start evicting businesses on Orchard, and renting to the businesses that Thompson would have brought in? Stores that need more space than the existing businesses use?"

Mark appeared thoughtful as he swallowed a bite of tomato. "She wasn't renewing Pauline's lease. And wasn't going to rent the diner space to Connie. It could have been the start of a trend. But Anna only stopped the deal Monday night. Who would know by Tuesday morning that she was going to turn Orchard upside down?"

"Claire, maybe. Or maybe Pauline told someone else she lost her lease and that person panicked and went to Anna's. Or maybe Anna had another meeting that morning. Maybe

238

someone else brought their rent check and got an eviction notice in return."

"That's a lot of maybes."

"And they're making my head spin. We'll have to find out just when everyone's lease is up," I said.

"I suppose, but not tonight."

I smiled. "Not tonight."

We didn't talk for a few minutes as we ate. I glanced out to the patio. All seemed well.

"I have to tell you something else, Mark," I said abruptly.

"Another theory?"

"I was offered a job in California."

The crestfallen expression on his face felt as good as his hand on mine. I realized right then why exactly I would not accept the offer. For all my contemplation that day of the pros and cons of moving to California, I knew my one true reason. The future I wanted was sitting right across from me. I'd had my fill of acting (I could still do community theater). I wanted a life with someone, and I knew the historian and Martin Van Buren biographer across from me was that someone. And I could tell he wanted the same life with me, as he struggled to pretend he was happy for me.

"Congratulations," Mark said with a weak smile. He took a sip of his drink and turned to check on Alex and Claire. "They look like they're having a good time," he said. He turned back and asked, "So what's the job?"

"It's a role on a soap that will be on the Internet."

"The Internet?" Mark asked.

"Yes. It's the new thing. There are already two soaps people can only watch online."

"That's interesting. I know people can watch television shows online, but I didn't know about shows that are entirely Web based."

"I'm not taking it."

Mark's jaw fell open. "You don't want it?"

"No." I jabbed my fork into a lettuce wedge. "It's in California, and what am I going to do in California?"

"Learn how to surf?" Mark cracked.

"No, thank you."

"So tell the truth, why don't you want it?"

"Because California will never be home. In every way that home is."

"Good."

"I'm not going to tell anyone else I got the offer. Just you. I'm going to sell my house in New City. It's Barton or bust. I'm going to buy All Things, if I can afford it. And if I can't, well then, I'll just work in the bookstore. Or find something else."

"You could deliver flowers for Carol."

"That's a fabulous idea. I've done that and I'm really good at it."

Mark looked down as he sliced a cucumber. "You could have a silent investor."

At first I didn't catch his meaning, and then I did. "If necessary," I said. I wanted to buy the shop on my own, not need help in any way.

I took a mouthful of salad and looked at him. His smile told me he had caught my meaning.

I took a glance around the dining room as I swallowed. The maître d', George, led Tim and Sue into the room and toward a corner table.

Tim grinned when he saw us and said something to George. He clasped Sue's hand and led her to our table.

"Hello," he said when he reached us. The huge grin that lit up his face pleased me immensely. He gave me a kiss on the cheek and shook hands with Mark.

Sue, who looked very happy herself, leaned over and gave me

a one-armed hug. "Welcome home, Veronica," she said.

"Thanks, Sue. What a great surprise to see you and Tim here." I gave her a look, hoping to convey my happiness at their reconciliation.

She understood; her smile was radiant. "Thanks."

Tim looked from Mark to me and grinned. "It's good to see you two here."

Sue nudged him. "Don't embarrass them, Tim."

"All I'm saying is it's nice to see them here together," he said. "And I hope you're behaving yourself, Veronica, and not snooping around where you don't belong." When Sue looked at him, puzzled, he explained, "Veronica's a bit too interested in her neighbor's murder."

Sue turned to me. "Be careful, Veronica," she said.

"Don't worry," Mark said. "I'm keeping her out of trouble."

"Good," said Tim.

Sue put her hand on my shoulder. "Will you still be in Barton when school starts? I lead the orchestra for school productions and I bet our drama club would love to meet you. Maybe you could give a talk one day." Sue was the music teacher at Barton High.

"I'd like that," I said, recalling the several occasions when I had met with students at the local schools.

"Great. I'll call you after Labor Day."

Tim took her hand. "Enjoy your dinner," he said as he escorted Sue to their table.

"You, too," I said, a warm feeling coming over me at the sight of their happy reunion.

"That's a nice sight," Mark said as a busboy took away our salad plates.

I agreed and took a peek out the window. "Still having fun," I murmured.

Indeed, Alex and Claire seemed like a regular couple enjoying a romantic Saturday evening.

Mark took a fast look. Leaning back, he asked, "What if we're wrong about Claire, and nothing at all happens tonight?"

"It will be no loss. We'd still have a delicious dinner and a fun time together."

Mark smiled and held up his drink.

"To nothing happening," he said.

I excused myself after dinner to visit the ladies' room. With Alex and Claire laughing and carefree, I began to wonder if anything at all would come of Alex's plan.

I was before the mirror, applying lipstick, when the outer door opened. I held my breath for a moment, watching the reflection in the mirror to see who entered. I prayed it wasn't Claire.

"Veronica!"

The appellation coincided with my first view at the newcomer. I turned and smiled. "Hi, Dana."

She joined me at the vanity mirror. "Fancy meeting you here."

I turned back to the mirror to finish coloring my lips. "Are you here on a hot date?"

Dana sighed. "No, I'm alone tonight. I'm sitting at the bar." She checked her own lipstick and opened her purse.

I noticed her eyes were a bit glassy. "Really? On a Saturday night?"

"Woe is me." She opened a lipstick and puckered her lips to apply it. "This is my hangout. I like to get away from the Orchard Street scene." She giggled. "I know, we're still on Orchard. But this is away from the main drag. You know what I mean."

"I do." I dropped my lipstick back in my purse and glanced at the mirror.

A smear of cranberry lipstick underlined Dana's lower lip.

"Uh-oh!" She leaned toward me and pointed at her mouth. "I colored outside the lines!"

The definite aroma of alcohol hit me. "Have you had dinner?" I asked.

"No. But I did have a shrimp cocktail about an hour ago."

I worried about her drinking on an empty stomach, and her later drive home. I didn't think Mark would mind (too much), so I asked, "Would you like to join Mark and me for dessert?"

She turned to me and grinned. "Ooh, *you're* on a hot date."

"We're just two friends having dinner."

"You're blushing," Dana said, cackling.

I was, but I didn't like having it pointed out.

"I don't want to intrude," Dana said.

"It's okay," I said.

She tugged a tissue from the box on the vanity and wiped away the errant lipstick. "Thanks. I'd like to join you. It is a little lonely at the bar."

I thought I saw a tear in the corner of her eye. I lightly touched her elbow and asked, "Is everything okay?"

"Yeah," she said as she put her lipstick in her purse. Her mouth closed into a tight smile. "It's just been a long week, you know? Anna's murder really shook me and Chloe. We're scared."

I embraced her. "It's okay," I said, gently patting her back. "The police will find who did it very soon."

"I know," she said, pulling away. "It's just so stressful until they do. You must be out of your mind, being right next door."

"There have been a few tense moments," I said.

Dana took another tissue and dabbed at her eye. "Okay," she said, checking her face in the mirror. "I'm ready."

We left and walked back down the hall to the dining room. George met us at the entrance and said, "Ms. Cafferty. Ms. Walsh. Are you enjoying your evening?"

"Very much, George. Dana is joining us for dessert. Can we

get an extra chair at our table?"

He smiled and gestured to several chairs lined against the wall. "I'll bring one right away."

As we wound our way around the tables toward the window, George following us with a chair, I watched as Mark turned and saw us. His momentary look of query fast turned into a smile.

Wow. He didn't mind that I was carting a third wheel to our table. He was becoming more of a keeper every minute.

He stood when we got to the table and moved to pull out my chair. "I invited Dana to join us for dessert," I said.

"Great."

As Mark pushed in my chair, I whispered to him, "She was alone at the bar."

"That's not good," he whispered in return.

He took his seat again as George set the chair for Dana along the outside edge of the table.

"This is nice," Dana said. "You don't mind me invading your date, do you, Mark?" she asked.

"Not at all," Mark said. "Only a fool would protest the presence of two beautiful women."

We lauded him for his wise choice of words as Doug came over with dessert menus.

"Put this on a separate tab," Dana said to him. "It's my treat."

"Oh, you don't have to do that, Dana," I said.

As Mark also protested, Dana held up her hand and said, "I insist on returning your kindness."

"Thank you," Mark and I said together.

Doug left and we glanced over the menu.

"Since I'm buying, I might get one of everything," Dana joked.

"I'll just have a slice of cheesecake," I said.

Dana set down her menu and leaned toward me. With a conspiratorial smirk, she said, "Your friend Alex and Claire are here tonight, too."

I feigned surprise. "Really? I haven't seen him all day because he had that golf tournament."

"They're out on the patio. I bet you can see them from here." She got up and walked behind me as Mark and I exchanged glances. "Yep, they're right down there." She poked me in the back and pointed out the window. I casually looked over and Mark turned and took a quick peek. It was eight-thirty and dark; the soft glow from the restaurant's outdoor lights and the glimmer of the white candles burning on each patio table cast a romantic luminance on Alex and Claire.

"Oh, yeah," I said.

Alex and Claire were having a grand old time. In the glance I took, I saw Claire throw her head back as she laughed at something Alex had said.

Dana returned to her seat as Doug came to the table.

"Have you decided what you would like for dessert?" he asked.

We nodded and gave him our orders. Once he had taken our menus and left, Dana leaned forward again.

"Do you think Claire had anything to do with Anna's death?" she asked in a whisper.

"My goodness, do you really think Claire is capable of that?" I asked in a naive tone.

"Anna was such a witch to her, always putting her down, making Claire follow her around like a dog on a leash. Maybe Claire had enough and snapped." Dana snapped her own fingers.

"Let's not talk about such a serious subject," Mark said.

"You're right, Mark," Dana said, flopping back against the chair. She turned to me and put both hands over my left hand.

"Are you sad about losing your job? Because you look sad." She pulled her mouth into a frown to dramatize how sad she was about my sadness.

"I'm okay, Dana," I said, patting her with my right hand. I glanced over to Mark; he was smirking with amusement.

"Oh, good," Dana said. "It's just so unfair when bad things happen to good people."

"Thank you," I said.

She removed her hands and started waving them through the air as she spoke. "It's just so unfair. You worked hard, you won awards, you were loyal to that show. And through no fault of your own, they just yanked the rug out from under you. All because they thought some stupid talk show could get better ratings." She folded her arms on the table and said emphatically, "It stinks."

"Thank you for your support," I said, thankful to see Doug headed our way with our coffee.

Dana sat quietly as Doug served us the coffee and our dessert. When he left, Mark asked her, "How did you and Chloe come to have your own coffee shop? It's an impressive accomplishment."

"Thanks, Mark," Dana said, leaning over and vigorously rubbing his arm. "You're so sweet." She ate a huge forkful of her tiramisu, chasing it with a sip of coffee. "Our grandparents owned a Dunkin' Donuts in Kingston. We would spend a month with them in the summer and help out in the shop. It was hard work, but we had a lot of fun. It's where we first tasted coffee and fell in love with it. Instead of playing supermarket at home, we'd play coffee shop with our parents' Mr. Coffee maker and mugs. Chloe and I knew by high school that we wanted to open our own shop. We were thrilled when that show *Friends* became a hit and coffee shops became popular. We did have a freak-out moment, thinking maybe it was just a fad that would be over by the time we opened our shop, but it didn't. So we went to college, majored in business, and worked and saved until we finally opened The Caffs."

"Good for you," I said.

"That's a great story," Mark added.

Dana smiled serenely and ate more tiramisu. Her cell phone rang in her purse; the tune was vaguely familiar to me.

"That's Chloe," Dana said.

I took a mouthful of coffee as she pulled the phone out, the ring becoming louder.

The caller's identifying ringtone was Elvis Presley's "Little Sister."

It was the tune I heard the morning Anna was murdered.

CHAPTER THIRTY-ONE

I set the cup down hard on the table, missing the saucer and spilling coffee over the white tablecloth. I coughed as I swallowed the coffee, causing some to go down the proverbial wrong pipe. I coughed harder as my throat burned from the hot liquid.

The friends list. Glenda's Brew, right at the top.

Mark reached over the table, grasping my hand as he asked, "Veronica, are you all right?"

Over my coughing, I could hear Dana on the phone, saying, "I'm at Giacinta's with Veronica and Professor Burke. I'll call you later."

"It went down the wrong pipe," I said, my voice strained. I coughed again, staring at Mark.

By now George and Doug were at our table, solicitously checking on me. I looked at them and nodded that I was fine as George patted my back.

Still holding my hand, again Mark asked, "Are you okay?"

"I'm fine, really. I just swallowed funny," I said, looking from face to face.

Mark, Doug, and George stared at me with comforting concern. Dana sat, stone-faced. Each side of her jaw slightly puffed out, a sign she was clenching her teeth.

"The coffee is not too hot?" a worried George asked.

"No, no," I reassured him. "It was my fault. Thank you."

George touched my shoulder and said, "Please let us know if you need anything."

"Thank you."

He and Doug finally left. The other diners were looking at me. Tim and Sue stared from their table, both looking concerned. I waved and gave them an embarrassed smile, mouthing, "I'm okay."

"That was scary, Veronica," Dana said. She slapped my back, hard, a couple of times. "Are you sure you're okay?"

"I am." I forced a smile. "The excitement's over," I said. I took a small bite of cake and a sip of coffee as proof.

"Be careful," Dana cautioned as she stared at me.

"I'll take small bites," I said, giving her a sweet smile.

I considered my options. I could leap up and shout "Murderer!" I could excuse myself and go outside to call the police. Or I could force myself to finish dessert and casually leave with Mark, acting as if everything were fine. And then I could call the police from the safety of Mark's car.

I took another bite of cheesecake. "That's a cool ringtone," I said to Dana.

She glanced down at her cell phone, which she still held. Shoving it back into her purse, she said, "Chloe has the same for me. Elvis doesn't have a song about big sisters."

"Neat," I said as I considered the possibility that it was Chloe at Anna's Tuesday morning. I committed myself to playing it cool.

"Getting back to the coffee shop. You should give your own college course on starting a business. Have you ever been asked to do that?"

"I've given talks at Barton High and at the community college. Arden's never asked me, though." She glanced at Mark as she took a bite of her dessert.

"I'm in the history department," he said with a chuckle.

"I'm just teasing you," Dana said, patting his hand. She picked up her cup and took a sip, watching me over the cup's rim. When she put the cup down she asked me, "So are you going to buy All Things?"

"I'm giving it serious consideration."

"That would be a big career change."

"Yes, but I'm ready for it."

"Really? It's a lot of work. Everyone thinks it's easy to just step in and buy a store, but it's not," Dana said, her tone rather aggressive.

"I know that." I looked over at Mark; he looked back with a furrowed brow of consternation at Dana's sudden mood change.

"I mean, it's not like on the soap opera. It looks easy there. This is real life. You don't get multiple takes if you mess up."

"I know that."

Doug was at the next table, serving the dinner course. Mark caught his eye and mouthed the word, "Check."

I gave a mental sigh of relief and changed the subject. "Have you taken a vacation this summer?" I asked Dana. "How do you and Chloe handle that?"

"We don't do everything together," she chastised me. "I mean, we need a break from each other once in a while."

"I understand. So, have you taken any time off this year?" I asked.

"In August I'm going to Lake George for a few days with a couple of friends. Their parents own a house on the lake."

"Very nice. That will be a well-deserved break for you."

Doug came over and handed Mark and Dana each a check. Dana, so insistent about treating just minutes earlier, pressed her lips together in a grimace.

Mark, a wonderful conciliator, held out his hand for her check. "Dana, let me do the honors."

Dana wasted no time in passing him the bill. "I thought you'd never ask," she said with a grin.

Mark pulled out his credit card and handed it to Doug, who

hurried away to finish the transaction.

"Thank you, Mark," I said as I folded my napkin and put it on the table. I couldn't wait to get out of there and tell him what the ringtone meant.

"Thanks, Mark," Dana said. She tossed her napkin on the table without thought.

"You're both very welcome," Mark said. He looked at me and said, "I look forward to doing it again soon."

"I'll have to join you for dinner next time," Dana said. Her laugh was a bit too loud.

Doug returned with Mark's card and the credit slip for him to sign. Mark signed it quickly and stashed the card and slip in his wallet.

"Thank you very much, Doug," he said as he shook the young man's hand. "We had a wonderful time."

"Thank you, Doug," I said.

"You're very welcome. I hope you all have a good night."

"We will," Dana muttered as she pushed her chair back and rose to her feet.

Doug left as Mark and I stood. I took a last glance out the window and did not see Alex and Claire at their table.

I noted how ironic it was that the evening started with Mark and me watching the pair, sure that Claire was involved in Anna's murder, and ended with the possible murderer at our own table.

And who was watching our back, as we had been watching Alex's?

No one.

Dana kept close to my side as we left the dining room. Mark walked behind us, his hand lightly on my back.

We stepped into the hallway just as Alex and Claire reached the top step of the staircase that led to the patio.

They wore wide smiles and had their arms around each other.

Claire looked stunning in a sleeveless lavender dress cut just low enough to accentuate her bosom. Alex, handsome in a white shirt, navy sports jacket and pants, had obviously had a wonderful time. His smile widened when he saw us. Claire's fell. I guessed she thought we had been watching her the entire evening.

"Hi, everyone," Alex said with exuberance. Of course, I knew why. He hadn't uncovered evidence against Claire, because she was innocent.

"Hey, you two," I said.

Mark and Alex shook hands and then Alex gave me a kiss on the cheek.

"Hey, pal," he said to me. And to Dana, "My caffeine supplier." He leaned over and gave her a kiss.

Dana, still practically glued to my hip, gave him a bland, "Hi, Alex."

"How was your dinner?" I asked Claire.

"It was lovely," she said coolly. "I didn't know you were here."

Mark stepped in and said, "I invited Veronica to dinner. I wanted us to catch up since I rarely see her. And Dana joined us for dessert."

"That's nice."

Alex stepped back to Claire's side. She slipped her arm through his and said to us, "Good night."

We said good night and Alex waved as Claire pulled him toward the door. I moved to follow them, but Dominic, the restaurant's owner, stepped into the hall just then to say goodbye.

"I hope you enjoyed your meal," he said, smiling at me as he and Mark shook hands.

"We did, thank you," I said.

Dominic gave me a slight bow and nodded at Dana. "Good night," he said to us all.

We walked to the door, Dana still very close to me. I began to grow nervous. As Mark held the door open for us, Dana linked her arm through mine and practically pulled me onto the outside step.

She held my arm tight with one hand and clutched her purse with the other. We descended the steps at a quick pace, Mark still behind us. I spotted Alex and Claire to the right, standing beside Alex's car. How could I convey that I, not Alex, was in actual need of backup?

"Good night!" Alex yelled to us.

As we passed, I caught Claire's eye. She stared back with an odd look on her face.

"Where are you parked?" I asked Dana.

"Over there," she said, making a dismissive gesture toward the road. "Mark, where's your car?"

"Up a few on the left," Mark said. "Do you need a ride?" he asked.

"Yeah."

When we reached Mark's car, Dana let go of my arm and thrust her hand into her purse. As we walked around to the passenger side, she pulled something from the bag and shoved it into my ribs.

"What?" I gasped.

There were several times on *Days and Nights* when my character, Rachel, had a gun pointed at her. There were a couple of times on set when I had a gun pointed at my head. Two or three times I had a gun pressed into my back.

So I knew what Dana was thrusting into my side. But this was not life imitating art. Dana's gun carried real bullets.

CHAPTER THIRTY-TWO

Dana put her arm around me, pinning my body against hers, and jabbed the gun into my abdomen.

"Shut up," Dana hissed as she turned me so Mark could see the gun. "Mark, unlock the door."

"Dana—" I began.

She opened the rear door on the passenger side. "Be quiet, Veronica."

"Dana, there's no need for this," Mark said calmly. "Let Veronica stay here and I'll take you wherever you want to go."

Dana ignored him. "Get in the car, Veronica," she demanded in a low voice. "Mark, drive."

She waited until Mark opened his door and got in the car. Then she shoved me into the backseat and climbed in next to me. She pushed the gun against my ribs and told Mark to drive back toward the heart of Orchard.

"Dana, why don't you just let us out and take the car," I suggested.

"No."

I glanced out the window as we backed out of the parking space. Claire and Alex were out of my view. I prayed they saw Dana's maneuver.

When we pulled onto the road, Dana mumbled, "This screws up everything. I should have changed that damn ringtone."

I tried to play dumb. "Dana, I don't understand this. Why are you doing this?"

Dana saw straight through my act. "Don't play dumb, Veronica. You've figured out that I killed Anna. It was written all over your face the second my phone rang. You literally choked on it. Damn it!"

My phone rang in my purse. Barked, actually. I wondered why Alex was calling. To tell us Claire was not the killer? Or to ask why we left with Dana? What had he seen? I prayed he had seen enough to raise his suspicions.

Dana grabbed my bag and threw it to the floor. The barking stopped after four rings. In a moment, Mark's phone began to bark.

"Don't even think about it, Professor," Dana said. She held the gun steady against my ribs. We continued along Orchard, listening until the barking stopped. I clenched my jaw at the ridiculousness of our synchronized ringtones.

"Who is that?" Dana demanded, her voice unsteady.

"Alex," I said. "We're supposed to meet him after dinner."

"Good try, Veronica. Alex just said good night. And from the way he and Claire were acting, I don't think they want to see anyone else tonight."

My cell began to ring again, but with the normal ringtone. Claire, perhaps?

"You're very popular tonight, Veronica," Dana said. "Turn on Primrose," she demanded of Mark.

The ringing stopped as Mark made the turn.

"Anna evicted you Tuesday morning, didn't she?"

"How do you know that?"

"I heard a few things. So Anna did tell you she was ending your lease?"

Dana stifled a sob. "Everything Chloe and I had worked so hard for, Anna was going to destroy. Just so she could make more money. She was such a greedy bitch."

"What happened?" Mark asked.

"I went over to her house Tuesday morning to thank her for blocking the farm sale. I brought her favorite coffee, a caramel latte. Chloe and I were grateful that the mall wasn't going to be built. We knew that would hurt us and everyone else on Orchard. A Glenda's would be in the mall. Everyone would be there, and not at our shop. The mall would get all the college kids. It'd be the new hangout. So I went over to Anna's. When I got there, she told me that she wasn't going to renew our lease when it's up in November." Dana stopped and let out a sob. "She was going to give the space to Glenda's."

We drove in silence for a few moments as Dana cried. I sensed that she was relieved to confess.

"It's okay, Dana," Mark said. "We understand. If we go to the police now, it won't be so bad."

"No," Dana said.

"So what led to—" I began.

"We fought. I told her I knew about her and Jason."

"You did?" I asked.

"Yeah. Connie told me. She saw them together at Sheridan's one night. She kept it to herself, because she's a professional, but she told me after Anna welshed on their deal. I told Anna I'd tell everyone if she evicted us. Turn on Sunrise Lane."

"So you're the reason the police brought Jason in for questioning," I murmured, talking more to myself than to Dana.

"I didn't know they brought him in. I just left a tip on their website that the two were *involved.*"

"How did Anna react when you told her you knew of the relationship?" Mark asked.

"She said go ahead and tell everyone," Dana said. "She didn't care. Then I slapped her and she hit me back. We kept shoving each other and she called me stupid and a failure. I got so mad, I grabbed the skillet and swung it. I didn't really mean to hurt her."

She wept for a few moments. Mark and I made eye contact in the rearview mirror.

When Dana's crying subsided, Mark asked, "No one missed you from your shop? That time of morning must be a busy time."

"I do a daily coffee run to the tellers at Chase and Andrea and everyone at the hair salon. I keep them happy, they keep me happy."

"Very smart," Mark said.

"I didn't tell anyone I was going to Anna's, not even Chloe, because that would be like spoiling a good deed. But then the shop got really busy, and she called to see if I'd be back soon."

I carefully asked, "Does Chloe know?"

"No," Dana said. "She doesn't know."

We turned on Sunrise and approached Pierce's. How ironic to be passing the scene that started it all.

"Turn here!" Dana shouted. When Mark pulled into the farm's parking lot, she ordered him to drive around the building and turn off the engine.

Mark did so and then turned to face us. "Dana, please think about what you're doing. We can just all walk away, right now. You can take the car and our phones if you want."

Dana put the gun to my temple. "Get out of the car."

Mark held up his hands in surrender and got out. Dana opened her door and yanked me out by my wrist, tugging me around to where Mark stood. She then gave me a shove. Mark caught and steadied me as Dana pointed the gun at us both.

"Dana, please," I said.

"Start walking," she said, pointing the gun at the cornfield.

The sound of a car turning into the gravel lot preceded by seconds the sight of that car's headlights. In the split second that Dana turned to the car, Mark grabbed my hand and pulled me down one of the rows and into the midst of cornstalks.

"Run," he urgently whispered. "Don't speak."

We were several feet in when we heard Dana hurrying behind us. Mark, still holding tight to my hand, swept our path clear with his free hand. He took a sharp right turn, raced a few yards, and then took a sudden left.

Dana thrashed somewhere behind us, muttering expletives. Mark and I continued to run through the maze of corn. The sliver of a crescent moon gave us barely enough light to see our path.

"Dana, stop!" It was Claire!

"Dana, give yourself up." That came from Alex. Softer rustlings of the stalks told me the pair was carefully moving through the field.

I heard a sob from Dana, and then, "I have a gun."

"So do I," Claire retorted.

Good grief. What was with all the Annie Oakleys on Orchard? Was a pistol the latest shop girl accessory?

"Get down," Mark whispered as he pushed me to the ground. I crouched as he put his arms around me.

I heard a soft rustling among the stalks. "Dana, you don't want to hurt anyone. I know you don't. Please, just come out," Alex said in a soothing tone.

"Dana, it's okay," Claire added.

"Dana, let's talk about this," Alex said.

Dana let loose another expletive directed at Claire.

"Nice language," Claire said with sass.

"Shut up, Claire," Dana hissed.

An eerie silence followed as no one moved; no one uttered a syllable.

Then Dana broke the quiet with a bomb of a curse as she again rushed through the field.

"Stay down," Mark whispered in my ear as he stood. He crossed a nearby row as Dana neared us.

Agonizing moments passed and then Dana screamed, "Let me go!"

"Drop the gun," Mark said.

I listened to their struggle. Someone fell to the ground. Mark groaned.

"Mark!" I screamed.

"Where are you, Ronnie?" Alex called. "I'm coming!"

Two yelps of a police siren did nothing to quell my fear.

Mark gasped for breath as footsteps came at me. The cruiser's headlights outlined Dana's figure a few yards behind me. She started to run along the row just feet from where I hid.

Still crouching, I steeled myself as I inched closer to the row. Just as she passed, I dove forward, grasped her ankles, and pulled her down. I scrambled on top of her as she tried to kick me. I slapped her, scratched her cheeks, and rubbed handfuls of dirt into her face.

"Over here!" I shouted. I sat on Dana's stomach and pinned her wrists to the ground. She mightily resisted, but thanks to a flood of adrenaline and my anger that she had harmed Mark, I was strong enough to hold her.

It will always seem to me that I had to wait minutes for help, but it really took just a few seconds for Alex to reach me. Tracey and Ron Nicholstone were there moments later, hauling Dana to her feet.

"Get your hands off me!" Dana screamed. "I didn't do anything."

"She killed Anna Langdon," I said.

"No, *she* did," Dana said in desperation.

"She has a gun!"

"I have it now," Ron said.

"What did you do to Mark?" I asked Dana as Tracey handcuffed her.

"I'm okay," Mark said. I turned and saw him limping toward

us. "Dana kicked me in a rather sensitive area."

Courtesy of Andrea's blasted self-defense lesson. But my prowess at the catfight saved the day.

"Say no more," Alex said with a sympathetic wince.

"Everyone to the parking lot," Tracey commanded.

We happily complied. I put my arm around Mark's waist and supported him as he hobbled through the field. When we reached the lot, I spotted Claire standing by Alex's car.

"Are you okay?" she asked when we reached her.

"Yes," Mark said.

Alex hugged me. "Are *you* okay?" he whispered in my ear.

"Yeah," I said. "Thanks."

"Thank Claire," he said as he shook hands with Mark. "She figured it out very quickly."

Surprised, I looked at Claire.

"Dana's car was on the other side of the lot from where Mark was parked. I just had a feeling something was wrong."

"You're hurting me," Dana screamed.

We turned and saw Ron guiding Dana into the backseat of the patrol car. Tracey walked over to us.

"You will all have to come down to the station to make statements and answer questions."

"We'll be happy to," Mark said.

"We have a lot to say," I said, glaring at Dana as we locked eyes. She glowered at me through the cruiser's closed window.

"Good. We'll see you in a few minutes." Tracey nodded and walked back to the patrol car.

We said a temporary goodbye to Alex and Claire.

As we headed for the car, Mark said, "You were right about that list." He put his arm around me and pulled me close.

"Thanks to Myrtle's loose lips."

"You never know what you're going to learn at a canasta game."

"Are you all right to drive?"

"I'm fine. Sore, but fine."

We reached his car. "Dinner was lovely," I said, trying to be jaunty and cool as I stilled my shaking hands.

"I certainly enjoyed dessert," Mark said as he opened the passenger door for me.

I stopped and put my hand on the door. "I'm sorry I brought a murderer to the table."

Mark, standing on the other side of the door, put his hand over mine. "You're forgiven, but try not to let it happen again."

He tilted his head forward and lightly kissed my lips.

"Well that made this whole thing worth it," I quipped with a probably silly grin on my face.

"Then I'm off to a good start."

I slid into the seat, saying, "Next time, let's not take the scenic way home."

CHAPTER THIRTY-THREE

An hour later, Claire and I were sitting on the hallway bench at the police station. Mark and Alex were giving their statements just down the hall from where Dana sat in a cell. Charlotte Farrell was also buzzing around, interviewing us all for what was probably the biggest story of her career. Tim was also present, summoned to represent Dana until she could get a criminal attorney.

Tracey had brought in Chloe. I met the two in the back hall as I left the conference room after giving my statement to Ron. Chloe, dazed and her eyes red-rimmed, gave me a blank stare as she passed me. I knew for sure Dana had told us the truth. Chloe had no idea her sister had killed Anna.

Claire sighed and said, "This is so surreal."

"That it is."

She swiveled on the bench so that she was facing me. "So, are you going to buy All Things?"

"Are you going to sabotage my every move and decision?"

"Will you put in a candy counter? There's a company in Saratoga that makes the most divine chocolate and candies."

"I don't know. Not many people like chocolate," I said dryly.

Claire stuck her tongue out at me. The perfect start to our new relationship.

"Is that all I need to do to make you happy? Put in a candy counter?"

She put on an angelic smile and nodded. "Yep."

"Done. But don't eat all our profits."

"You won't fire any of us?"

"Of course not. That's not my style. Unless you eat all the profits."

She turned and leaned against the hard bench. "I always knew I couldn't afford it. It's a pipe dream." There was a wistfulness in her voice that matched the melancholic look on her face.

I put my hand on her arm. "Don't give up on your dream. Keep saving your money. You never know what will happen."

"Thanks, Veronica." I'm sure I saw a tear in her eye. "There's another thing."

"Yeah?"

"I'd love to get back to the store's roots of selling local craftsmen's work. Anna really moved away from that and started selling the magazine lifestyle. Not that there's anything wrong with that, but it wasn't Mr. Frazer's intent."

"I agree."

"I'm not saying we go completely local. That would be retail suicide because we have a lot of customers who love the stuff Anna brought in, but let's increase our made-in-the-Adirondacks inventory."

"Absolutely. Let's make amends for Anna's snub of our homegrown talent."

Claire said, "I'm also thinking of ways to capitalize on your fame. We'll notify all the soap magazines and maybe that TV channel devoted to soaps will do a feature on you."

I laughed at her enthusiasm. "Maybe."

We leaned against the bench and contemplated our grand plans. After a few minutes, I said, "There's something I'd like to know." I stopped, wondering if I really wanted to make my own confession. "What happened at Anna's Tuesday morning?" When Claire gave me a querulous look, I made my admission.

"I was in the house yesterday when you were there. I heard you and Pauline."

"You were? Where? And what were you doing there?"

"Looking for that stinking rent check."

Claire stared at me for a moment, then burst into laughter. "This is all so ridiculous. So where exactly were you?"

I gave her a step-by-step account of my movements. When her shoulders continued to shake from the hilarity, I said, "I know. Ridiculous. And it doesn't matter now, but I'm very curious about what happened Tuesday morning among the three of you."

"Pauline was there when I arrived, arguing with Anna. Anna had just told her that she wouldn't be renewing Pauline's lease when it was up in December. Pauline was crying, yelling, pleading with Anna. She said Anna was ruining her family's life. That they could lose their house. That her children wouldn't have shoes or food. Pauline brought the high drama. You would have given her one of your Emmys. Pauline begged Anna to change her mind. Anna said no. I calmed Pauline down and got her to leave. I asked Anna what she was up to, and she just said she was taking care of her business. I didn't want to hear anymore, so I gave her the pastries and she gave me the check. And then I left."

I told Claire about the list I found on Anna's desk and about Anna's phone call to Myrtle.

She nodded and said, "Anna moves fast when she has a plan. And it's making sense to me now why she wanted to sell you All Things."

"Why?"

"It's all about the money, Veronica. All Things is worth a lot, but Anna was bored with it. She'd get the money upfront from you and be rid of the shop. She probably would have given you a one- or two-year lease, and then doubled the rent at renewal time."

"The Worm of Orchard," I mumbled.

"What?"

"Dotsie Beattie's nickname for Anna."

"She was."

"So when did you next see Pauline?"

"After I left Anna's, I immediately went to the store to check on Pauline. The door was locked and she didn't answer when I knocked. The car was parked around the corner—"

"Is that the only car she and Glen have?"

"No, they have a nicer car that Pauline usually drives. But Glen will take it when he's going to show a house to a client."

"I see."

"So, anyway, I couldn't find Pauline. I worried that maybe she had walked back to Anna's. I went over to All Things to open up because everyone would be in soon for work. After a half hour or so I called Pauline. She was calmer and said maybe it was for the best that the store closed."

"When you heard about Anna, did you think that Pauline murdered her?"

Claire sighed. "I did, and I was really worried. I went over and told Pauline as soon as I heard. She freaked out and swore up and down she didn't go back to Anna's. I believed her."

"But you would have told the police about her eviction."

Claire spoke defiantly. "Only if I had to defend myself. I thought I might have to when Pauline suggested she would tell the police that I wanted to buy All Things and was p.o.'d Anna was going to sell it to you. I'm so relieved this is all over and I don't have to worry about it anymore."

"Do you still have her rent check?"

"I shredded it Tuesday morning, after I heard about Anna. Pauline needed the break."

"That was nice of you. Thanks for listening to your instinct and following us from the restaurant."

"At first I thought you were giving Dana a ride because she had been drinking. Then you both got in the backseat and it just seemed strange. And then I remembered seeing Dana walk by the store Tuesday morning. She was carrying a Caffs bag, so I figured she was on her daily coffee run. I had just walked in and was headed upstairs. My mind was still on the fight. So I thought nothing of it, and completely forgot by the time I heard about Anna."

"Our memories work in funny ways."

"They certainly do."

After another silent pause, Claire said, "So that's why Alex was hovering around the hedge. He was your *lookout*."

I snorted. "Some lookout." Then I realized what she said. "You saw him?"

Claire nodded. "When I was leaving. He said he was looking for your earring."

I was speechless, but only for a few seconds. "What?"

"He said you were missing an earring and thought maybe you had lost it on the driveway. He said you were turning your house upside down, looking for it."

"Son of a—"

"That's when I invited him to dinner."

"You what?"

She gave me a sly look. "I wanted to see what information I could get on what you were up to. And have some fun. He's a very attractive man."

"Son of a—"

"It wasn't a coincidence that you and Mark were at Giacinta's, was it?" she asked, suddenly indignant.

"We planned it, yes," I said, mortified. "Actually, it was all Alex's idea, down to programming our phones to bark."

Claire stared at me for a moment, and then grinned. "Alex is a very interesting man," she muttered.

"You do know he's not staying? He's moving to California. I don't want you to get your heart broken."

"Oh, I know. He told me all about his new role. He's really not my type, anyway. He's a bit too self-absorbed."

"Don't I know it."

"But interesting."

We were quiet for a few moments and then I asked, "Do you always carry a gun?"

"I don't own a gun. I just said that to scare Dana. Thank goodness she didn't test me on it."

I sighed with relief. "Good. I don't want my manager packing heat."

Mark and Alex walked into the hallway. "Are you talking about me?" Alex asked.

Claire and I looked at each other and shook our heads. We were going to do fine working together.

"Claire told me all sorts of things," I said.

"All true, if good," Alex said. "Mark and I thought we should all repair to The Hearth for a drink."

"Perfect," Claire said.

Chief Price and Tracey came into the hall.

"Not so fast, Ms. Walsh," the chief said.

My pulse thumped. "Yes, Chief?" I stood, feeling like a child caught doing mischief. Claire stood close beside me, in solidarity.

"You're very lucky you didn't get hurt. If you plan on staying in Barton, leave the crime-solving to the police."

"Yes, sir," I said. "You do such a good job, I doubt there will be any crime to solve." I thought that was just enough butter to please the chief.

He chuckled and cracked a slight smile. "Have a good

evening," he said before disappearing into the station.

"Good night, all," Tracey said.

The four of us said good night and started to walk to the door.

"Impressive tackling, Veronica," she said.

I looked back; she wore a clever grin. "I excel at catfights." I winked and left with my crime-solving crew.

I called Carol as Mark drove to The Hearth. I had called my mother when we got to the police station. I wanted her to hear about the "incident" from me.

"You won't believe the night I had," I said when Carol answered. After giving her a brief summary of dinner with Mark, I told her every detail of what happened, starting at the moment I met Dana in the ladies' room.

"You actually ended up in the cornfield?" she asked, dumbfounded.

"Yep."

"Unbelievable."

"Yep."

"And you tackled Dana?"

"Yep. Can you believe it?"

"Yes, I can."

Carol asked me several times if Mark and I were okay. I reassured her again and again that we were.

"Oh, and there's something else. Mark and I are going steady."

Mark let out a low rumbling chuckle.

"You sure don't let a crisis go to waste," Carol said.

"Nope." I glanced over to Mark. "I'll talk to you tomorrow, Carol."

Mark turned into The Hearth's lot and parked. We went into the restaurant and found Alex and Claire in the bar area, sitting comfortably beside each other in a booth. A bottle of wine and four empty glasses stood in the center of the table.

"We were just wondering if The Caffs will be open tomorrow," Alex said as Mark and I slid onto the bench across from them.

"Probably not," Mark said.

"There will be quite a few grouchy people around if they don't get their caffeine fix," Claire said.

"I'm switching to tea," I said.

Alex poured wine into each of the glasses. "To the future," he said, holding his glass up so that the light beautifully highlighted the wine's deep scarlet hue.

"To new beginnings," I said.

I touched my glass against Mark's, tickled by his wink. I then turned to Claire and held my glass above the center of the table. She brought hers across to touch mine and finally permitted me a warm, genuine smile.

CHAPTER THIRTY-FOUR

Although Carol's shop is normally closed on Sundays, we met there the next morning for our daily meeting. The beautiful flowers around me served as a reminder of how close Carol came to having to create arrangements for my wake.

"I'm sorry," I said to her as I hugged her.

"For what?" she asked.

"I almost sent a lot of business your way. Though I shouldn't flatter myself. Who knows how many people would have sent flowers of condolence."

"Flatter yourself," Alex said as he pulled the lid off a cup of coffee. "You are much beloved. Carol and every florist in a twenty-five-mile radius would have sold out."

"Thanks, Alex," I said.

"There would have been no flowers left for my funeral," Mark teased.

Carol patted his hand. "I would have found some," she soothed.

"Where did you get the coffee, Alex?"

"The bakery. The Rizzutos were debating the purchase of a new coffee machine."

"They should," Carol said. "The Caffertys' customers will have to go somewhere."

"I still can't believe Dana killed Anna," I said.

"It makes me rethink what a crime of passion is," Carol said. "I always connected it with romantic love. But it's really about

270

a crazy love for anything. Money, status, fame. Anything."

"I think in Dana's case, it was a crime of protection," Mark said. "She was protecting her livelihood. The investment she put into it in money and hard work. And she was protecting her sister, in a way."

"That's true," Carol said.

We all nodded in agreement and drank our coffee in silence for a few moments.

"How did you do in the tournament?" I asked Alex. "I completely forgot about it."

"I shot a seventy-five."

"Not bad," Mark said.

"Thanks." Alex looked at his watch. "I should probably get going," he said.

Mark slid from his stool and extended his hand. "It's been great getting to know you, Alex," he said as they shook hands. Alex then pulled Mark into a loose hug. Mark's jaw clenched; he obviously wasn't a "man hug" kind of man.

"I plan on being back next year for the tournament," Alex said. "Maybe I'll see you out on the course, Professor."

Mark grinned. "Maybe."

"Good luck with your book on Martin Van Buren. Our eighth president, and a governor of New York."

"You did your research," Mark teased.

"I expect an autographed copy of your tome," Alex said.

"Consider it done."

Carol stepped from around the counter and hugged Alex. "Send this one a dozen of your best roses," he said, nodding at me. "Make it two dozen."

"Will do," Carol said.

Alex hugged Carol again and kissed her cheek, prompting me to say, "She's married, Alex."

"All right, I know," Alex said, releasing Carol. "I'll call you later to settle the bill."

"Have a safe trip," Carol said.

"Thanks."

I felt a sudden surge of emotion when Alex turned to me. "Walk me back to the inn?" he asked, nodding toward the door.

I glanced at my watch. I had plenty of time before I had to meet Mom for ten-thirty Mass. "Sure."

I blinked away my tears as we walked outside. Alex put his arm around me, resting it on my shoulder. I wrapped my arm around his waist.

"I'm glad you visited."

"Me, too. I prevented you from buying the farm."

I groaned. "So, when do you move to California?"

"I'm flying out on Thursday to look for a place to live. I'll probably move at the end of the month."

"It's going to be wonderful. I'm happy for you."

"What I said the other night, about you staying here. I didn't mean to insult your home. It really is a terrific place to live."

"I know you didn't mean it."

We walked in comfortable silence for a few minutes and then he asked, "Am I making a big mistake? What if I move all the way out to California and get settled, and then they cancel *Passion* in a year?"

"It's what you love. You have to take the chance."

"I hate change."

"But it's good."

When we reached the inn, Alex stopped and turned to face me. Grinning, he said, "Maybe I'll move to Barton if they do cancel the show. Set up a coffee shop."

He put his arms around me and held me close. We held the hug for a long minute. Tears ran down my cheeks, and I'm certain Alex sniffled.

"We'll keep in touch," I finally managed to say.

"Of course we will."

I patted his cheek, saying, "Thanks for always having my back."

Alex kissed me. "I enjoyed being married to you," he joked.

"It was rather fun."

I watched Alex walk into the inn and then slowly walked back up Orchard. I put my sunglasses on to hide my tears. It would be the last time I cried over losing *Days and Nights,* over missing all my friends from the show. I would always miss them, but my mourning was complete.

I stopped in front of Pauline's shop. Through the window I could see her setting up the register, getting ready for the day's work. She caught my eye and waved, a genuine, cheerful smile brightening her face.

It felt good to no longer suspect her. I waved to Pauline and turned to face All Things.

"Behold, my future."

I stood, staring at what would be mine very soon. I was suddenly very excited about this new, shiny future I had and all the possibilities it offered. I started to think of changes, small, that I would make to the shop. I knew I wanted to do what Claire wanted—go back to the store's roots of supporting local artists. I wondered where exactly I would get a candy counter.

"From that look I'm guessing you're truly all in?"

I turned and found Mark beside me.

"My soap character was a brilliant businesswoman. It's time I put all that I learned from her to use."

"But not the six husbands part, I hope."

"Most definitely not the six husbands part."

Mark's smile mirrored the contentment I felt. I put my arms around him and kissed his lips. Not a soap opera kiss. A real one.

ABOUT THE AUTHOR

Jeanne Quigley grew up reading mysteries, watching soap operas, and vacationing in the Adirondacks, never imagining these pleasures would be the foundation of her debut novel. Her love of characters—real and fictional—led her to study Sociology and English at the University of Notre Dame. Jeanne has never been a soap star (alas), but she has worked in the music industry and for an education publisher. She lives in Rockland County, New York, where she is writing her second Veronica Walsh Mystery.